"A thriller that you won't put down until you've reached the last page." —Kids' Picks, *Odyssey Magazine*

"*Trapped* is a complete thrill ride." —TCM Reviews

"This adventure will keep kids turning the pages... perfect for middle grades." —*Teaching Pre K-8 Magazine*

"Highly recommended for both boys and girls. Wonderful and unique." —Discovery Journey

"My class loved it. They were totally engaged. It's a hard book to put down."
—Jeff Montag, 5th Grade Teacher
As Quoted in the *San Diego Union-Tribune*

"Cinematic. Readers will surely be reminded of Eleanor Cameron's *Mushroom Planet* series, as well as Heinlein's *Have Space Suit—Will Travel,* and even Clarke's *2001.* Vividly speculative. Able to capture the imagination of any teen." —*Asimov's Science Fiction* magazine

"Keeps you turning the pages. It had me hooked by page two of the first book." —The Children's Book Review

"Captures that pulse-pounding excitement you remember from your *Have Spaceship Will Travel* and *Postmarked the Stars* days. Crisp, clean, and delivers what it promises."

—SFReader.com

"Brings to mind the classic young reader's novel A *Wrinkle in Time*. An adventure story for young and old alike."

—Associated Content

"Fun and suspenseful. Highly recommended."

—*Kirkus Discoveries*

"An entertaining novel . . . that reads in a flash."

—Bookloons Reviews

"The gripping storyline will make young readers read this story in one sitting and want a sequel. I strongly recommend this book." —The Midwest Book Review

"I did not want to stop reading."

—8th Grade Student
Published in the Newsletter of the ISTA

"If you have a middle schooler that is into science or sci-fi, buy this book. If you have a reluctant reader who has an interest in science or adventure stories, buy this book."

—Amateur de Livre Book Reviews

"I read this book with my class for the first time this year and my class loved it."

—President, Idaho Science Teachers Association

"Brilliant. Perfect for a class reader for 9-13s, and a 'must' for any school library. These books are, I hope, the first of a long series!"   —*Primary Science* (UK Journal)

"Nonstop action adventure . . . You really can't put the book down for very long. A thrilling read."

—California Science Teachers Association

"Would make a great read-aloud and would foster much talk among families."   —*The Old Schoolhouse Magazine*

"A suspenseful thriller that you will not want to put down. . . . vividly written."   —*The Science Reflector*

Praise for
THE PROMETHEUS PROJECT: CAPTURED

"A page turner that kids—and their parents—will love reading . . . thrilling adventure."

—Catherine Hughes, Sr. Editor
National Geographic KIDS magazine

"Will keep you on the edge of your seat while begging you to read on . . . full of fast paced action (that) keeps the reader wanting more. I eagerly await the third book."

—Steve Fielman, Director-at-large,
Intermediate Science, New York State

"Holds even an adult readers attention to the very end. I look forward to his next offering in the series."

—AAAS

"With *Captured,* the author continues to tell a story that leaves the reader reaching for chapter after chapter with plenty of suspense and cliff hangers. This is a fun and adventurous story."

—California Science Teachers Association

The Prometheus Project

Book 3

Stranded

The Prometheus Project

Book 3
Stranded

Douglas E. Richards

Paragon Press

Copyright © 2009 by Douglas E. Richards

Published by Paragon Press, 2010
ParagonPressSF@gmail.com

ISBN: 978-0-9826184-0-0

Library of Congress Control Number: 2009944189

Printed in the United States of America

First Edition

Contents

Contents

The Prometheus Project

Book 3

Stranded

Chapter 1

Zero Chemistry

Ryan Resnick squirmed in his seat and struggled to pay attention to Mr. McPherson, his tall, wiry chemistry teacher, as he droned on and on. So far Ryan had managed not to lapse into a coma, but he knew he couldn't hold out forever. Ryan loved chemistry, but Mr. McPherson could probably find a way to make a daredevil attempt to jump across a wide, alligator-filled river on a rocket-propelled motorcycle seem routine and uninteresting.

It wasn't so much that Mr. McPherson was Ryan's least favorite teacher: always in a foul mood and always delivering lectures so mind-numbingly dull that they would be considered torture in every free country in the world. It wasn't even that Ryan knew the material so well. The main problem was that it was *Friday*. The closer it was to the weekend, the harder it was for Ryan

3

to pretend to be interested in the ordinary part of his life when the totally *incredible* part of his life was about to begin.

His life outside of school hadn't always been extraordinary. He and his sister Regan, two years younger, had once been normal kids leading normal lives. But a few years earlier, when their family moved from San Diego to Brewster, Pennsylvania—a wooded town in the middle of nowhere—this had changed forever.

When their parents had behaved suspiciously after the move, they had investigated. They soon learned their parents were members of a top-secret team of scientists assembled to explore the greatest discovery ever made—an immense, abandoned underground city, in *perfect* condition. A city built by an alien race, filled with such fantastic structures and advanced technology that the greatest cities on Earth seemed like a collection of straw huts and Bronze Age tools by comparison. A city codenamed Prometheus.

The entire city was contained within a hockey-puck shaped hole that had been hollowed out a mile beneath the woods of Brewster, surrounded by a thin force-field. This energy barrier was so impenetrable that only the genius of Ben Resnick, Ryan and Regan's father, had enabled the team to finally break through.

When the team entered the city they had discovered its most astonishing feature of all: Prometheus was far larger than the hole it was in! This *should* have been impossible, but there was no denying it was true. While the hole was about a mile around and thirty feet high, the city inside covered nearly as much ground as *Manhattan* and its ceiling was almost *fifty miles high*. If not for the absence of the sun in its bright, cloudless sky, visitors to the sprawling metropolis would have sworn it was above ground.

After Ryan and Regan had discovered the buried city, their involvement should have ended. Dr. Harry Harris, the head of the Prometheus Project, had refused to let them join the team. But just as they were about to be banished from the city forever there had been an emergency, during which they had saved their mother from almost certain death. They had also made a key discovery—that a race called the Qwervy had built Prometheus using automated nano-robots, with the intention of visiting Earth every hundred years or so to check in on human progress. Dr. Harris had been so impressed with their accomplishments he had allowed them to join the team after all.

Now they spent almost every weekend, and several nights each week, inside the remarkable city. They assisted top scientists who were attempting to unlock the secrets of Qwervy technology. They were part of the most important project in history, one that had already led to numerous scientific breakthroughs.

No wonder Ryan found it nearly impossible to stay focused on Mr. McPherson as he delivered information Ryan already knew with all the excitement of a robot. Ryan's eyelids slid shut three times and each time he managed to jerk them open again, shaking his head to bring himself back to life. Finally, despite his heroic efforts, his eyes closed for good, his chin fell against his chest, and he drifted into unconsciousness.

"So who can tell me the definition of 'absolute zero?'" said the tall teacher in bored tones.

Thirty-three students sat at desks in the front half of the class. Behind them were rows of long black chemistry benches, each with a sink, evenly spaced gas lines that could be connected to Bunsen burners with rubber tubing, bottles filled with chemicals of all kinds, and beakers and flasks in various shapes and sizes.

Several eager hands shot up immediately as Mr. McPherson surveyed his class. His eyes narrowed as they settled on Ryan Resnick in the second row. He ignored the few still-outstretched arms that stood out like tall, thick weeds in a well-trimmed lawn of students, and walked quietly over to Ryan. Mr. McPherson stood as close to him as he could get and folded his arms irritably.

Ryan's chin remained glued to his thin, black sweatshirt as his subconscious mind failed to notice how unnaturally quiet the class had become and awaken him. After ten seconds of hovering over his motionless student, Mr. McPherson made an exaggerated show of looking at his watch, which elicited a roar of laughter from the entire class.

The laughter broke Ryan from his nap, and when he opened his eyes to find Mr. McPherson's scrawny, goateed face staring at him from point blank range, he was so startled that he actually pushed his chair—with the desk attached—six inches backward.

"I didn't wake you, did I?" snarled Mr. McPherson.

"Uh . . . sorry," said Ryan, as the class laughed once again.

"Okay, Ryan, now that you're with us in mind as well as body, why don't you tell the class what I mean by the phrase, 'absolute zero.' "

The definition, and much more about the topic, flashing into Ryan's brain in an instant. He had learned about this subject from a member of the Prometheus team who had won a Nobel Prize in chemistry. Absolute zero was the coldest temperature anything in the universe could ever be. It was $-273°$ Celsius or $-460°$ Fahrenheit, a temperature at which even the microscopic movements of molecules virtually stopped, frozen in place.

"Absolute zero?" repeated Ryan, as if stalling for time.

"That's right," said Mr. McPherson.

Ryan shrugged stupidly and gritted his teeth. "Uh . . . my chance of getting an A in participation this week," he said with just a hint of a smile.

The class erupted in laughter yet again, the exact reaction for which Ryan had been hoping.

"No," said Mr. McPherson seriously. "That's *absolutely* zero, not *absolute* zero. But you're not wrong about your participation grade, that's for sure."

The grim-faced chemistry teacher moved away from Ryan and called on another member of the class.

Ryan could have easily given a dazzling answer that would have blown Mr. McPherson away, but more and more lately the existence of a certain girl was affecting his every behavior.

He had just turned fifteen and was in his first year of high school. As much as he loved being a part of the Prometheus Project, it was a curse socially. In San Diego he had had numerous close friends. He had played soccer and baseball, and kept up with the latest video games. But now that he spent almost every weekend in Prometheus, he had been forced to give up on these other activities. He was generally well liked and there were a lot of kids he was friendly with at school, but close friends did things together *outside* of school, and he just didn't have the time for that.

Without close friends or any outside activities he could talk about, he knew that if showed off his scientific knowledge too much the other students would classify him as a single-minded nerd, whose only interest was studying. He had never cared about this before, but then again, he had never met the girl of his dreams before, either. Next week he was determined to ask her on a date, so it wasn't such a bad idea to practice being a little more normal, even though his secret life made him anything but.

"Ryan, are you there?" came a telepathic broadcast from his sister.

Okay, thought Ryan, shaking his head, maybe his secret life on the Prometheus team wasn't the *only* thing that made him different. He should probably count the whole, *telepathy with his sister* thing also. He was confident the first few dates with a girl would be okay, but he wondered how long he could keep almost everything about his life hidden before a girl decided he was about as normal as a two-foot elf with a foot growing out of its forehead.

"Yeah," Ryan broadcast back. *"What's up?"*

Ryan and Regan's telepathy stemmed from their interactions with Prometheus's super-advanced central computer, which they had activated during their first adventure within the city. Since they had been inside an alien schoolhouse at the time, the computer had introduced itself simply as the *Teacher*. It had connected with them telepathically, and afterwards they found they could communicate with each other in the same way! Over a range of about fifteen miles. Since this ability was due to their interactions with the Teacher, and they had promised to keep its identity secret, they had decided to keep their telepathy secret as well.

"My teacher just told me that Mom called the front office. She's pulling us out early. She'll be here soon and wants us to meet her at the front desk."

"Any idea why?" asked Ryan as he absently closed his book and began loading up his tan backpack.

"No," answered his sister. *"But who cares? As long as we get to start the weekend early."*

Ryan was about to reply when he realized the mistake he had made. But it was too late. Mr. McPherson's beady eyes had already locked onto his fully loaded backpack like two laser-guided missiles. Ryan groaned. How could he be so stupid?

"Going somewhere, Ryan?" snapped Mr. McPherson.

Ryan decided in a flash his best strategy was to pretend he had no idea what his teacher was talking about. He put a bewildered look on his face and pointed at his own chest as if to say, "Who, me?" when the phone on Mr. McPherson's desk began to ring. The tall chemistry teacher put the receiver to his ear, listened for a short time, and then returned it to its cradle.

Mr. McPherson stared at Ryan long and hard, and then shook his head in disapproval. "That was the office asking me to excuse you from class," he told Ryan. "Which you *obviously* expected," he added, gesturing toward Ryan's fully loaded backpack in disgust while thirty-two thoroughly entertained students looked on in fascination. "Next time, Mr. Resnick, if you know you'll be leaving my class early, I expect you to tell me about it *before* we start. Is that understood?"

Ryan stood up and hoisted his backpack to his shoulder. "Absolutely," he said as he exited the class. "It won't happen again."

He may have recently decided he didn't want his classmates to see him as nothing but a science nerd, but being seen as a troublemaker wasn't exactly what he had in mind either.

As Ryan thought about this he began to laugh at himself. He was taking things far too seriously. It was only school after all. He would find a way to get it right.

Ryan made his way through the hall toward the front office to await his mother's arrival, his mood improving with every step. He had no idea what was in store for him the rest of the day, but he was sure it couldn't be any worse than his morning had been.

CHAPTER 2

Leaving School

The large, old-fashioned circular clock on the wall of the school's front offices read 10:42 as Ryan signed himself out of school. When he finished, he handed the pen to Regan who was standing beside him.

The outer door flew open, but instead of their mother, a girl who was in Ryan's English class, Alyssa Cooper, stepped inside the school's main entrance. She wore jeans, a yellow sweater, and brown flats. She held a small book in one hand and walked toward the front reception area, where Ryan and his sister were now standing. Ryan's heart skipped a beat and his breath shortened. How incredibly lucky! Since he was leaving school early he had thought he wouldn't see her until Monday.

"Hi Ryan," she said cheerfully. Her perfect blond hair hung below her delicate shoulders and bounced slightly as she moved. Her skin was as smooth as silk.

"Hi Alyssa," said Ryan, his green eyes locked on hers. He moved over to let her reach the sign-in sheet, happily breathing the delicate perfume she was wearing.

While she was signing in, Ryan quickly tried to straighten his brown hair with his fingertips, although his hair was so short it was difficult to imagine just how out of place it could possibly ever be. Ryan had undergone a growth spurt recently that had not only added inches to his height but had filled out his thin frame nicely. All in all, he had grown into a confident young man that many would find handsome.

Regan watched her brother's reaction to Alyssa Cooper with utter fascination. Even his stance was more rigid than usual, and he seemed to be tightening his stomach and broadening his chest just slightly. Regan grinned. Now she knew the reason he had started doing pushups every day for the past few months, and flexing his arm muscles in front of mirrors just as regularly.

"You've got a crush on her!" transmitted Regan telepathically while Alyssa finished signing in.

"What are you talking about?" snapped Ryan. *"We may be able to talk telepathically, but you can't read my mind."*

Regan smiled. *"I don't have to. You've got it bad."*

"Could you just stay out of my head right now," he shot back.

"So are you and your sister leaving early?" said Alyssa as she finished her task and returned the pen to the counter.

Ryan nodded. "Yeah. My mom will be here any minute. What about you?"

"Just got back from the dentist," she said with a broad smile that lit up her face and revealed perfect teeth. "No cavities."

"Congratulations," said Ryan.

Alyssa beamed. "Thanks."

The school's main offices were temporarily deserted. The nurse was helping a student who had injured an ankle and the woman who usually manned the reception desk was using the restroom. Principal Lyons was in her office with the door closed. Given this, Alyssa didn't appear to be in any hurry to rush off to her class, which was already in session.

Regan had wandered a few yards away and was pretending to read a brochure on the counter, but Ryan knew she was still listening intently.

"So how long have you liked Alyssa Cooper?" asked Regan.

"Would you leave me alone already!" he yelled into her mind.

Ryan smiled at Alyssa. "So are you starting to like Brewster any better?" he asked. Alyssa had moved from Chicago only four months earlier, and Brewster Pennsylvania took some getting used to. Especially for someone who had come from a big city.

Alyssa attempted a halfhearted smile. "A little." She

paused and then sighed heavily. "Your parents work at Proact, right Ryan?"

"Right," replied Ryan, even though this wasn't—exactly—the truth. Proact was a company established by the government as a cover for the scientists on the Prometheus team. Included within its twenty-acre grounds was the only means of reaching the underground city—an elevator housed within an exceedingly well-protected concrete bunker. In addition to Prometheus scientists, Proact employed top scientists from every field who had no knowledge of the city a mile beneath their feet. These scientists worked on advanced projects using human science and technology.

"Do you ever get to *see* them?" continued Alyssa with a frown.

Ryan titled his head slightly in confusion. "Yeah, why do you ask?"

Alyssa hesitated, and from the expression on her face Ryan could tell she was deciding just how much she should open up to him. Finally she said, "Well, you know my parents are divorced. My sister and I live with our mom and grandmother. But for the past three months we've barely seen my mom. And the few times we have she's been *really* stressed out. You can barely talk to her. I know Proact's a big deal, but is that how your parents were when they first started working there?"

For just a moment, Alyssa's face revealed the true

depth of the anguish behind this question. Ryan suspected her mother was part of Prometheus, not just Proact.

"Regan, do you know if her mom's on the team?" he asked.

"You're kidding me, right?"

"Come on, Regan, the team's growing like crazy and I'm horrible with names."

"You can be such an idiot, Ryan. Not only is she a member of Prometheus, but she works for our mother! How can you not know that?"

"Really?"

"Absolutely."

"Well," said Ryan aloud. "You know there's more important and fascinating work going on at Promethe . . . um . . . at Proact than just about anywhere else in the world. Your mom's probably just excited to be a part of it. She probably finds it almost impossible to leave work. Give her some time. She'll come around."

Alyssa thought about this for a moment. Her grand-mother was suffering through her mom's absences and moody behavior as well, and had told Alyssa and her sister, Kelsey, the same thing Ryan just had. "Yeah, you're probably right," she said, looking hopeful but not entirely convinced. She put her hand on Ryan's arm for just a moment and electricity surged through him. "Thanks Ryan."

There was an awkward silence for several long seconds. Finally, Ryan pointed to the book Alyssa held at her side. "What are you reading?"

She lifted the book to show him. Small pictures of a number of different animals appeared on the cover along with the title, *Classical and Operant Conditioning: Advanced Research Methodologies.*

"Okay then," said Ryan playfully. "Classical and operant conditioning: advanced research methodologies. Good choice. I mean, I almost picked that one up at the bookstore the other day." He grinned broadly. "But I decided to wait for the movie."

Alyssa laughed, a sound that was like music to Ryan's ears.

"Actually, it's for a Science Fair project I'm working on," she explained, wincing just a little, hoping Ryan wouldn't think she was a total geek.

"That's great," said Ryan enthusiastically. He paused in thought. "Didn't I hear that you went the furthest of anyone in Chicago in the Science Fair competition last year?"

Alyssa brightened, surprised he had known this. "Well," she responded almost shyly. "I got lucky."

Ryan smiled. This girl just got more and more awesome every single day. She was smart, but also modest. She was friendly to everyone and had an easy, infectious smile that brought a sparkle to her eyes and could light up an entire room. Most importantly, she wasn't the least bit fake, which is something he couldn't stand. He had never liked a girl *nearly* this much before.

"I'm hoping to do really well this year too," she continued. "Since there's nothing else for me to do here in Brewster, I've been spending a ton of time on the project. My sister Kelsey is helping me."

An idea burst into Ryan's head. Maybe this was his chance to be with Alyssa outside of school; to have something in *common* with her; something to talk about that wasn't classified. He might have to postpone asking her on a date for a few weeks, but so what? He had already waited *this* long. "You know, maybe I can help too," he offered eagerly. "I don't have a lot of time, so I wouldn't want to be an official member of the team, but I know classical and operant conditioning really well."

Actually, while he remembered that Regan had discussed this subject with their mother a few months ago, he hadn't listened to a word, and he knew absolutely nothing about it. If Alyssa took him up on his offer he would have to learn very quickly. But as he gazed into her soft blue eyes he knew it would be more than worth it.

"I was thinking of doing a project in this area myself last year," he added.

"*You liar,*" broadcast Regan, still pretending she was reading. "*You were never thinking of doing a Science Fair project last year. And you don't know anything about the subject.*"

"Get out of my head!" insisted Ryan. *"And stay out!"*

"Really. That is so cool!" said Alyssa. "No one else I've talked to even knows what classical and operant conditioning *are*. What's your favorite experiment?" she asked excitedly.

Ryan's outer expression remained calm, but inside he was panicking. He didn't know enough to even guess at an answer.

"Regan, help!" he pleaded.

"I thought you wanted me out of your head," she replied with a grin.

"Hmmm," said Ryan aloud, stalling for time. "Let me think about that for a second."

"I'll give you two dollars," offered Ryan.

"Ten."

"Five," broadcast Ryan frantically. *"It's all I have."*

"Done," agreed Regan. *"Tell her Pavlov's Dog is still your favorite, because it started the entire field."*

Ryan had no idea what Regan was talking about, but he had no other choice but to trust her. He tilted his head and smiled at Alyssa. "There have been so many fascinating experiments done in the field," he said. "But I would have to say Pavlov's Dog is still my favorite, because this really started it all."

Alyssa nodded. "I get why you would say that one," she said. "But my favorite—"

She stopped in mid-sentence as the door to the principal's office began to creak open.

"Better go," she said and rushed off to her class.

Just as Alyssa was out of sight, Ryan and Regan's mother entered the school and greeted them warmly. Regan looked more and more like her mom with every passing year. Both were petite, with soft, attractive features, and bright, expressive eyes. While Mrs. Resnick's hair was brown and relatively short, Regan had long, vibrant hair that had darkened from a reddish-blond to a reddish-brown. Unlike her brother, Regan hadn't grown in over a year, and now seemed unlikely to reach five feet tall. She had a delicate bone structure that matched her small size, and those who didn't know her were always surprised by the enormity of energy, personality, and intellect contained within her slender, eighty-pound frame.

The kids lifted their backpacks to their shoulders, preparing to leave, when the school's principal, Lynda Lions, exited her office and hurried over to them.

"Good afternoon, Principal Lyons," said their mother.

"Good afternoon, Dr. Resnick," said the principal. She knew that Ryan and Regan's parents had both earned a Ph.D.—which stood for Doctor of Philosophy—their mother in biology and their father in physics. They had earned the right to be called *Doctor* every bit as much as had medical doctors, and Principal Lyons insisted on using their proper titles even though she knew they didn't care. Perhaps if they were prouder of their accomplishments their kids wouldn't be such underachievers.

"I see you're pulling Ryan and Regan out early again," said Principal Lyons disapprovingly.

Mrs. Resnick nodded.

"I certainly don't mean to judge," she said, and all three Resnicks knew that was *exactly* what she was doing. "But Ryan and Regan's attendance record is the worst in the entire school."

Amanda Resnick raised her eyebrows. *"Really?"* she said, almost with a touch of amusement. "Ahh . . . sorry about that. I hope their grades haven't suffered," she finished innocently.

The principal's frown deepened. "Well, they both get A's, that's true. But A minuses. The lowest A minuses possible—just a hair above B plusses. It's as if they've worked out how to do the absolute minimum to get low A's."

The principal had seen the siblings' standardized test scores and they were both off-the-charts bright—not entirely surprising when considering their parents were both world-class scientists. Bright students were at an epidemic in Brewster, Pennsylvania. The school and the town only existed because of the Proact research facility, after all, and even those Proact employees who weren't brilliant scientists believed passionately in the value of education.

But as talented as many of the students were, none tested as well as Ryan and Regan Resnick. None. And yet numerous students outperformed these two siblings in class. The principal had spoken with the kids the year before about finding a passion and working to their potential but apparently this had not done much good.

"I just think they're capable of a lot more," said Principal Lyons. "And I don't think missing all these classes helps matters, either," she added.

Amanda Resnick fought off the instinctive urge to defend herself. In normal circumstances the principal would have been right. She just didn't know that the kids were being exposed to far greater learning opportunities as part of the Prometheus Project than any school could possibly offer.

"I appreciate your concern, Principal Lyons," said Mrs. Resnick pleasantly, making her way to the door with her kids in tow. "I'll try to limit their absences in the future," she added in a tone that made it clear she had no time, and no interest, in further discussion.

The principal watched the three Resnicks rush through the door and shook her head. She had long ago decided there was something not quite right about this family. But for the life of her she couldn't put her finger on just what this something might be.

CHAPTER 3

Isis

Mrs. Resnick had parked the family car, a boring blue four-door sedan, along the curb at the entrance to the school. It was desperately in need of a bath, but the adult members of the family kept so busy inside Prometheus they rarely found enough time to even send it through an automatic car-wash. As they approached the car, Ryan pulled a crumpled five-dollar bill from his pocket and held it behind his back so his sister could see it but not his mom. She snatched it from his hand, her green eyes shining happily. "*Nice doing business with you, Ryan,*" she thought at him, amused.

Ryan took the passenger's seat while his sister slid into the back.

"Guess what, Mom?" said Regan excitedly. "Kimberly Grimm got a new cell phone today. It's *really* cool."

Mrs. Resnick sighed loudly as the car growled to life

and they began to roll forward. Regan seemed to find a new way to introduce the subject of cell phones almost every week. "I thought kids weren't allowed to bring their cell phones to school."

"Well . . . not technically. But it was brand new," said Regan, as if this explained everything. "And she was very careful to only show it to her friends when none of the teachers were around." Regan removed an elastic tie from her hair. "But here's the thing. Kimberly told me I could have her old one if I erased its memory and changed out the number."

"Regan, how many times do I have to tell you? You're not getting a cell phone for two more months. The cost has nothing to do with it. You know that."

"How can you not see how unfair you're being?" complained Regan. "Just because Ryan didn't get a phone until he was fourteen shouldn't mean I have to wait that long."

"You're not," said her mother. "We've compromised a lot already, so stop pretending you don't know that. In two months you won't even be to thirteen-and-a-half. Barely thirteen-and-a-quarter."

"But why start with the age Ryan got one and then compromise from there? If it wasn't for him, you'd get me one *now*. Ryan didn't *care* if he had a phone when he was twelve or thirteen. I do. We're *different*. He never asked you to buy him a dress, either, but that didn't stop you for buying *me* one. Besides, Ryan's already told you he's okay with me getting a phone at a younger age than he did."

"Regan, I'm not having this conversation again."

"Mom, you'll let me use Qwervy technology that's thousands of years more advanced than ours, but you won't let me use Earth technology that *everybody* uses. I just don't get it. Do you know that I'm the only kid in my entire class without a cell phone?"

"I doubt that," said her mother with just a hint of amusement. "But even if you're right, so what? You're unique."

Mrs. Resnick knew that her daughter's arguments were stronger than hers, but she and her husband had decided it wasn't good for their children to always get everything they wanted the instant they wanted it. Besides, they had already moved the date in by almost a year.

"So I'm old enough to be on the Prometheus Project," said Regan, trying yet another angle of attack. "I'm old enough to meet the President of the United States. But I'm not old enough to have a cell phone?"

Her mother smiled and shook her head. "Regan, you are the most relentless human being I have ever known," she said, although there was more approval in her tone than criticism. "Your father and I have made our decision. It's only two more months, which will fly by. Besides, you can't use cell phones at school and you can't get reception inside Prometheus, so it isn't like you're giving up all that much."

Regan was about to reply, but Ryan jumped in first. "As much as I would love to listen to this same old argument forever," he said sarcastically to his mother beside him, "I'd kind of like to know why you took us out early."

His mother nodded, glad for a change of topic. "Because it's Friday and we need to get a jump on things," she replied, turning onto a road that cut through the heart of a woods, one that had only recently been paved. "I know you and your sister have been dying to see the Enigma Cube," she continued. "Well, your father has finally decided that being in the same room with it is safe. As long as you don't get so close that you might accidentally touch it. So this is your chance."

"Awesome," said Ryan happily.

The team had discovered the bizarre cube a few months earlier, but their father was terrified of it. He didn't know what it was, but his instincts told him that it had the potential to be the most dangerous alien object they had yet discovered.

"I'll take you there once we're inside Prometheus," said Mrs. Resnick. "But there's no time to waste. At 1:00 your father and I are leading a group off-planet, with plans to stay for the weekend."

Ryan and Regan had discovered a small building inside Prometheus that served as a galactic zoo. Small though it was, it contained numerous doors, or portals, that each led to a different primitive planet. The kids had learned that the Qwervy only allowed visitors on planets that didn't contain intelligent life. Force-field barriers, similar to the shield that surrounded Prometheus but far smaller, completely surrounded the portal entrances on each planet. These served to protect visitors from dangerous animals, but a tram could be used to cross the force-fields to explore.

"So is Grandma coming to stay with us this weekend?" said Ryan in disappointment. He loved his grandmother, but if she was taking care of them they couldn't spend any time inside the city since she wasn't in on the secret.

"Nope," said Mrs. Resnick cheerfully, having hoped they would jump to this conclusion so she could surprise them. "Actually"—she glanced at her unsuspecting kids and raised her eyebrows—"we've decided to let you come *with* us."

"*Really?*" said Regan excitedly, immediately forgetting all about the injustice of not having a cell phone. She and Ryan were always pushing to go on extended field-trips to other planets, but their parents had only ever let them go off-planet for four or five hours at a time, and only while heavily supervised.

"I wouldn't kid you about something like that."

"Fantastic!" said Ryan. "Thanks, Mom." He scratched his head in confusion. "But I don't get it. Why didn't you tell us about this *before* we left for school?"

"We had planned to leave tomorrow, and we were going to surprise you with the news tonight."

"So what changed?" asked Regan.

"When we got here this morning and began to think about everything we wanted to accomplish on the trip, we realized we needed more time. By leaving just after lunch we'll give ourselves an entire extra day."

"Great!" said Regan. "The longer we have the better. So what planet are we going to?"

"Isis."

Regan tilted her head in thought. "Isis? Isn't that the planet where Carl was almost killed by a native animal?" she asked. Colonel Carl Sharp was the head of Prometheus security and someone with whom the kids had become very close.

Her mom hesitated and then blew out a long breath. "That's the one," she replied finally, and while she said it in a casual tone suggesting this didn't trouble her, the haunted look in her eye communicated something very different.

"So what *did* happen to Carl anyway?" asked Regan, now more intrigued than ever. "You never really told us. All you would ever say was that he had a close call."

Mrs. Resnick hesitated as she struggling to decide just how to answer this question. "Well, it's not a pretty story," she said finally. "But I suppose if you're going to be on Isis you have a right to be told," she added, clearly not happy about it.

There was a long silence in the car.

"Well?" prompted Ryan. "Are you going to tell us?"

"Yes, Ryan. I was just trying to decide where to begin." His mother sighed. "First, let me give you some background on the planet. We started studying it about six months ago. Isis has been shaped by numerous active volcanoes; with regions of lush rainforest right next to barren areas littered with lava rock. Very much like Hawaii."

They were now driving under a thick canopy of autumn leaves that extended over the road: leaves that had changed into a beautiful assortment of colors but had not yet begun to fall.

"The planet is teeming with animal life. Most of the species are either mammal-like or reptile-like, and while many of them are strikingly different from anything on Earth, they tend to share many general similarities with our animal life. Two or four legs. Same general body structures. A dozen different types of light-sensing organs, mostly in the form of simple or compound eyes. Numerous styles of mouths, claws, tentacles, ears, fur, scales, what have you. With one notable exception: we couldn't find evidence of an olfactory sense."

Regan wrinkled her forehead in thought. She remembered olfactory meant smell. "You mean none of them have noses?"

"Well, many of them don't. Some have noses that serve as a second breathing passage. But we're pretty sure they can't smell anything with them. We went right up to some of the species—the ones *with* noses—and opened vials of everything from onion to concentrated skunk spray. Nothing. We didn't try it with the ones that didn't have noses. Perhaps some of these can smell with their tongues like snakes, or through some other mechanism. But it's also very possible that the sense of smell just never evolved anywhere on the planet."

"How can that be?" asked Ryan. "Doesn't that make it tougher for them to survive?"

"You would think so, but apparently not. A dog can sense an odor at concentrations millions of times lower than a human can. So compared to a dog, *we* don't have a sense of smell. And a dog's hearing is far better than ours as well. Every species has their own set of senses that works for them. If an animal on Isis had a combination of senses that left them at too much of a disadvantage, they would have gone extinct. Evolution can be cruel."

Regan was fascinated by evolution and had recently made the decision to become a biologist like her mother. Evolution didn't explain everything about Earth's biosphere, but it was astonishingly simple and did explain a lot. If, because of a mutation, an animal was lucky enough to be born with a trait that would help it survive—like better eyesight or greater strength—it would live to pass this trait on to its offspring. If it was unlucky enough to be born with a trait that hampered its survival, it would not live long enough to pass it on.

Cruel indeed, but also awesomely powerful in perfecting a hawk's vision or a cheetah's speed.

"We have five senses," continued Mrs. Resnick. "Taste, smell, hearing, sight, and touch. I wouldn't be—"

"What about the sixth sense?" interrupted Ryan impishly. "Seeing dead people."

"Very funny, Ryan," said his mom.

"I don't get it?" said Regan.

"That's because you've never seen the movie," said Ryan. "I guess you have to be old enough to own a cell phone," he teased.

Regan leaned forward and punched her brother in the arm, which only made the grin on his face grow wider.

"As I was about to say," continued their mother, her tone serious once again, "I wouldn't be surprised if the animals of Isis rely on other senses that we aren't familiar with."

"Like what?" asked Regan.

Mrs. Resnick shrugged. "It's hard to know without further study. Bats use sound waves to locate objects and navigate. Sharks can sense electricity. Certain birds can sense the Earth's magnetic field. We've discovered a number of animals on Pegasus Four that can sense radio waves. There are bound to be dozens of other senses we can't even guess at. I suspect that during the early history of life on Isis, another sense that helped animals in their struggle to survive came along before smell, and this other sense was perfected at smell's expense."

They arrived at the guardhouse just before the Proact parking lot and Mrs. Resnick stopped the car. A guard checked their badges and then waved them through.

"I visited the planet several times with different groups of biologists," continued their mother. "And a member or two of security as well, of course, as Carl insists whenever we go off-planet. The planet has more than its share of predators, so at first we took extreme precautions. We didn't leave the tram, or if we did we took the portable force-field generator that your dad's team developed."

Mrs. Resnick pulled into a reserved parking space and killed the engine. No one made any move to leave the car.

"But the strangest thing happened," she continued. "The wildlife ignored us. I mean *completely*. As if we didn't exist. After a while we got comfortable walking among the most lethal predators without the slightest fear. We experimented and it soon became clear that they could see and hear us, they just didn't care."

"That *is* weird," said Ryan.

"It still doesn't make any sense to me. On every other planet we've visited the predators either hold their ground or try to attack us. And the prey animals run from us. It's the most unusual thing I've ever experienced." She shrugged. "Anyway, the last time we visited

Isis was three months ago. Carl was providing security, and I took three other biologists, Bob Zubrin, Eric Morris, and Michelle Cooper."

Ryan's eyes widened. The woman he knew as Michelle, who worked for his mom, was Michelle *Cooper*. Alyssa's *mother*. Regan was right. He *was* an idiot.

"Are you kidding me," he complained to his sister. *"Michelle is Alyssa's mom! Why did it have to be her? She pretends to be nice but I get a strong feeling she hates my guts."*

"She probably thinks kids shouldn't be part of the team," replied Regan. *"She doesn't like me, either. Then again,"* she added with a laugh, *"at least I don't have a thing for her daughter."*

Regan's laugh interrupted her mother in mid sentence. "What's so funny, Regan?" she said with an annoyed look on her face.

"Uh . . . nothing. Sorry Mom. My mind wandered for a second. Can you repeat that?"

"As I was *saying,*" continued Mrs. Resnick in a tone that made it clear she wasn't happy about Regan failing to pay attention to a story *she* had asked to hear. "Once we arrived on Isis, we took a tram out about a mile from the portal. Eric and I began observing a powerful predator that looked like a combination between a bear and a T. Rex. Michelle took up a position lying on the ground to observe a two-legged creature, with a neck longer than a giraffe, rip fruit from a tall tree. She was surrounded by orange lava rocks and even had her feet resting on one of the larger ones. Carl was near Michelle, keeping an eye out for trouble."

Their mother had been relaxed while she spoke about the planet and its wildlife, but she was now visibly tense. She swallowed hard. "I walked over to ask Carl a question but he didn't see me," she said. "He was watching something in the distance and he decided to jump on a lava rock, about the size of a truck tire, to get a better view."

Mrs. Resnick blew out a breath. "Only it wasn't a lava rock," she said with a visible shudder. "It was a deadly predator! Perfectly disguised and lying on its back. Carl's weight crushed its chest cavity. But it still managed to bite Carl's calf with a set of long, razor sharp teeth and then pull like a crocodile. The force of the bite and the strength of its jaws were *incredible*. Carl screamed in surprise and agony—a scream I'll never forget."

Mrs. Resnick stared straight ahead for several seconds and then continued, almost in a whisper. "The lower part of Carl's leg was fractured and a good part of his calf muscle was torn from the bone."

Their mother spared them a description of the blood that must have gushed or maybe even sprayed from Carl's wound, but this didn't prevent these vivid images from appearing in Ryan and Regan's minds anyway. Neither could keep their upper lips from curling up in disgust as they envisioned the attack.

"How horrible for him," said Regan earnestly.

Mrs. Resnick nodded solemnly in agreement. "At that moment I thought for sure Carl was dead."

She paused in thought, as though she were considered the incident from several different angles. "It all happened so fast," she said finally. "Almost in the blink of an eye. We had run across this same species many times before, but never in its camouflaged state. They were magnificent mimics. We had no idea they could make themselves into absolutely perfect replicas of lava rocks. When we had interacted with them, they had ignored us, like all life on Isis." She shook her head miserably. "We got careless. *I* got careless."

"Mom, there was nothing you could have done," insisted Ryan, realizing that as the leader of the expedition his mother still felt responsible for what had happened.

She nodded grimly, as if she wanted to agree with him but wasn't quite convinced.

"But go on," prompted Ryan eagerly. "How did Carl get away?"

An amused look crossed Mrs. Resnick's face as she realized just how poor of a place she had chosen to stop her narrative, but her expression quickly darkened as she prepared to resume. "How did Carl get away?" she repeated. "Well, the animal that was ripping his leg to shreds died almost immediately from having its chest crushed. But even in death its jaws refused to unlock. Still, Carl somehow managed to pry them open—which was remarkable considering that all the blood had made Carl's hands slippery and he had lost a lot of strength."

Mrs. Resnick shook her head. "Not that that was the end of it," she added. "Just before Carl freed himself, four other animals we had thought were lava rocks suddenly sprang to life. Including one that Michelle was touching! She had had her feet resting on it for twenty minutes. That's how harmless they were. But not anymore. Reacting to Carl's perceived attack on their companion, they attacked back. Michelle jerked her legs away from the animal just as its jaws snapped down on where they had been resting. If she had been just one second slower in reacting she would have lost them both. She jumped to her feet and scrambled away as fast as she could. Carl followed, although how he managed to get away after losing so much blood and having one of his legs turned into hamburger I'll never know."

"Did the animals go after them?" asked Ryan.

"Oh yes. All four of the remaining creatures did. Like enraged lions. And they didn't just go after Carl and Michelle but after all of us." Mrs. Resnick paused. "As you might imagine, we raced for the tram. Luckily, it was only thirty yards away. We were about to reach safety when Carl turned and shot all of the animals behind us, one after the other." Strangely, instead of sounding grateful for this act of courage on Carl's part her tone was one of disgust. "He killed them all," she finished accusingly.

Ryan and Regan exchanged a confused glance. "Isn't that a *good* thing?" asked Regan for them both.

Mrs. Resnick shook her head. "No. Because it wasn't necessary. Carl said if he hadn't shot them they would have killed us. But he's wrong. The first two, maybe. But the last two had backed off after the shots. There is no way they could have reached us in time. He killed those out of pure revenge," she added, severe disapproval in her voice.

Ryan's eyes narrowed. He and Regan were extremely fond of the head of security. "Maybe you're right about Carl," said Ryan. "Maybe he didn't need to shoot them. But what if *Carl* was right? In that case, he saved your lives."

She shook her head. "No, he was out of line. I'm sure of it."

"Don't you think you're being a little hard on him, Mom?" said Ryan.

His mother didn't answer for several long seconds. "Maybe," she admitted. "It's complicated. It wasn't the creatures' fault they attacked us. We started it, after all. Yes, I know they were only unintelligent animals. As a biologist I have a great appreciation for life, but you know I'm not a vegetarian, and I've done research that has resulted in the deaths of scores of rodents over the years. But the deaths of those two animals on Isis were *senseless*. They were backing off and we were almost in the clear. Carl didn't kill them in the name of research, or food, or clothing. He just killed them out of hatred. Out of revenge." She paused. "I just thought Carl was better than that."

Ryan remained silent, unsure of how to respond. The parked car had become stuffy so Mrs. Resnick gave the key a half-turn and powered the windows down a few inches. Cool autumn air entered the car along with the scent of fallen leaves.

"Wait a minute," said Regan, changing the subject. "We saw Carl fairly soon after this happened. His leg seemed fine."

"We got him back to Prometheus and to a surgeon fairly quickly," said Mrs. Resnick. "And I hunted down a Med-Pen and used it on him within twenty minutes of our return."

The Prometheus team had found three of these amazing alien medical devices a year before in one of the Prometheus buildings. Cigar-shaped and resembling bloated pens, they could provide complete pain relief and perform other medical miracles such as speeding wound healing and eradicating infections. Another remarkable feature of these alien devices was that their colors and patterns changed instantly whenever they were moved. Not to match their surroundings, but to do the opposite: to stand out in sharp contrast to whatever they were near. How this was accomplished was still unknown, but the designers of these life saving devices had clearly wanted to make them easy to locate at all times, even in a clutter. The team had kept one Med-Pen to study and voted to give the other two to its two youngest members whenever they were in the city. The Resnick siblings had spent many an hour whisking the devices past different objects and watching in fascination as they changed instantly, trying to guess the counter-color and counter-pattern the devices would adopt.

"It didn't heal him instantly, of course," continued their mother, "although doctors agree that without it he would have *never* healed properly. But miraculously, because of the Med-Pen, Carl healed in only a few weeks. Completely and perfectly. Those devices are truly amazing. He wasn't even scarred." She considered this further and then shook her head. "At least not physically," she added gravely.

CHAPTER 4

Collision Course

Mrs. Resnick powered the windows back up and they exited the car, each lost in their own thoughts. Mrs. Resnick's mood remained somber, but she began to snap out of it at the first security checkpoint—drawn out by the guards who, as usual, chatted pleasantly with her and the kids while they worked. The guards carefully inspected Ryan and Regan's backpacks and let them pass.

Six weeks earlier, the Med-Pen the team was studying went missing for a day. While it had only been misplaced, security had been stepped up. Now, team members were scanned and backpacks checked on the way *out* of Prometheus as well as in, to make sure no one left with an alien object, purposely or accidentally. Security had also installed a number of sensors that were keyed to detect chemical, material, or energy signatures that were out of the ordinary. This made it even more difficult to sneak anything of alien origin by the guards.

They next entered a structure called the decoy building. It was nothing but a shell that had been built around the reinforced concrete bunker that housed the Prometheus elevator. The decoy building looked normal from the outside. Its spacious lobby even had a reception desk and a receptionist, so anyone from Proact who entered the building by mistake would not be suspicious. But anyone who wasn't part of the Prometheus Project would find it easier to break into Fort Knox than to get beyond the reception desk.

They passed though several additional checkpoints, provided additional passwords, and had their fingerprints and retinas scanned electronically. Finally, after ten minutes, they entered the massive Prometheus elevator, slightly larger than a three-car garage and several stories high. Their mother was upbeat by nature and her mood had now fully returned to normal.

"After what happened to Carl," broadcast Ryan as the elevator began its long descent, *"I can't believe Mom and Dad are letting us go with them."*

"Me either. But whatever you do, don't say anything about it and jinx us."

"You two really owe me for this, by the way," said their mother as if reading their minds. "Dad was originally against you coming with us."

"Really?" said Regan, as if she couldn't imagine anyone being so unreasonable.

"Really. I was finally able to convince him that Isis was safer than most of the planets we've let you visit, despite what happened to Carl. I reminded him that I've been on Isis eleven times before this tragic incident and I never got as much as a scratch, and not a single animal ever paid us the slightest attention—including the species that could disguise themselves as lava rocks. I pointed out that the few individuals from this species that finally did react to us only did so because Carl crushed one of them—and none of these survived to hold a grudge."

"Sounds safe to me," agreed Regan enthusiastically.

"Well, as safe as any primitive planet can ever be, I suppose. But even so, we'll be taking precautions. We're bringing a portable force-field generator, just in case. And the guards going with us will have guns—this time filled with tranquilizer darts," she added pointedly, intent on ensuring that no further senseless killing of Isis wildlife would be possible, regardless of the provocation. "But *whatever* you do," she instructed her children firmly, "*don't* step on any lava rocks."

Ryan rolled his eyes. "Thanks, Mom," he said sarcastically. "If you hadn't warned us just now that would have been the first thing I did."

At last the elevator stopped and they stepped off into a massive, manmade cavern, the size of a baseball stadium, illuminated by powerful electric lights and filled with machinery and high-tech equipment. They said a warm hello to two heavily armed guards, both dressed casually. Carl had not wanted Prometheus turned into a military base and insisted the members of his security team not wear uniforms or use military titles. In fact, everyone on the team used first names with each other, decorated colonels and Nobel Prize winning chemists alike. Dr. Harris was the only exception, despite his objections, because he was the head of the entire project.

They entered the city through a rainbow-colored section of the force-field wall their father had managed to hold open with a furious onslaught of precisely tuned energy.

"So is Dad just coming to keep us company?" asked Regan.

"Actually, it's *his* expedition. I decided to go and bring along some of my staff to keep *him* company." Amanda and Ben Resnick were among the first few members of the Prometheus Project and had recruited dozens of scientists who now worked for them.

"I don't get it," said Regan. "You're the one who studies alien life. What does a physicist want with a primitive planet?"

"Isis is about 25,000 light years away. Less than 900 light years from a massive black hole in the center of our galaxy."

A light year was the distance light could travel in a year. And since light was insanely fast, screaming along at 670 million miles per hour, 25,000 light years was some *serious* distance. Einstein had shown that nothing in the universe could travel faster than light—but obviously the Qwervy had found ways to circumvent this rule with their portals.

"According to your father, when stars are sucked into black holes and annihilated, X-rays are emitted into space. He's calculated that the X-rays from one of these events that happened many, many years ago will be close enough to Isis for him to measure sometime tomorrow or Sunday. He says this data has the potential to greatly enhance our understanding of black holes. He'll set up the equipment tonight, and baby-sit it for the rest of the weekend to make sure nothing goes wrong." Mrs. Resnick shook her head and an amused smile crossed her face. "He's pretty excited about it."

"Who wouldn't be?" teased Regan, unable to keep a straight face.

Her mother's smile broadened. "Since the animal life on Isis is so interesting," she continued, "and since I haven't had time to return since the incident, I thought we could make it a family outing. With a few others along for the ride. It'll be fun."

The familiar rows of fast, oversized electric-powered golf-carts were parked beside the entrance along with a half dozen electric trucks. The trucks were huge, with expansive cargo beds. They were called *Haulers* by the team since they were used to haul heavy scientific equipment around Prometheus. Despite their size their electric engines were almost whisper quiet. The trio jumped into a large golf-cart at the end of the row. This time Regan took the front seat next to their mother while Ryan took the back.

They drove past buildings that shimmered and others that changed colors depending on the angle from which they were viewed. Buildings that appeared to be floating and others that sparkled brilliantly as though made of diamonds. The city was magnificent. No matter how often the kids visited they continued to find it awe-inspiring.

Several minutes later their mother stopped the cart in front of a four-story building in the shape of a complex three-dimensional snowflake. "I need to speak with Lou Holmgren," she announced. "Wait here. This should only take a few minutes. Then we'll go see the Enigma Cube."

As they waited, one of the buildings off in the distance began changing shape, something that was always fun to watch. They exited the cart and walked toward one edge of the snowflake building to get a better view.

"Hold on," said Regan when they were ten feet from the building's edge. "I need to tie my shoe." She knelt down to begin tying.

Ryan turned toward her to ask her a question.

And then a low hum hit his ears. The hum from a Hauler!

Ryan's heart jumped to his throat! He turned back

around just in time to see a massive runaway Hauler shoot around the corner of the building. It was headed right for them!

The driver—a scientist who had been working around the clock for days—had fallen asleep at the wheel. Ryan absorbed the entire situation in an instant, but it was too late.

Before he could begin to warn his sister or launch himself out of the way, the twelve-ton vehicle was on them.

Ryan didn't even have time to close his eyes as the Hauler slammed into his chest.

CHAPTER 5

The Enigma Cube

The exact instant the Hauler made contact with Ryan's sweatshirt, he felt a powerful force acting on his body that he couldn't possibly describe, threatening to pull him apart. And then the driver's face was less than a foot in front of him.

Impossible! The front of the Hauler should have crushed his chest and thrown him under the tires already.

Even more impossible, he could see inside the driver's *face*!

Ryan could clearly see his brain, a three-pound mass of wrinkly material. He could see the backs of his eyeballs; huge orbs set into his skull, riddled with a complex network of blood vessels. And he could see inside of the blood vessels as well. And inside of the individual cells that made up the blood. And he could see through the truck to the driver's chest, and through this to his heart, and through this to his cells. He could see all of this in a single instant, and knew that his mind couldn't hold it all in and would soon become overloaded.

And then the truck was past him! Instantly his vision returned to normal.

With a start, the driver of the Hauler awakened and jerked the wheel to straighten the vehicle. Realizing he had dozed off for several seconds, he shook himself awake and drove on, completely unaware he had just hit two kids.

Only he hadn't. He had passed right through them.

Ryan felt faint and dropped to a sitting position on the ground next to Regan as the Hauler receded in the distance. Both were now white as ghosts—which is apparently what they and the truck had become.

"How can we be alive?" said Regan, her heart pounding thunderously in her ears. "I looked up and the Hauler was on us. We didn't have a chance."

Ryan nodded. "Just as it hit us, it became transparent somehow." He paused. "No, that's not the word for it. It became, I don't know—not solid. Like a cloud or something. I think we did too."

Regan nodded her agreement. "It was *so* freaky. I could see inside the tires. And inside the front hood—I could see the engine. And *inside* the engine. Somehow we and the truck passed right through each other."

Both kids looked down and pressed on their arms

and stomachs, half expecting their hands to pass through their bodies.

"Well, we're solid enough now," said Ryan. "And the truck became solid again once it passed us." He shuddered as the memory of the massive steel Hauler bearing down on him replayed itself in his mind. Never before had he felt so totally helpless and so certain that he had taken his last breath.

"That was like some kind of miracle," said Regan, shaking her head in disbelief.

"Yeah," said Ryan, nodding thoughtfully. "It was." The slightest of smiles played over his face as he reached an inescapable conclusion. "So who do we know that can pull off miracles?"

The answer came to Regan immediately. "The Teacher," she whispered, her eyes widening. Of course! The city's central computer—so advanced it made a human supercomputer seem like a primitive adding machine. There could be no doubt it had saved them from certain death.

"*Thanks,*" broadcast Regan to the Teacher with as much power as she could.

There was no reply, which didn't really surprise them.

The existence of the Qwervy's observation post was *supposed* to remain a secret, off limits to humans and aliens alike. When the Qwervy discovered that humans had managed to find and enter their city, they considered expelling them and erasing their memories. While the Qwervy thought humanity was very promising, they knew the species had a dark and dangerous side it needed to master. They finally decided to let the team remain, but would not allow the Teacher to have any further contact with Ryan or Regan or help the team in any way. The human race would be on its own. The Qwervy wanted to see if humans could learn from the city's technology rather than destroy themselves with it. Humanity had thrown itself into deep water, and now it was time to see if the species would sink or swim. Only Ryan and Regan knew the exact nature of the Qwervy's decision and that they were keeping tabs on the team.

Ryan scratched his head. "This had to have been the Teacher's doing, all right, but I still don't get it. It's under orders not to help us. Call me crazy, but doesn't saving our lives count as helping us?"

Regan thought about this for a moment. "Maybe not. I mean, it *did* help us, but I think the idea was it wasn't supposed to help us if we got into trouble while messing around with Qwervy technology. We're supposed to be on our own with that. If we decide to play with fire and burn ourselves, that's our problem. But being hit by a runaway Hauler? Come on—that has nothing to do with how we use their technology. I bet that's why it saved us."

"Whatever the reason," said Ryan, "I'm not complaining." He paused. "At least we've figured out *who* saved us. *How* the Teacher did it is another story. We'll probably never know that."

"Dad might know what happened," said Regan hopefully. "You know, come up with some kind of weird physics theory."

"You think we should tell him?"

"Yes!" said Regan emphatically. "Why wouldn't we?"

Ryan considered. At first, harboring important secrets like the Prometheus Project and their telepathy had been fun, but this had quickly become a burden they were very tired of carrying. "I can think of a reason," he said finally, not looking at all happy about it. "If we told him what happened, we'd also have to tell him about the Teacher—about the Qwervy monitoring the team. We promised the Teacher we wouldn't do that." Ryan didn't know what would happen if they broke this promise, but he didn't want to risk finding out. He wouldn't be surprised if the Qwervy changed their mind and refused to allow them to explore the abandoned city any further.

"We wouldn't *have* to tell him about the Teacher and the Qwervy," said Regan.

"Yes we would. In the end we would. Dad's not stupid. He would know the timing couldn't be a coincidence. What are the odds of us turning into ghosts the exact instant the truck was about to hit us? Dad would figure out we're being monitored pretty fast—it's the only conclusion that makes any sense."

"We could lie and tell him it just happened out of the blue."

Ryan thought about this. He wondered if his father would even believe them. Solid objects just didn't become non-solid. That was even more impossible than the other impossible stuff they had seen. Heck, *he* almost didn't believe it, and it had happened to *him*. But this wasn't even the issue. "I don't think we should risk it, Regan," he replied at last. "Whatever the Teacher did to save our lives, it probably *shouldn't* have. It may have used an ability the Qwervy don't want humans to know about. I think we should keep this to ourselves."

Regan's eyes glistened as if she was holding back tears and severe disappointment was written all over her face. After having looked certain death in the eye her emotions were running high. Ryan knew exactly how she felt.

"I'm really sorry, Regan," he said softly, putting his hand on her shoulder. "I hate the idea of keeping this secret as much as you do."

They sat in silence for several minutes, each reflecting on their traumatic experience and trying to get their nerves back under control.

Mrs. Resnick emerged from the building and walked over to them, wondering why they had decided to plop themselves on the ground at this particular spot. Her eyebrows came together quizzically. "Having a picnic," she said. She looked more closely at them. "Are you two okay? You look pale."

After staring death in the face, Regan didn't doubt it. "We're fine, Mom," she said, barely managing to fake a smile. "Must just be the lighting."

Ryan rose unsteadily from the ground and gestured toward the cart. "What are we waiting for?" he said, although with more weariness than enthusiasm. "Let's go see the Enigma Cube."

Five minutes later they parked the cart near a cylinder-shaped building with a surface as reflective as the finest mirrors on Earth. They watched themselves approach. The curved wall of the building distorted their reflections like a funhouse mirror. As they neared an opening appeared in the seamless structure and then disappeared once they were inside.

The floor was made from a smooth, polished material, pure white in color, that was one of several dozen building materials the Qwervy seemed to favor. It was similar in many ways to marble, only much harder. There were concentric rings etched into the floor spreading out from the center of the building, which had about as much space inside as a large gymnasium. The far wall was totally transparent, providing a massive window onto the sprawling city. Three foot by three foot cubes were sprinkled throughout the room and holographic projections, often used by the aliens as controls, appeared at different locations. The cubes were alien chairs, and would instantly reform themselves around any body type to provide unmatched comfort.

"Dad says this room is as perfect a circle as anyone has ever measured," said their mom as they walked toward its center.

The small alien artifact sat on the floor at the precise center of the room. The trio approached it carefully and crouched down to get a better view.

It was every bit as astounding as the kids had been told.

It had an outer shell of edges linked together to form an open, cubical cage, about the size of a Rubik's cube. Small indentations appeared at even intervals along this outer cage, possibly controls of some kind. It didn't have a color, but it shined with such unearthly brightness it seemed almost to be made of pure light. Within this outer cage was cradled a smaller, solid cube—but this was anything but normal. It was a cube yet not a cube. It was motionless but at the same time spinning furiously—their minds couldn't decide which of these distinct visual impressions to believe. It pulsated with a strange energy, as if it had a heart beat. Energy that seemed limitless. It changed back and forth continuously between a cube and other geometric shapes. Now it was a cube. Now a diamond. Now an impossible shape that was indescribable and unsettling to look at. The pulsating cube was almost hypnotic, drawing them in with its unearthly power. Yet they were unable to look at the object for more than a few seconds at a time without looking away.

Mrs. Resnick held out an arm in front of her kids as they began leaning forward for a closer look. "Not too close," she warned.

Their dad's team had learned that the cube was made of an unknown material and pulsed with an unknown energy—an energy they sensed was vast but that they had been unable to measure.

It also weighed 200,000 pounds! Slightly more than your average Rubik's cube.

When the cube had been found, Ben Resnick insisted on proceeding with extreme caution. Before it was touched or anything that might be a control was tried, he intended to contain it within the strongest force-shield Earth technology could manage. Human equipment that was to be used to accomplish this feat had been gathered and stored against one wall.

They would soon be ready to begin experiments, but Mr. Resnick had recently changed his mind about the cube. He was now arguing that it shouldn't be studied any further, no matter how great the precautions. The team had long talked about the danger of playing with advanced technology they didn't understand. How even an innocent electrical outlet could be lethal to a cave-man who decided to stick a finger inside to investigate. But in the case of the Enigma Cube, Mr. Resnick believed they were more like cavemen who had stumbled upon a *nuclear warhead*, and that it was best to leave it completely alone.

Ben Resnick worried they might accidentally trigger the Enigma Cube to unleash some horror upon the world. He was a scientist who had dedicated his life to the pursuit of knowledge, but he was also absolutely terrified of this alien artifact.

After seeing the cube for themselves, Ryan and Regan couldn't blame him. The power throbbing away inside this unearthly object would scare any sane person.

CHAPTER 6

Entering Other Dimensions

Mrs. Resnick drove the electric cart to the silver, octagonal building that housed both her and her husband's labs. Both kids were unusually quiet during the two-mile journey.

"We're on a bit of a tight schedule," said Mrs. Resnick as they arrived. "So why don't you two grab an early lunch while I finish packing for the trip."

"What kind of food are we bringing to Isis?" asked Ryan, trying to hide his concern but failing.

"Don't worry, Ryan, since it's only a weekend trip everyone is bringing their own food. I'll make sure you don't starve. I'm bringing enough peanut butter to last a week."

"What about pizza?" said Ryan.

"Sorry. Unless you can figure out how to keep it cold or cook it over an open fire, frozen pizza is out. I'm pretty sure you can survive two days without it. I guess we're going to find out," she said in amusement.

Ryan and Regan were almost complete opposites when it came to food. Regan ate very little but made healthy choices and actively sought out new and un-usual dishes to try. Ryan consumed more fuel than a blast furnace but was probably the pickiest kid on the planet. Aside from junk food, he lived almost entirely on pepperoni pizza, peanut butter, and hotdogs. If it weren't for peanut butter, one of the world's most nutri-tious foods, his parents were convinced he would now be only three feet tall.

A small kitchenette had been built in the corner of Mr. Resnick's lab. While their mother packed, the kids entered the lab to find their father seated in front of his computer eating a submarine sandwich. He was short and what Regan termed *cuddly-looking,* with a few strands of white hair now at his temples where a uni-form lawn of brown used to be. Unable to keep his hair from pointing in a dozen directions or his shirts tucked in and unwrinkled, he had finally given up. Now he kept his hair short and wore nothing but wrinkle-free polo shirts and black jeans.

"So what did you think of the Enigma Cube?" asked Mr. Resnick after greeting them.

"It's the coolest thing I've ever seen," replied Ryan.

"I'm glad you got to see it before we put a vault over it and locked it away forever."

Ryan raised his eyebrows. "When are you going to do that?"

"Hopefully on Monday. That's when the Managing Committee will take a vote. I think I've convinced a majority of members that it's too risky to study any further." He sighed. "At least I hope I have."

"What about Dr. Harris?" asked Regan.

"Even though he's the head of the project, he only gets one vote. That's not to say his opinion doesn't carry a lot of weight. The good news is that I think he's leaning toward my point of view. He told me he was going to visit the Enigma building one last time today and make his final decision."

Mr. Resnick held up his nearly finished sandwich. "Is Mom going to make you lunch?"

"No," said Regan. "She said she needed to finish packing for the trip. We're just gonna find something for ourselves."

She and her brother headed off toward the kitchenette, but they were blocked from their destination by five large whiteboards that had been pulled together like train cars. The boards were covered with equations, strange symbols of every type, and indescribably strange geometric shapes. And four words—"stadium in a barrel".

"Sorry about that," said Mr. Resnick, rolling two of the boards apart so they could get through.

Regan pointed to the upper left corner of the board nearest her. "Stadium in a barrel, Dad? What does that mean?"

Mr. Resnick laughed. "It's the result of a quick side calculation I did for fun. You know how Prometheus is far bigger than the hole it's in. Well I calculated that when we enter this city, it's the equivalent of stepping inside a barrel and finding a full-sized football stadium inside. A pretty neat trick."

"Yeah, but we've known about that forever," said Ryan.

"True. And I've always been pretty sure the key to pulling this off involves other dimensions. Well, I'm finally getting around to trying to understand this better mathematically."

"Wait a minute, Dad," said Ryan excitedly. "Back up for a second. Are you saying this city exists in another *dimension*?"

"Well, yes and no."

"What does *that* mean?" said Ryan. He ran a hand through his hair. "And for that matter, what does *another dimension* even mean? You hear about traveling to other dimensions in science fiction all the time. But where exactly *is* that?"

Mr. Resnick looked at his watch. "Well, I suppose we have enough time before we need to head out. If you want, I'll explain it to you. What do you say?"

"Are you kidding?" said Ryan. "I would *love* to hear this."

Regan nodded in agreement.

"Okay," said their father. "Why don't you get something to eat while I erase a few of these white boards."

"We'll be right back," said Ryan eagerly.

Once inside the kitchenette, Regan removed a bottle of water and a small container of low-fat yogurt from the refrigerator. She opened the yogurt, thrust a white plastic spoon inside, mixed in the strawberries on the bottom, and walked back to her father. Ryan eyed a frozen pepperoni pizza hungrily but knew he didn't have the time to cook it. Instead he grabbed a bottle of water, an entire jar of peanut butter, and a plastic spoon before rushing to join his sister.

"Ready?" asked their father.

"Ready," said Ryan for both of them, plunging his spoon into the jar and removing a brown, heaping mound of super-chunky peanut butter.

Regan shriveled up her nose as if a skunk were in the room. Ryan had eaten his favorite food straight out of the jar like this for years, but she wasn't usually nearby when he did. What he was eating may have *tasted* great, but Regan thought it looked like something that should be coming *out* of his body rather than going in. "Ryan, why can't you make a sandwich like everyone else?" she complained. "That is *sooo* disgusting."

"Well I think *yogurt* is disgusting," he replied, biting off the top portion of the brown lump loaded with countless bits of chopped up peanuts.

"Do you want to hear this or don't you?" said Mr. Resnick pointedly. He waited for both kids to give him their full attention and then began. "Okay, here we go. But I warn you. You'll be pulling your hair out before I'm through and your brain will hurt. Don't expect to understand everything I'm about to tell you. Believe me, *I* don't fully understand everything I'm about to tell you." He paused. "So what is a dimension in the first place?" he asked. "How would you even define the word?"

Both kids thought about this for a while. Finally Regan shrugged. "I don't know. Something you can measure?" she said uncertainly.

"Okay," said Mr. Resnick. "Something you can measure. That's a reasonable definition, and as good a place to start as anywhere. So a line represents one dimension. Because you can only measure *one* thing about it: its length. That's all. It doesn't have any width or height. So then what figure would represent two dimensions?"

"A square," said Ryan.

"Yes. Any flat shape would do, but a square works well. You can measure its length and width. But it still doesn't have any height. So what figure would have three dimensions?"

Regan swallowed a spoonful of yogurt that the strawberries had turned pink. "A cube," she replied. "You can measure three things. Its length, its width and its height."

"Good," said her father. "So these are the three dimensions we can perceive in our universe. And while you can think of a dimension as something you can measure, you can also think of dimensions as directions you can travel in. So let's imagine for a moment that Brewster, Pennsylvania is the entire world."

Ryan and Regan both groaned at the same time. "Are you trying to give us nightmares, Dad?" said Ryan with a grin.

Mr. Resnick laughed. "How about San Diego, California?"

"Now you're talking," said Regan.

"Okay," said their father. "Suppose you were a conductor on a train going due north through San Diego. How many different directions could you go in?"

Regan tilted her head in thought. "Only one," she said, wondering if this was a trick question. "You'd have to stay on the train track. So you could only go north."

"Right. You can think of the train track as a line. A one-dimensional figure. And your options for travel in a one-dimensional world are extremely limited." He paused. "Now let's suppose you're driving an off-road vehicle in the center of San Diego. What directions could you travel in?"

"Any direction you wanted to," said Ryan. "North, south, east or west. Or anything in between."

"That's right. So the flat city of San Diego is like a two-dimensional figure. And you have *lots* of options for traveling in this two-dimensional world. Just adding a single dimension gives you a lot more freedom to move, doesn't it?" He paused once again to give the kids time to digest this idea. "Now suppose you're piloting a *helicopter* in the center of the city. What directions could you travel in now?"

"Well, you could travel north, south, east and west," said Regan. "*And* up and down. And anywhere in between."

"You've got it," said Mr. Resnick. "So obviously, San Diego and the airspace above it represent a 3D figure. And once again, you have far more directions you can travel in."

Mr. Resnick paused. "Okay," he said. "So far this has been fairly simple. But it gets impossibly hard very quickly. Don't worry if you don't understand the rest of this. No one really does. Not completely. But I'm hoping you understand enough of it to at least get a sense of the possibilities." He raised his eyebrows. "So what is the fourth dimension? And while 'time' can be considered a dimension, that's not what I mean. I mean the fourth dimension of space."

Both kids just stared at him blankly. Ryan even lowered his second mountainous spoonful of peanut butter to his side, and away from his mouth, for this first time.

"Well," said their father. "Maybe we should review. To go from the first-dimension to the second, you have to move in a side to side direction. And to go from the second to the third, you have to move in an up and down direction. So what direction would you have to move in to get to the fourth dimension?"

They thought about this for about thirty seconds before giving up in total frustration.

"I think you've lost your mind, Dad," said Ryan.

"Ryan's right," said Regan, taking a sip from the plastic water bottle in her hand. "There isn't a fourth dimension. It's a trick question. The universe ran out of dimensions after three."

"You may be right," said her father. "But then again, one of the most popular theories in modern physics suggests there are as many as 10 or 11 dimensions." He smiled. "So I'll tell you the answer. You would have to move in a direction that no human has ever been able to visualize. A direction that no human has ever moved in. A direction that isn't north, south, east or west. Or up and down. Or anything in between."

Ryan frowned. "There *is* no such direction," he said in annoyance. "It's ridiculous."

"Just because we can't imagine such a direction doesn't necessarily mean it doesn't exist. But even if we can't visualize the fourth dimension, there are still ways we can understand some of its properties. Understand how beings living there would interact with us—with poor humans that can only sense three dimensions."

Ryan shook his head. "I'm still going with the 'you lost your mind' thing," he said.

Their father looked amused. "The best way to grasp some of the possibilities," he said, "is to try a thought experiment."

"A thought experiment?" repeated Ryan questioningly.

"Yes. An experiment you do in your mind only. Using nothing but your imagination. It's an enormously powerful tool in physics. Some of Einstein's greatest breakthroughs were the result of using this technique. The thought experiments we'll be doing first appeared in a book written by an English schoolmaster, Edwin Abbott, in 1884. A book called *Flatland*.

"Abbott figured the best way to understand how we would appear to fourth dimensional beings," continued Mr. Resnick, "is to think about how beings living in *lower* dimensions would appear to *us*. So he imagined a kingdom that existed in a universe with only one dimension. He called this Lineland. And he imagined a kingdom that existed in a universe with only two dimensions. He called this Flatland."

Mr. Resnick raised his eyebrows. "So if there were a kingdom of people that existed in a universe with only one dimension, what would that kingdom be like?"

The siblings looked at each other perplexed. "I have no idea," said Ryan for them both.

"Well, in Lineland, all the inhabitants would be line segments. And they could never change their order. Here, I'll show you what I mean."

He picked up a black marker and pulled off its cap with a loud pop. He went to the whiteboard and began writing squeakily.

TWO MEN
THE COURT JESTER
THE QUEEN
A GUARD
CHILDREN
THE KING

Ben Resnick gave his kids a few seconds to digest his drawing and then, pointing to the line segment labeled, "The Queen," he continued. "For example, if you were the Queen, you'd be stuck between the Court Jester and the King. *Forever*. Without any width dimension you couldn't pass anyone—if you tried you would just slam into them. Like two trains trying to pass each other on the same track. Now if you could make use of the second dimension—move side to side—you could just move to a different track, so to speak, and easily get by. But a Linelander can't. Their entire universe exists on a single line and they have no awareness of anything outside of this line."

Mr. Resnick capped the marker and slid it onto the tray at the bottom of the whiteboard. He motioned to his desk. "I'm not a very good artist, so let's move to my computer," he said.

They walked a few yards to his glass-topped desk, on which sat a sleek laptop computer connected to a thirty-six inch monitor. In less than a minute of searching he found a cartoon drawing that would demonstrate his point and put it up on the screen.

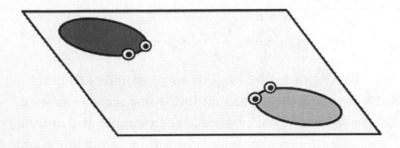

Both kids smiled broadly and barely managed not to laugh when they saw it.

"Dad couldn't draw that?" broadcast Ryan. *"Really?"*

"We're lucky Dad has such a powerful computer," replied Regan sarcastically.

"So this brings us to Flatland," continued Mr. Resnick, unaware that his kids were teasing him telepathically. "Flatland exists in a 2D universe. So think of Flatland as a giant piece of flat notebook paper. And Flatlanders—who appear as circle-people in the figure—are totally, well . . . *flat*. Flatlanders have no idea there is such a thing as up or down. They can only look and move in sideways directions. So if a Flatland dad suggested to his kids there might be another direction to move in, other than back and forth and sideways, they would tell him he was crazy. Impossible, they would say.

There is no such direction, they would say. To us 3D beings, the up direction is obvious. But to the poor 2D Flatlanders, no matter how much you told them about the up direction and described what it was like, they couldn't even *begin* to imagine it."

"Like we can't even begin to imagine what direction the fourth dimension would be in," said Regan.

"Exactly," said Mr. Resnick happily. "And since their universe exists in only two dimensions, Flatlanders are completely unable to lift themselves off the page. Not even a billionth of an inch. Just like we're unable to move even a billionth of an inch in the direction of the fourth dimension. Whatever direction *that* is. But unlike people living in the line universe, at least Flatlanders can move *past* each other."

Regan raised her eyebrows. "That must be a relief," she said playfully.

Regan dropped her empty yogurt container and spoon into a small wastebasket nearby. Ryan decided he was done eating also and did the same with his spoon, screwing the lid closed on the jar he had been holding and setting it down on one of the few empty spaces on his father's desk.

Ben Resnick walked to the whiteboard once again and motioned for his kids to follow. "The key point is that the fewer dimensions you perceive and can operate in, the more limited you are." He hastily drew another diagram on the board.

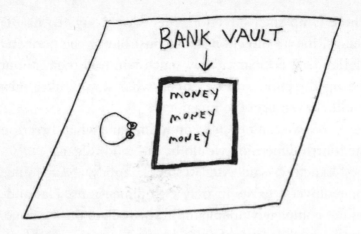

"So here you see a Flatlander eyeing a bank vault."

"How is that a bank vault?" protested Ryan. "It's just a square. And it's not enclosed."

"Good point," said Mr. Resnick. "It doesn't have a roof. Why do you think that is?"

Regan's eyes widened. Could it be that this was finally beginning to make some kind of bizarre sense to her? "Because it *can't* have a roof," she said. "Because you can't have any height in Flatland. A roof has to go *over* something. But there is no such thing as over or under in Flatland."

"You've got it," said her father. "But it doesn't need a roof. Flatlanders have no way to see what's inside the vault. And they can't climb over the line blocking them from the money. So unless they can break through one of the walls there is no way they can get into this vault. But *we* live and move in the third dimension. So we could get the money.

Easily," he said. "We could just reach in from above and grab it. Everyone in Flatland would think the theft was impossible. Like magic. But what seems impossible in one dimension can be laughably easy in a higher dimension."

Ryan scratched his head. "So everything you're saying about Flatland would be true for us also."

His father nodded. "Yes. That's exactly the point of this thought experiment."

"So someone living in the fourth dimension could rob one of *our* locked vaults," said Ryan. "Just as easily as we could steal from a Flatland vault."

"Very good," said Mr. Resnick, nodding enthusiastically. "Even if our vault had four walls, a floor and a ceiling that were all made of three-foot-thick steel. The Flatlanders can't possibly imagine that their vault is wide open from above. To them there *is* no above. Same with us. Our sealed vault seems absolutely closed and impenetrable to us. But it would be wide open when viewed from the fourth dimension. And when our money disappeared from a closed vault, we would think it was magic."

"*Are you understanding any of this?*" asked Ryan.

"*I don't know,*" replied Regan. "*But Dad was right. This stuff is making my brain hurt.*"

"So let's perform a thought experiment that wasn't in Abbott's book," continued Mr. Resnick.

He scribbled on the board once again and said, "Here I've drawn a three-dimensional object, shaped like a wedge of cheese.

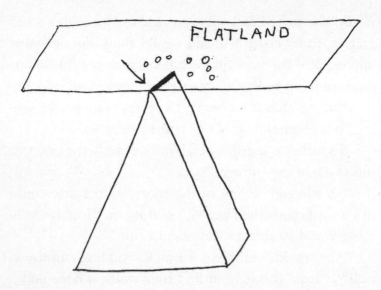

"Notice how only its top edge is touching Flatland. So which part of this 3D object would the Flatlanders see?"

Regan rolled her eyes. "Dad, you drew one of the lines thicker than the rest and you have an arrow pointing to it. So I'm going to say they'd only see that." She pointed to her father's drawing. "Are those little circles supposed to be Flatlanders?" she said in amusement.

Mr. Resnick smiled with his eyes. "I'm afraid so. Now you see why I went into science and not art. Anyway, that's right, the Flatlanders would see only a line. Now if you and I were standing on Flatland, we could look down over the edge and see the cheese wedge. But not Flatlanders. They can't perceive anything above or below them. The wedge is there—they just have no way of looking in that particular direction. Are you with me?"

Both kids nodded.

"Let's suppose that one day a few Flatlanders stumble upon this line and measure it very, very carefully. Suppose they even name it." His eyes twinkled. "Let's say they call it *Prometheus*."

He drew a second figure next to his first.

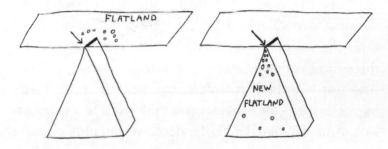

"So now they enter this line right where I have the arrow pointing, and spread out. Notice that the precise point where they enter is part of both Flatland and the surface of the cheese wedge that is facing us."

Mr. Resnick capped the black marker and slid it onto the tray at the bottom of the whiteboard once again.

"So now, as far as the Flatlanders know, they're still on Flatland. They still perceive everything as being in two-dimensions. They have no idea they're now on the surface of a *three-dimensional object*. One that is touching their realm. All they know is that they're stepping onto a small line that they've measured over and over again. And when they do they're suddenly roaming around a surface that gives them hundreds of times more space than they expected when they entered."

Ryan was straining so hard to understand he thought his head would explode. "So you're saying you think this is what is going on with *us*. That *our* Prometheus touches upon the very edge of a higher dimension."

"Exactly. The Flatlanders in the drawing are roaming around on a two-dimensional surface of a three-dimensional object. We're roaming around on a three-dimensional surface of a four-dimensional object. And just like the Flatlanders, we perceive a city vastly bigger than the measurements we take of it from the out-side. And also like the Flatlanders, we can only perceive the three-dimensional piece that's touching us. Which is a hollow, hockey-puck shaped hole carved out of the earth far under Brewster."

Ryan scratched his head, perhaps hoping to stimu-late his brain, and his sister appeared to be in a trance as she considered all that their father had said.

"I think I'm getting some of this," said Regan, "but there's a lot that still isn't sinking in."

"Same here," said Ryan.

"Don't worry," said their father. "If *any* of this makes sense to you you're doing well. Flatlanders can't imagine an up or a down direction. How can they? They live in a two-dimensional universe. Only if you lifted them off the page, so they could see Flatland from above, would they be able to understand. Well, we're just like them.

Our minds can't possibly imagine where this fourth spatial dimension might be. And there's no one to lift us off the page, so to speak." He paused. "So you see—"

An outer door burst open and the tall, athletic figure of Captain Dan Walpus charged into the lab. His blue cotton shirt was in tatters. "There's been an emergency, Ben," he said breathlessly. "I need one of your Med-Pens right away."

Mr. Resnick stared at Dan with his mouth open. "Amanda has them," he said, trying to shift mental gears as quickly as he could. "She's packing them for our trip to Isis."

"Where is she?" asked Dan urgently.

"I'll get her," said Ryan, rushing off without waiting for a reply. As much as he wanted to know what had happened there was clearly no time to waste, and he was the fastest member of his family.

"Hurry!" called Dan after him. He turned back to Ben Resnick. "Dr. Harris has been shot," he said, deeply shaken. "In the Enigma building."

Regan gasped while her father shrank back in shock and disbelief. "What?" he croaked thinly. "How can that be?"

As far as Mr. Resnick knew, Dr. Harris didn't have an enemy in the world. He was unanimously seen as a great man with a brilliant mind and gentle soul. A wise and sensible leader who was respected by all. But even if he was widely hated, everyone who was part of the Prometheus Project had undergone extensive psychological testing. All those who had the slightest violent tendencies or were the slightest bit unstable had been weeded out. Or at least they were *supposed* to have been.

"Will he make it?" whispered Mr. Resnick, unable to keep from wincing as he prepared for the worst.

Dan shook his head. "It doesn't look good," he said grimly. "And, Ben . . . there's something else you should know."

From the expression on Dan's face it was clear he was about to deliver more bad news. Ben Resnick took a deep breath and mentally braced himself for another shock.

The tall, square-jawed captain stared at him without blinking. "The Enigma Cube," he said uneasily. "It's missing."

CHAPTER 7

Lockdown

The entire Resnick family returned to the Enigma building with Dan Walpus. Dr Harris's body was well concealed behind a row of equipment. His thick glasses had been dislodged from his face when he had fallen. Splattered blood had turned parts of his white hair and beard a dirty red.

When Dan had discovered Dr. Harris, he had torn strips of cloth from his shirt and tied them over the gaping bullet wound in Dr. Harris's shoulder. Amanda Resnick knelt over him and pointed a Med-Pen at these blood-soaked, makeshift bandages, far too horrified and focused to marvel at the uncanny color changes that danced across the alien device. Without the Med-Pen his chances of survival were zero. Even with the device, Mrs. Resnick knew that his chances were not good.

A tear escaped the corner of her eye and rolled slowly

down her face, and the eyes of her husband and two children were moist as well. They all held great affection for Dr. Harris, and now there was a chance they would lose him forever.

Dr. Frank Lopez, one of the team's three medical doctors, raced into the building wheeling a gleaming stainless steel gurney. He pushed two fingers into the carotid artery in Dr. Harris's neck for five seconds. "I'm feeling a pulse," he announced, "but it's very weak." He fitted an oxygen mask over Dr. Harris's face and Dan helped him to gently lift the leader of the Prometheus Project onto the gurney. Without another word Frank Lopez rushed his patient outside to a Hauler that had been outfitted as an ambulance.

Two other members of security now manned the door, each carrying an automatic weapon, ensuring the Resnick family and Dan Walpus wouldn't be disturbed. Ben and Amanda Resnick had become the highest-ranking scientists on the team after Dr. Harris, and this was the only reason Ryan and Regan were allowed to stay in the building.

All in all, Dr. Harris had been lucky. Dan had just happened to be near enough to the Enigma building to hear the gunshot. Whoever had pulled the trigger was gone when he arrived, but he had had no time for pursuit. Because he had heard the shot he had searched the entire room and found the well-concealed victim. He did the best he could to bandage Dr. Harris's wound, but knew he had to get an alien medical device as quickly as possible.

And that meant the Resnicks.

Since there was no cell phone reception deep underground, team members were issued personal walkie-talkies with individual frequencies. But the Resnicks had theirs turned off. Fortunately their labs were only two miles away. He had rushed to get them, barking orders to the security team and calling for a doctor as he drove.

"Where's Carl?" asked Mr. Resnick, forcing himself to focus on the emergency at hand and not the fate of Dr. Harris.

"At his parents' anniversary party in Colorado. I'm the ranking member of security in his absence."

"Is he on his way here?"

Dan shook his head. "No. I've put us in lockdown mode. No calls in, no calls out. No one enters Prometheus. No one leaves. Frank will be allowed to take Dr. Harris topside once he's stabilized so he can be flown to a hospital. But that's the *only* exception. The head of the project has been shot. And if that's not bad enough, an alien artifact that is potentially the most dangerous yet discovered is missing. This is a threat of unknown proportions," he said. "And I'm taking it very, very seriously."

"Good," said Mr. Resnick approvingly. "I couldn't agree more." He looked over to where the Enigma Cube had rested on the floor less than an hour before. "I know the word impossible is overused in this city, but the Enigma Cube simply can't be missing. It *can't* be. We estimate it weighs *200,000* pounds. It's not the sort of thing you just put in your pocket and run off with."

"What kind of equipment would it take to lift something like that?" asked Dan.

"None that we have around here," replied Mr. Resnick. "Some of the heavy duty machinery used to dig out the cavern next to Prometheus might be capable of it. *Might* be. But you could never fit it through the entrance."

Dan Walpus clenched his teeth, unable to suppress his fury any longer. "Then we'll just have to ask whoever moved it how it was done," he growled. "Because I'm going to find the person responsible for this before the weekend is out."

"How can you be so sure?" asked Mrs. Resnick.

"Whoever did this is still in the city. And they're not going *anywhere*. Our computers keep track of the number of people within Prometheus at any given time. As of this moment, there are 628 people here. One of these 628 is the shooter. If we can't account for someone, we'll sweep the city with sensitive heat and motion sensors and find them. There will be no hiding from us."

"What if they go off-planet?" asked Regan.

Dan shook his head. "They would have to go through the zoo building. I posted a guard at the entrance within minutes of hearing the gunshot. I also had Miguel, who was manning headquarters, verify the location of all my security personnel. None of them were near the Enigma building when this happened. I'm positive."

"That was smart," said Mr. Resnick. "At least now we know we can trust security. A lockdown isn't very effective if the person guarding the exit is the bad guy."

Dan sighed. "Well, we're sure no one from security shot Dr. Harris. It's still possible that someone from security is working with the person who did."

"Thanks," said Mrs. Resnick, rolling her eyes. "Now I feel better."

"We need to keep this bottled up," said Dan. "Other than the members of my security team, your family and Frank Lopez are the only ones who know this happened. I'll ask all of you to keep it that way. I was lucky to find Dr. Harris so quickly. The longer the culprit thinks we haven't discovered the crime, the better."

Dan frowned. "And there's something else," he said. "If word gets out there's a killer among us, it will incite panic. Everyone will suspect everyone else. And whoever did this might think their only chance of escape is to take hostages."

"So now what?" asked Mr. Resnick.

"We need to question everyone in Prometheus while they're hooked up to a lie detector. Everyone here has agreed to submit to such questioning in emergency situations. I'll want to do this one at a time—again, to reduce the chances of hostage-taking. And I'll need to be as careful as possible so as not to arouse suspicion. This might take a while, but it can't be helped."

"What about people trying to leave the city?" asked Regan. "Or anyone who goes near the exit? They'll know we're locked down."

"No they won't. We're not posting guards on the Prometheus side of the entrance. That would be too obvious. We're posting them inside the cavern. The elevator is the only way to the surface. The guards enforcing the lockdown will be posted there. So no one will know we're in lockdown until they've entered the cavern. If they pass the lie detector test, we'll keep them in the cavern and ask them to do their part to keep the investigation secret until we've found the shooter."

"It's going to be tough to keep this secret for long," noted Mr. Resnick. "No matter what you do."

"I know. But the longer the better."

"Well, under the circumstances, I think it's an excellent plan," said Mr. Resnick. "But I'd like you to question me first. Then, when I pass, I can help you with your investigation. I think you know how much the Enigma Cube scares me."

Mrs. Resnick turned to her husband. "Don't you need to set up your equipment on Isis?" she asked. "I thought you said this was the chance of a lifetime."

"I'll have to miss it. This is just too important."

"No, Ben," said Dan Walpus. "Go. I read about your

proposed expedition to Isis this morning when I was deciding who to assign for off-planet security. I don't want to offend you, but right now you'll just be in the way. And canceling a trip this important would be highly unusual. We don't need that." He paused. "The group that was scheduled to go should do so. Don't worry, we'll know exactly who's there. If we need any of you, we know where to find you."

"And what if whoever did this is in our group?" said Mr. Resnick.

"It's a small group so that's not very likely. But you'll be taking the same risk that everyone else in the city is taking whenever they're around others. If we haven't found who's responsible, we'll know it's one of you and come calling."

Ben Resnick thought about it. He knew Dan was right. "Okay," he said. "You win. We'll go as planned." He directed a long, hard stare at the tall captain. "But I expect you to catch whoever did this and find the Enigma Cube," he added with grave intensity. "When you do, make sure the Cube is well guarded. *Whatever* you do," he insisted, *"don't* touch it."

Dan nodded solemnly. "Understood," he replied.

Mr. Resnick held the stare for a moment longer and then turned to his wife and kids, his expression and voice softening. "We'd better get moving," he told them. "We don't want to hold up the rest of the group."

As much as he hated leaving the city during a crisis, the trip to Isis would at least get his family half a galaxy away from an unknown shooter. His eyes swiveled to the spot Dr. Harris had fallen, still stained with blood, and he sighed heavily, as though the weight of the world were resting on his shoulders.

CHAPTER 8

Arrival

D ue to the Resnicks' unusual tardiness, the eleven members of the Isis expedition assembled twenty minutes behind schedule. Along with the four members of the Resnick family there were two other physicists, Donna Morgan and Nathaniel Smith. Amanda Resnick had long before decided to bring the same three biologists who had been with her on her last, fateful visit to the volcanic planet: Bob Zubrin, Eric Morris, and Michelle Cooper. A return to Isis would help them put the harrowing events they had experienced behind them once and for all. Dan Walpus had assigned Lieutenants Miguel Sanchez and Cam Kincaid to provide security for the group.

They loaded overstuffed backpacks, sensors for detecting X-ray levels in space, a portable force-field generator, self-inflatable dwellings, and stores of water into the back of a Hauler and pulled up in front of the zoo building. As usual, the building projected an endless series of realistic holograms of alien animals near its entrance, advertising its function as a zoo.

Dan had already instructed the guard manning the zoo building, Lieutenant Lebron Williams, to blend in as much as possible so as not to arouse the suspicions of anyone passing by. When the Isis expedition neared, Dan ordered him to stay out of sight and watch carefully through binoculars to be sure that only the eleven people authorized for the trip went inside. He didn't want to tip off anyone on the expedition that anything was out of the ordinary. After they had entered, Lebron could man his post once again.

After several trips back and forth through the portal, the team's belongings and equipment were safely stowed in two trams parked within the dome-shaped shield on Isis. These were the only two trams on the planet, but they were large enough to easily accommodate both the team members and their supplies. While the trams were standard alien equipment on each of the zoo planets, each planet seemed to have them in different sizes and different numbers. Some had only one. Some had dozens.

Mr. Resnick, the two other physicists, and Miguel took the lead tram. They would be on the lookout for a good location at which to set up the X-ray detector.

Mrs. Resnick, Regan, Cam Kincaid, and the three biologists piled into the one behind.

Mrs. Resnick had put one of their two Med-Pens in her backpack, but she pulled the other one from her pocket. She inserted it into a canvas emergency kit they had brought with them, letting everyone know that she had done so. In addition to a Med-Pen, the emergency kit contained bandages of every type, gauze, several flares, and a variety of human medications.

"Hey Ryan," said his sister telepathically. *"Looks like there's an empty seat next to Michelle Cooper."*

Ryan glanced at Michelle Cooper's steely blue eyes. Now that he realized who she was, he could see the similarities between her and Alyssa. She was a million years older, of course, and not nearly as pretty. She was also decidedly less friendly.

"Um . . . that's okay. I think I'll go with Dad," he broadcast back.

"Chicken! This is your chance to get on her good side. Don't blow it."

"Are you coming?" said Mrs. Resnick to her son.

"Sure," said Ryan. He wished it weren't true, but his sister had a point. He exhaled loudly and took a seat beside Alyssa's mother. Maybe he was just imagining that she didn't like him. The first few times they had met she had treated him like a celebrity. Although she hadn't been there when the alien invader named Tezoc Zoron had captured the entire team, she had heard all about it. She had told Ryan that his actions during that crisis were legendary, and deservedly so. She had really liked him then. He had no idea why this had changed.

"Hi," said Ryan, smiling pleasantly.

Michelle gave him the slightest nod. "Hi Ryan," she said. She wasn't outwardly hostile, but something about her body language made it clear to him that she wasn't open to further discussion. It was as if he had a really nasty case of body odor but she was too polite to tell him; turning ever so slightly and moving as far from him as she could without being obvious about it, instead.

Could it be that she had *always* disliked him? Maybe she had only been *pretending* to like him in the beginning because she worked for his mom? Regan thought she just didn't approve of having kids on the team, and Regan was usually right. Maybe Michelle Cooper had just forgotten some of the contributions he and his sister had made.

He glanced at the red crystal medallion in the front of the vehicle that hung down from the roof like a circular rear-view mirror. These crystals allowed the trams to pass through the force-fields. Without one of the red crystals, the shield could only be breached using a furious onslaught of energy from high-powered lasers and other advanced power generators. Their father had been convinced that the shield opened when it detected a tram trying to pass. But Regan had proved him wrong. She had discovered that the crystals were the key, not the trams. These crystals were like universal garage-door openers, able to get through *any* force-field barrier.

It was possible that Michelle Cooper hadn't heard about this contribution. If not, maybe she could use another reminder that kids could play an important role on the team. And since it was Regan who had been responsible for the discovery, he wouldn't be bragging.

Everyone else in the tram was now engaged in conversation except for Alyssa's mother—and Regan, of course, who wanted to eavesdrop on his efforts to win the woman over.

Ryan took a deep breath and turned to the icy woman next to him. "You know," he began, "Regan actually discovered how these trams get through the force-fields. This was when Tezoc was threatening to—"

"Thanks, Ryan," she interrupted, "but I know all about your sister's discovery." While her tone was pleasant enough, Ryan saw nothing but contempt in her eyes. She flashed a quick smile that Ryan was convinced was fake. "Sorry to cut you off, but I'm not really up for discussion at the moment. I'm trying to focus on *Isis* right now," she added pointedly. "I'm a biologist who studies alien life. And here we are on an alien planet. You get that, right?" she finished, as if speaking to a five-year-old.

"Yeah. I get that," said Ryan. "Totally."

"Real smooth, Ryan," broadcast Regan as their parents each activated a holographic control and the cara-

van of two trams began moving forward. *"What are you thinking? How about starting a conversation by asking her how she's doing or something?"*

"I know. I always act like an idiot around her. Even when I had no idea Alyssa was her daughter. Knowing she doesn't like me stresses me out."

"Maybe it's time to find some other girl to like."

Ryan frowned. *"No. I could still be okay,"* he broadcast hopefully. *"Aren't girls supposed to be attracted to guys their parents don't like?"*

Regan laughed. *"You've been watching too many bad movies, Ryan. And I don't think you'd fall for a girl like that."*

Ryan was about to reply.

But he couldn't!

The strange force he had felt when the Hauler had hit him was back. His body seemed to stretch out and threatened to pull completely apart. He wanted to gasp, but he couldn't do *that* either.

But he realized in horror that there was one thing he *could* do.

He could see the heart, lungs, and ribcage of the person in front of him with perfect clarity.

CHAPTER 9

An Ideal Location

In less than a second it was over.

Ryan patted his own body once again to be sure he was solid as his heart pounded away furiously in his chest.

"*Did you feel that?*" he asked anxiously.

"*Uh-huh,*" replied Regan, her mind reeling in shock.

"*It was like when the Hauler hit us. Exactly the same. I felt like I was being stretched apart in some weird way and I could see through things again.*"

"*Yeah, me too.*"

"*What's going on?*"

"Mom," said Regan out loud. "Did you just feel anything funny?"

Mrs. Resnick shook her head. "No, Honey. But I'm in the middle of a conversation, okay," she added.

"Sorry," said Regan.

"I don't get it," she broadcast. *"This is even freakier than before. The Teacher didn't do it this time. The Teacher isn't even on the planet."*

"So whatever happened to us in Prometheus, it might keep happening. What if we're not stable anymore? What if this happens more and more often? Until ... I don't know ... we become ghostlike—permanently."

"But it wasn't random," pointed out Regan. *"It happened exactly when we were going through the shield. That has to be important."*

Ryan hadn't been paying attention to where they were when it happened, so he hadn't been aware of this. What could this mean?

"Maybe becoming not-solid is the way we always get through the shield," he suggested. *"How anything gets through. Maybe that's what the crystal really does. It makes objects ghostlike for an instant until they pass through."*

"Then why didn't we ever experience this before?" asked Regan. *"And why were we the only ones who experienced it now?"*

"Good question."

Regan tilted her head in thought. *"I have an idea,"* she broadcast excitedly. *"Maybe the Teacher changed our brains again. It talked with us telepathically—did something to our minds so we would have a compatible frequency—and then we became telepathic. The tele-*

pathic signals were always there, we just couldn't pick them up."

"So you're saying that the crystals have always caused our bodies to become ghostlike and pass through the shield, we just didn't sense it before. But when the Teacher had to jerk our bodies into this state, it changed the structure of our minds again."

"Exactly," she replied. "We weren't telepathic. Now we are. We couldn't sense being turned into a ghost. Now we can."

Ryan considered. "I guess it's as good a hypothesis as any," he broadcast finally. "We'll have to see if it happens again the next time we cross the barrier."

With that the siblings stopped talking, telepathically or otherwise, and focused on their surroundings.

The gravity on Isis was slightly lower than on Earth and the air contained slightly more oxygen. The temperature was comfortable, if not a little chilly. The sky wasn't blue but instead had a reddish cast to it; similar to how parts of the sky could appear when the sun was setting on Earth. And while the vegetation was similar to tropical vegetation on Earth, yellow replaced green as the most popular color.

The Isis portal was within a section of rainforest, but they had exited this to a more open area fairly quickly. To their left, a towering volcanic mountain range seemed to go on forever. Three peaks, rising above all others, gathered rain clouds around themselves like blankets. These clouds would provide the water to quench the thirst of the broad swaths of rainforest.

Barren landscapes broke up the rainforest periodically—areas that were in the path of lava flows. The flows were usually a few yards below the surface, but even so, little or no vegetation would grow anywhere nearby. And there were no roots to break up the array of pink, orange and black lava rocks. After the incident with Carl, the expedition knew to steer well clear of these. And other than the half-mile section they had passed through when exiting the Isis shield, they avoided the rainforest as well.

A half-mile to their right, dozens of miles of cliffs stood guard over a reddish-hued ocean far below. Glowing orange lava, mostly traveling through underground lava tubes, burst through the cliff face at dozens of locations hundreds of feet above the surf. From there it fell to the sea in thick, molasses-like waterfalls. Where it entered the ocean, thousands of gallons of seawater were turned instantly into blistering steam that rose and formed billowing sea-monster shapes above the cliffs.

Isis teamed with large wildlife of every kind, as their mother had told them. The variety was astonishing. It was as though all the animals of Africa, North America, and Australia were concentrated on a single land mass. And judging by the number of species with massive jaws, fangs and other spiked natural weapons, the planet appeared to have more than its share of carnivores.

But as their mother had promised, the humans were

completely ignored. Not a single animal attempted to approach the tram—not that this would have done them any good.

Although there were no detectable force-fields around the trams, no animal had ever been able to get within ten yards of one on any planet. No animal, that is, except humans. Whether the trams recognized humans specifically, or intelligent life in general, was unknown, but highly advanced alien technology was clearly behind this inexplicable effect.

Taking Regan's lead, their father had experimented on the trams and discovered a small white crystal that provided power to the vehicles. The power of these crystals seemed limitless, like batteries that never died. When the white crystals were removed the trams wouldn't move. But even without their power source, the trams somehow still managed to provide a zone of safety around themselves, keeping all animals at bay.

After they had traveled for about thirty minutes Mr. Resnick called a stop. They were about three miles away from the portal on a large, barren stretch of land that was roughly in the shape of a rectangle. One side bordered a rainforest. Behind another side a mountain range rose majestically into the red sky until it was out of sight behind wispy Isis clouds. Yet another side looked down on valleys that ended at the cliffs above the ocean. The land was flat and didn't contain lava rocks. It was protected from the wind by several natural features. Because it overlooked two valleys, the biologists could observe any number of species in the distance interacting with one another.

An ideal place to set up camp.

Everyone emptied out of the trams. The three physicists removed large cases in which sensitive equipment had been carefully packed in Styrofoam. They hauled the cases thirty yards away—within sight of the rainforest on that side of the clearing but not too close. They immediately unpacked and began to assemble the X-ray detector under Cam's protective eye. He held a tranquilizer gun in one hand and the canvas emergency kit in the other.

The four biologists pulled pad computers from their backpacks, with built-in camcorders, and wandered off in search of the perfect place to observe their favorite wildlife. Miguel watched carefully for any signs of trouble.

Ryan and Regan wandered off on their own, but their mother caught up with them ten minutes later. "I want to show you something," she said. She pointed to a valley below them to the south and motioned for them to follow her. "I've spotted a herd of animals that are very unique. We call them—"

A scream pierced the reddish alien air! A shrill shriek that was earsplitting in its intensity.

The members of the expedition were spread out, but

everyone jumped at once as though they had received an electric shock.

The scream repeated.

It was coming from just inside the rainforest.

And it was unmistakably human.

Chapter 10

Attack

Everyone rushed to the rainforest to investigate, with Miguel and Cam in the lead, putting on an impressive display of pure speed. The unnerving screams continued as the two members of security passed the tree line and entered the thick yellow forest. They searched frantically for whoever was doing the screaming but saw no one.

Where was the screamer? The screams were coming from the area in which they were now standing. They were sure of it.

Within thirty seconds the other members of the expedition, who had come from different parts of the large clearing at different speeds, had all joined the two men.

The screaming stopped abruptly. As quickly as it had begun.

Yet they had still failed to find it source.

"Are we sure it was a human scream?" asked Cam anxiously.

"No doubt about it," said Donna Morgan, still breathing hard. "It was a woman's scream. But it wasn't one of us. Was another expedition here ahead of us?"

Cam shook his head. "There's no one else here. I'm positive." He raised his eyebrows. "No one from the Prometheus Project at any rate."

"Could whoever was screaming have been dragged off by an animal?" asked Miguel.

"No," said Amanda Resnick. "The animal life here ignores humans completely."

"Let's spread out and comb the area," said Miguel. "Look for anything that might help us understand what just happened."

The search had only begun when Bob Zubrin shouted, "I found something."

He was under an exotic tree, with circular yellow leaves the size of Hula Hoops. Everyone joined him in seconds. He picked up a strange, tan-colored object that was roughly spherical and about the size of a soccer-ball and handed it to Miguel.

It seemed to be nothing more than a makeshift, uneven ball of padding. Miguel examined it. A black electronic device was buried inside this cushioned cocoon, which was open on one side so a speaker on the device would not be blocked. Miguel reached in and ripped it free of the tape that held it.

It was digital tape recorder! It was on but no sound was coming out. Miguel reset it to the beginning and hit the "Play" button. Nothing. He moved it ahead five minutes and tried again.

A shrill scream emanated from the recorder at such high volume it almost deafened him.

Miguel had a sick look on his face as he quickly hit the "Stop" button.

Someone in their group had done this! They had neared the tree line, activated the padded recorder, and tossed it into the dense growth. It had run for four or five minutes until it reached the long stretch of pre-recorded screaming, which it had broadcast with chillingly realistic sound quality.

But why would someone do this? There were only two reasons Miguel could think of. As a sick practical joke. Or to create a diversion!

Miguel had a very bad feeling about this. He hastily took an inventory of the people around him. Two were missing: Michelle Cooper and Nathaniel Smith. "Let's get back to the trams," he ordered. "Now!"

As the group turned to retreat, three animals emerged from behind trees, heading straight toward them. They were about the size of wolves with thin gray fur and gleaming silver eyes. Unlike wolves, they didn't have elongated snouts—or snouts of any kind for that matter—which only seemed to leave more room for massive mouths filled with sharp, jagged teeth. They had four legs that ended in feet that were padded and clawed like those of a leopard. They issued a low-pitched clicking sound that was as intimidating as a rattlesnake's rattle.

Cam and Miguel pushed the others in between them and raised their tranquilizer guns.

"So the animals here ignore humans, Amanda!" said Miguel angrily. "Is this what you call being ignored!"

"Shut up and pay attention!" she shot back as four more of the animals emerged. "We've seen these a dozen times. They've ignored us completely. They're pack animals," she added as five more animals joined the rest, circling the group of humans threateningly.

"No kidding!" snapped Donna Morgan. "Thanks for the news flash!"

No one other than Cam and Miguel were armed. Ryan had the same pocketknife he always carried on camping trips in his right pocket, but knew it would be useless in this situation. Instead he searched the ground around him hastily. There were a number of fallen branches in the area and he scooped one up to use as a club. Bob Zubrin and Donna Morgan noticed this and did the same. With the only useful sticks taken the others looked for rocks to use as potential weapons.

More and more of the clicking gray predators continued to emerge from deeper in the woods until there were seventeen in all. The circle of carnivores tightened slowly around the humans. Their silver eyes gleamed with an unearthly malevolence and they bared their ferocious teeth, leaving no doubt as to their deadly intentions.

Miguel shot one in the chest with a tranquilizer dart. It yelped and backed off along with its pack-mates but they returned to their positions only minutes later. Miguel and Cam quickly squeezed off six more shots. Again the animals backed off, but only temporarily. The tranquilizers had no effect.

"Who chose the tranquilizer that was put in these darts?" shouted Cam.

"I did," said Bob Zubrin. "It's very potent."

"Maybe on Earth animals, you idiot!" yelled Cam. "Next time test it on *native* animals! It doesn't do *squat* here!"

As he yelled, he and Miguel continued to fire into the pack until they had run out of darts. Several of the animals now looked like pincushions, but the darts did little more than get them even angrier. Their clicking grew louder and louder and they continued to tighten their circle.

"Didn't you bring any real guns as backup?" yelled Ryan from within the mass of humans that had crammed together ever more tightly.

Before Cam could answer a few of the creatures leaped at him. He knocked one to the ground but the other bit deep into his arm. Screaming in pain, he dropped the emergency kit he had been holding and slammed the animal against several others, knocking it off his arm and stunning its mates. Blood streamed down his arm and poured onto the forest floor.

Miguel was kicking at the nearest beasts and began to wade into them in a blind rage, twirling around to block attacks coming from multiple directions.

Miguel and Cam had ceased being human and were now creatures of pure instinct, battling the threat with animal ferocity. They were protecting the rest of the expedition for now, but the pack was relentless. And when the pack broke through Cam and Miguel, the clubs and stones held by the others wouldn't hold them off for long. In only a matter of minutes the entire expedition would be torn to pieces.

And there was absolutely nothing anyone could do to stop it.

CHAPTER 11

Stranded

Regan was terrified, but also angry for some reason she couldn't quite understand. Perhaps it was just determination. One thing the past few years had taught her was to never give up. They needed to find a weapon and they needed to do it fast. She forced herself to ignore the powerful emotions boiling inside her and concentrate.

Her mind raced. Early man had managed to survive in a world filled with deadly predators. With weapons almost as pathetic as the ones they were using. But how? How could any primitive human have survived in the wild for even a week?

Regan gasped as the answer hit her squarely between the eyes. Of course! She knew exactly what she had to do.

She reached for the emergency kit that Cam had dropped to the forest floor as the battle raged on around her. She snatched it off the ground. But as she was pulling her arm back one of the predators managed to slash at her with its front claw. The claw stabbed through her cotton jacket and shirt and deep into her forearm. Regan ignored the blood and the explosion of pain and managed to continue her motion and hang onto the canvas bag.

"Ryan, give me your stick!" she demanded telepathically.

"Get your own!" he snapped back.

Regan reached into the emergency kit and grabbed a self-igniting flare. She yanked the cap off and fire shot from its end. Billowing orange smoke gushed from the flare an instant later and rose in the sky. She held the flare out and waved it at the nearest predators that were attacking Miguel. They backed off immediately and considered this new threat.

"GIVE ME YOUR STICK! NOW!" shouted Regan telepathically at her brother.

Ryan shoved the two-foot long fallen branch he had been holding into his sister's open hand. Regan handed him the flare and unzipped and removed her punctured jacket. She wrapped it around the stick four or five times, snatched the flare back from Ryan, and lit the jacket on fire. She lunged into the front edge of the pack with the flaming branch, intent on setting them all on fire if she could.

Miguel, still on the front lines, was weak from blood loss but there was still plenty of fight in his eyes. He ripped the blazing torch from Regan's hand, pushed her back behind him, and lashed out at the nearest attackers. The rest of the group caught on immediately and began removing jackets and tearing clothes, creating makeshift torches of their own, using the flare to ignite them.

The tide was turning.

Thrusting their few torches at the horde of attacking predators, the group was able to slowly push them back. As they gained new ground they found additional fallen sticks, dry leaves, and other flammable materials with which to create additional torches.

Soon all nine of them had raging torches and formed a circle, facing outward. The pack now backed off, showing a healthy respect for this human circle of flame.

"Back to the trams," ordered Mr. Resnick, and the group slowly emerged from the rainforest, maintaining their defensive circle as they did so. "We need to get back to Prometheus and regroup. Treat the injured. Try to determine what happened."

As they made their way across the field toward the trams, they came upon four powerfully muscled reptilian creatures that had recently been shot. And not by a tranquilizer. They had been shot by a nine-millimeter automatic weapon at close range. *Somebody* on Isis had brought more than tranquilizer darts with them on the expedition.

Representatives of a variety of species were now gathering in the clearing and each eyed the group with a predatory bloodlust. If the predators of Isis had ignored humans before, they were more than making up for this oversight now.

This was all some sort of nightmare, thought Regan. But she was more enraged than scared. She wanted to lash out at these ruthless creatures. Beat them back with her bare hands. If only she had the necessary strength.

The torches kept all of the animals back, but none of them retreated far. Even in the face of fire.

The unwieldy human circle continued to move awkwardly to where they had left the two trams.

But now there was only one!

The other tram was missing. It was nowhere in sight.

The nine remaining members of the Isis expedition finally reached the single tram. They snuffed out their torches against the ground, dropped them near the tram, and poured inside, hastily pushing out equipment and supplies until there was plenty of room for everyone.

Carnivores of all types, each one more lethal than the last, formed a circle around the protective tram at distance of about ten yards. No animal on any planet had yet been able to approach a tram any closer.

"Let's get out of here," said Mr. Resnick, activating the holographic control to begin the return journey.

The tram didn't respond!

Mr. Resnick's eyes widened. What was going on?

He scanned the front compartment of the tram and his heart nearly stopped. The white crystal that powered it had been removed. Without it, the alien vehicle wouldn't move an *inch*. And if they left the tram, they would be torn to pieces by the ever-growing collection of predators straining every muscle to get at them.

But their problems didn't stop there.

The tram's red crystal was missing as well! The crystal that would allow them to pass back through the shield that encircled the portal home.

Without this crystal the shield was impenetrable; returning to Earth impossible.

They were stranded! Stranded on a primitive planet that had suddenly turned extraordinarily hostile to humans.

CHAPTER 12

Hate Mail

Mr. Resnick decided not to tell everyone the devastating news until after the injured had been tended to. Amanda Resnick was already hard at work patching Miguel Sanchez using bandages from the emergency kit. Eric Morris was doing the same with Cam Kincaid. Both members of security had severe bites and slashes up and down their arms and legs. Both had lost considerable blood. Mrs. Resnick removed the Med-Pen from the kit and she and Eric traded it back and forth, each training it on every wound they found, moving it so quickly across so many backgrounds that the device became a flashing kaleidoscope of colors.

Regan and her father were also bleeding from cuts and lacerations but their condition was not nearly as bad as was Miguel's and Cam's. They were able to bandage themselves up, borrowing the Med-Pen only after

Miguel and Cam had been treated. Although the effects of the alien device on wound healing weren't immediately apparent, the Med-Pens pain relief function acted instantly, and they now felt no pain whatsoever.

Of the eleven members of the Isis expedition, two were missing and four had been wounded. Two severely so. Only five had come through untouched. At least so far.

Native beasts continued to converge in a circle around the tram. Everyone in the tram felt as though their nerves were being drilled on by a crazed dentist, and their tempers were getting short.

Mrs. Resnick noticed that some of the backpacks had been opened and began searching through them to see if anything was missing.

"Why aren't we moving?" muttered Miguel woozily from the back of the tram.

Mr. Resnick sighed. "We can't," he said. "This tram has been sabotaged. It can't move. And the crystal we need to get back through the barrier is gone."

He waited for the commotion this announcement caused to die down.

"Michelle and Nathaniel must have taken the other tram," he continued. "There's little doubt they were also responsible for the trick with the tape recorder. And for leaving us stranded here."

"But only for a few days," said Regan optimistically, her nerves now back under control after the indescribably potent fury she had felt while fighting for her life. "We're scheduled to return on Sunday afternoon. When we don't show up, Carl will send a team looking for us."

"Don't count on it," spat Donna Morgan. "We don't know why Michelle and Nathaniel did this, but they're both very smart. They can tell Carl anything. That we were torn to pieces by hostile animals. That we were killed in an earthquake. That we fell into a lava flow. Anything."

"Hold on," said Mrs. Resnick before her daughter could respond. "One of the Med-Pens is missing." She held out her backpack as if this were proof. "In its place is an envelope. An envelope with your name on it, Ben," she said.

She handed the white envelope to her husband without another word. On its front was written, "To Ben, From Nathaniel." He removed three typed pages and straightened them out.

"Everyone listen up," he said loudly.

He waited a few seconds until he was sure he had everyone's attention and then he began reading out loud.

This letter is to all the worthless members of this pathetic expedition to Isis. But it's especially directed to Ben Resnick, a man I have come to loathe. Ben, if you're reading this letter, it means that my simple little plan has worked. I knew if I tossed a recorder out of sight, playing a time-delayed scream from a horror movie, all of you hero types would rush over and pounce on it like hungry dogs on a steak. And when you did I'd have all the time in the world to steal a Med-Pen, sabotage your tram, and even take a hostage—whoever happens to be nearest to me when you all rush off to save the day gets to be the lucky volunteer.

Why am I doing this? Let's just say I've grown sick of the entire Prometheus team. The biggest collection of pompous fools the world has ever seen. And I've grown especially sick of you Ben. Especially sick. So smug. So arrogant. So sure you're a better physicist even than Albert Einstein. Well I've got news for you, Ben, you're not even a better physicist than *me*.

What you are, Ben, is spineless. Always so careful. Always so cautious. You're sitting on the greatest treasure chest in history and you're afraid to open it. Oh, I'm scared. Oh, let's not study anything in case it's dangerous. Where would we be if the Wright Brothers had had this attitude, Ben? No guts, no glory.

So I thought it would be fun to strand you all on Isis. Forever. And make no mistake, Ben, for reasons I will make clear shortly, you have no hope of ever being rescued. Stranding you on a primitive planet is the ultimate torture; knowing the portal home is so close, yet so far away. You can see it, but we both know you have no way to ever cross the barrier to reach it. This way you get to suffer for the rest of your lives. You get to find out if you're all as smart and resourceful as you *think* you are. My only regret is not seeing the looks on your faces as it sinks in that you will never be going home.

But look on the bright side, Ben. The Isis wildlife is no threat to humans so your group should be able to survive for at least a few years. Sure, the conditions are primitive, but civilization is overrated anyway. I just hope you packed plenty of toilet paper.

Just to be clear, I'm not stranding you on Isis *only* for my own amusement. There are other reasons, too. You see, Tezoc Zoron has become an idol of mine. I wasn't on the team during his attempted invasion, but the story is legendary. This was one smart alien, Ben, and I've taken a number of lessons from him. First, hostages can be very useful. You never know when one might come in handy. Second, planning is everything. For example, as soon as I finish writing this letter, I plan on stealing the Enigma Cube and then rushing off to Isis as part of your team before anyone knows it's gone. If you're reading this letter then I've succeeded. Imagine how surprised security will be when I return from Isis two days early with the Cube—and a hostage. And since you always bring one or two Med-Pens with you on expeditions, I get to steal one of these while I'm at it. How's that for great planning?

I also decided not to underestimate your exceedingly irritating kids. Tezoc did this and it cost him. Personally, I don't see what the fuss is all about. They just aren't that special. But while I don't see any way in a million years they could possibly stop me, or even slow me down, neither could Tezoc. And we all know how it ended for him. So when you announced a few weeks ago you planned to surprise them by letting them join the Isis expedition, you saved me the trouble of having to find a way to kill them. Thanks. Sorry kids, no heroics this time. Unless you can find a way to stop me from countless trillions of miles away. Good luck with *that*.

Finally, I learned one other trick from Tezoc as well. As powerful as he was, he knew that even *he* couldn't do everything alone. So like him, I've recruited a team of mercenary soldiers to help me out. Remember when we lost a Med-Pen for a day? That was me. I needed it to demonstrate the power of alien technology to my mercenary friends. After I did they believed everything I told them about Prometheus and couldn't wait to do their small part to help me become the wealthiest and most powerful man on Earth.

Which brings me to the point of all this. I've experimented with the Enigma Cube after midnight—when even scientists are asleep—every night since it was discovered two months ago. I can play the controls like a violin. Ben, while you were afraid to let your kids even look at the thing, I was man enough to start pressing the buttons. And guess what. I'll be the most feared man on Earth while you're spending the rest of your pathetic life on a primitive planet. See how far a little courage can get you.

So what does the Enigma Cube do? Well, I've told you I'll have taken it by the time you read this. So here's clue for you, Ben. Even though I've been working out I probably don't have the upper body strength for the job. So how could I possibly steal an object that weighs 200,000 pounds? There's only one way I know of—reduce its weight. Change it so it's as light as a feather.

Get it Ben? The Enigma Cube controls *gravity*.

Every night since my experiments began I've carried that extraordinary little cube out of the Enigma building *in my pocket*. Imagine that. If only we could unlock its secret, it would be worth trillions. But we all know we never will. The team has had a Med-Pen for over a year and still doesn't have the slightest idea how it works. Good thing those dumb mercenaries didn't consider that. They think it's worth a fortune.

So antigravity won't be making me rich. But don't worry about me, Ben. I'll get by. Turns out the Enigma Cube makes the perfect weapon. And I mean *perfect*. Point a certain of its corners or edges at something you want to affect, use another control, and presto—you've changed its gravity in any way you want. For whatever duration of time that you want. Someone bothering you? Send them floating. Or perhaps *increase* the pull of gravity on them so they're pinned to the ground for a few days, unable to lift themselves. You can aim it at a single object, like a gun, or set it to affect the gravity of everything in a circle around you, without changing how gravity affects you at all. Just dial in a radius and press a button. But here's the best part, Ben. How great is this? If you want, you can set it to affect gravity for *living things only*.

Imagine what this means. It has a range of almost twenty miles. So if an entire army has you surrounded, you can send them all floating at the touch of a button. Presto, they are no longer affected by gravity. Or better yet, increase their gravity so they can't lift themselves from the ground, or lift a finger to control a tank, plane, or submarine.

Yes, it's true that gravity is the most ridiculously weak force-that-isn't-a-force in the universe. But still, when you have total control of it, well . . . let's just say that capturing Prometheus—and keeping it forever—won't even be a challenge for me. And that will be just the beginning. I have big plans, Ben. Big plans. I'm going to succeed where Tezoc failed.

Unfortunately for you, this means that no rescue party will be coming for you and your team. Ever. But look on the bright side, Ben, at least you don't need to waste time worrying about what I'm doing on Earth. After all, you're a citizen of Isis now. So enjoy your stay. It's going to be a very, very long one.

Nathaniel B Smith

CHAPTER 13

Cut Off

There was a stunned silence after Mr. Resnick finished reading the letter, but it didn't last long.

"Are you kidding me!" screamed Eric Morris. "This guy's a raving psychopath!" He turned to Miguel and Cam who were each lying across several seats in the back of the tram. "Isn't it security's job to make sure a psychopath doesn't join the team? You people tested *me* enough."

"Pointing fingers at each other isn't going to help us," said Mr. Resnick. "We need to decide what we're going to do from here."

"Yeah, who died and made you king!" snapped Donna Morgan.

"I'm in charge of this expedition," said Mr. Resnick.

"Well maybe you shouldn't be," said Eric. "You're

the one who sent Nathaniel over the edge, after all. If it wasn't for you we wouldn't be in this mess."

"We need to pull together," said Mr. Resnick. "This is no time for petty arguments."

"Oh *really*," said Donna. "When *is* a good time, Ben?" she demanded. "And what does it matter? We don't have a chance anyway. Your brilliant wife led us all to believe the wildlife was harmless." She waved at the formidable beasts surrounding them, dying for the chance to rip them to shreds. "Do they look *harmless*? We won't last a week."

"Please," said Mr. Resnick. "Not in front of the kids."

"They're not stupid," said Eric. "They can see the situation we're in."

"Would you two shut up!" thundered Mrs. Resnick.

"All of you stop it!" shouted Ryan. He had never been so bold as to shout at a group of adults like this before, but his anger was so intense he didn't even question it. "If we can't work together as a team we won't last a *day*."

Regan was shocked by her brother's outburst. "*What are you doing?*" she snapped at him.

"I have an idea," said Eric through clenched teeth. "How about staying out of adult business! No kid's going to tell *me* what to do."

Regan frowned. She wasn't surprised by Eric's reaction at all—Ryan had brought it on himself. Even so, as one of only two kids on the team, she felt the need to defend him. "If it wasn't for a kid," she pointed out in as calm a voice as she could manage, "we'd be dead already. Remember who started the torches going."

"Great," said Eric. "Congratulations. We'll give you a medal if we survive 'till morning. Instead of a quick death, now we get a slow one. Thanks for nothing."

"Enough!" screamed Mr. Resnick at the top of his lungs. "Here's what we're going to do. We're going to stop arguing. We can't live the rest of our lives in this tram. So we're going to relight the torches and set up another—far bigger—protected area using the portable force-field generator. Once we've set up camp, we'll gather as much flammable material as we possibly can. If we ever want to expand our territory, we'll need plenty of fires."

Bob, Donna, and Eric glared at him bitterly for several long seconds.

"Okay," said Donna finally, a scowl on her face. "It's as good a plan as any. I'll follow you . . . for now. But just because you and your wife outrank us back at Prometheus—back on *Earth*—doesn't mean *anything* here. What are you going to do if I don't carry out an order—fire me?" She laughed bitterly.

It was clear from the hard expressions on the faces of both Bob and Eric and their grim nods that they agreed with her completely.

"If fire is our best source of protection," said Eric, "the two flares we have left won't help us for long. Please tell me someone thought to pack some matches."

Mr. Resnick nodded. He rooted through an over-stuffed backpack and pulled out a container with fifteen small lighters inside. "These are better than matches," he said. "Waterproof, and easier to use."

"Well aren't you the Boy Scout," said Donna, grabbing a blue one.

Mr. Resnick passed the rest of the lighters around until everyone had one, including his two kids. There were six remaining, which he stowed carefully away.

"Use these only when you have to," said Mr. Resnick. "Light torches with other torches. I didn't bring any extra lighter fluid. Once it's gone, it's gone."

With the lighters distributed, the group prepared to carry out Ben Resnick's plan. They located the case with the portable force-field generator inside. They gathered their torches and prepared to relight them so they could fight their way through the vicious horde beyond the tram.

Only the horde was gone. All of the predators had left. Every last one.

They hadn't bolted off, as if they had spotted a more dangerous predator. They had just calmly left the area, until none of them remained.

Ben Resnick scratched his head. "Where do you think they went, Amanda?" he asked.

His wife shrugged. "I'm not sure. But the way they all dispersed is very unusual behavior."

Not that she was complaining. With the circle of claws, fangs and deadly horns gone, she finally felt as though the drilling on her raw nerves had stopped.

The portable shield was based on secrets Mr. Resnick's team had learned from studying alien technology. It was far, far weaker than the force-fields that surrounded Prometheus and the zoo planet portals. Any animal with the strength of an Earth bear could break through with enough effort, so Mr. Resnick had made sure it was also electrified. After getting a significant shock no animal would push on it long enough to break through, and would quickly learn not to touch it at all.

The generator formed an energy bubble with a diameter of about thirty yards and was very energy efficient. It could operate for up to twenty hours on a single charge and it could recharge using solar energy. If the sun wasn't out, a hand crank on the generator's side could be turned manually for about an hour to recharge it.

Mr. Resnick chose a flat, open area about forty yards from the tram and activated the force-field. A greenish flicker gave its location away so those inside wouldn't accidentally touch it and shock themselves. Along with the water and most of the supplies, they carefully carried Miguel and then Cam inside the large, protective dome of energy and laid them on the ground near one of its edges. Only two hours had passed since the group had arrived on Isis, but so much had happened, so much had changed, that it seemed like a lifetime ago.

"Ryan, give me a hand," said Mr. Resnick. "We need to bring the last inflatable habitat over from the tram."

Even though half the food and water had disappeared with the second tram, there were two fewer bodies to feed and most members of the troop had packed far more food than they needed for just a weekend. If they pooled their provisions and exercised careful rationing they could make them last three or four days. The biologists who had been on the planet before knew of a freshwater stream five or six miles away. They would need to relocate there before they ran out of water. Then, if they wanted to survive, they would have to learn to hunt with primitive weapons; an exercise that was bound to prove more than just a little challenging given that the closest most of them had ever come to hunting was picking out steaks in a grocery store.

Ryan walked to the edge of the barrier with his father, who deactivated it with a small silver remote, about the size of a cell phone. They stepped outside its protective confines, each carrying a burning torch, and Mr. Resnick reactivated the shield behind them.

Not a single native animal had returned since they had left ten or fifteen minutes earlier, but Mr. Resnick wasn't about to take any chances.

As they neared the tram a strange odor hit their nostrils. They sniffed and glanced at each other questioningly.

A jagged, three foot tear opened in the ground between them!

They both darted to opposite sides of the opening as the tear grew. Ryan didn't feel an earthquake but the growing split in the earth behaved as if it were being caused by one.

"Ryan, move farther away!" shouted his father as he took his own advice and backpedaled in the direction from which he had come. "Hurry!"

Ryan quickly backed away from the lengthening trench that separated him from his father just as bright orange lava spewed from below the ground and began pouring into the new channel.

Another tear opened suddenly near Ryan's feet and he retreated even farther, dropping his torch. He was now twenty yards away from his father. He scanned the area and was able to find a lava-free path that would allow him to return—provided no further breaches occurred.

He was moving toward a crossing point when his father shouted, "Ryan, the mountain! Look up!"

Ryan did so and his heart jumped to his throat. A massive river of molten lava was racing down the mountain as if a dam had burst.

And it was headed directly toward him!

It was as if Ryan was in the middle of a dried up

river bed that was about to become filled once again after a flash flood. Instantly. Filled with a liquid fire that would kill him on contact.

He bolted toward the edge of the multiple rips in the ground and kept sprinting away even after passing this boundary, farther and farther away from their makeshift camp. The river of lava surged over the ground he had just occupied. Additional fissures opened up and spat lava, and Ryan was forced to keep running at full speed to be sure he was completely in the clear. It was almost as if the fissures were following him. The ground didn't settle for several hundred yards. When it did, Ryan continued to race away from the area for several minutes, just to be on the safe side.

"Ryan," broadcast his sister frantically five minutes later. *"Ryan. Are you okay?"*

He was now much too far away for her to see or hear, but well within the fifteen-mile range of their telepathy.

"I'm okay," answered Ryan finally, although he knew this was a very temporary condition.

Ryan could sense the relief in his sister's mind.

"What about you?" asked Ryan.

"It was close, but we got away. We had to move the camp in a hurry, but only to a spot thirty yards from where we were. We were on the very edge of the flow. Unfortunately, it kept getting wider and wider in the direction you went."

"And Mom and Dad?"

"Both okay. Dad almost got splattered by lava. But he was carrying the force-field generator to the new location and it saved him. The generator is melted in a few places but working fine. Cam and Miguel made it too. While Dad was running with the generator, the rest of us carried them to the new camp."

"Can you see the lava river from where you are?" he asked.

"Yeah."

"Is there any break in it? Anyplace I could cross and get back to camp?"

There was a long pause, and Ryan knew he had his answer.

"I'm really sorry, Ryan," she replied at last. "But there isn't. The lava starts at the very top of the mountain and flows down to the cliffs and the sea below."

"So you're saying I'm totally cut off from the rest of you. By myself. Without any food, force-fields, or weapons. On a planet whose predators have developed a taste for humans. Is that about right?"

Regan didn't answer, but then again, she didn't have to.

He had summed up his hopeless situation perfectly.

CHAPTER 14

Death Awaits

There was a long silence, and then Regan's telepathic voice returned.

"Mom and Dad were freaking out about you. So I told them you were okay. That you had managed to outrun or dodge all the cracks in the ground and all the lava flying around."

"Then you must have told them about our telepathy."

"No. I can't see why keeping this secret matters anymore, but I didn't. I told them I spotted you far off in the distance before you disappeared behind a hill."

"Did they buy it?"

"Of course. Why would I lie about that?" She grinned. *"I mean, if you forget for a moment that I was actually lying."* She became serious once again. *"They're working on some way to rescue you. But they haven't had any luck so far."*

"Because there isn't a way."

Ryan couldn't believe it would end like this. All alone on a savage planet trillions of miles from home. *"How could this happen?"* he broadcast angrily. *"I've studied volcanoes. Lava doesn't act like this. It's usually thick and moves slowly enough for you to jog out of the way. And the volcano didn't erupt and shoot gas and lava into the air like it's supposed to. I mean, we had absolutely no warning. So how do you get a river of fresh lava flowing down the mountain without an eruption?"*

"Hold on for a minute," she replied. *"I'll ask Dad."*

A few minutes later she returned. *"Dad pretty much said what you just did. He has no clue how the lava acted this way, and how it could be so thin and travel so fast. But he reminded me that a volcano on Isis doesn't have to work the exact same way as one on Earth. And lava doesn't either. He said that even without an eruption, we should have had some warning from smoke and burning plants. But, apparently, there were no plants of any kind in its path."*

"Just my luck," broadcast Ryan bitterly. He sighed. *"Look . . . Regan . . . I have to go. I'm not sure how many hours I have until it gets dark, but I have to come up with some sort of plan long before then. I'll contact you with an update later."*

"Good luck, Ryan," she replied. And with that their connection ended.

Ryan looked around. He was still on a barren section of the planet. So far he hadn't seen any native wildlife but this wouldn't last forever. They had seen their share of big game in areas like this on their way out from the portal. He guessed that even the planet's most fearsome carnivores didn't want any part of the raging river of scorching lava and were keeping as far away from it as possible.

But Ryan knew he wouldn't stay lucky forever. Soon enough he would encounter a predator and it would attack. It would have speed, strength and other formidable physical weapons that evolution had perfected over millions of years to allow it to survive in a hostile environment. And he would have his fists, a lighter, and a red pocketknife that contained two blades, a screwdriver, and a bottle-opener. The bad news was that he had no hope of survival. The good news was that if he needed to open any *bottles,* he was in great shape.

He had to find protection and he had to find shelter. A cave might be ideal, but he doubted he would be lucky enough to find one—at least not right away.

He needed a torch. The tiny flame from a lighter wouldn't scare off a rabbit. More than that, he needed a roaring fire to protect him and to keep him warm during the long night.

And that meant going back into another forested section of the planet for wood and other kindling. Into the habitat of the gray-furred, silver-eyed pack animals they had just finished battling. Ryan didn't want to go anywhere *near* where they might be, but he knew he didn't have a choice.

The nearest section of accessible rainforest was the area they had traveled through when they first exited the Isis shield. He began jogging in that direction. He needed to have his fire raging and a large pile of kindling gathered by dusk.

As Ryan ran, it occurred to him that his best bet was to spend the night with his back against the force-shield. This way no animals could approach him from behind. If he built a semicircle of fire in front of him, he might be protected. He could use his pocketknife during the night to fashion a spear or two from broken branches.

He jogged about two miles to the very edge of the forest, for once glad of all the running he had been forced to do in Phys Ed. He skirted the tree line, not wanting to enter until he had found a stick nearby to use as a torch. He soon found one and with the help of his lighter had it flaming only a few minutes later. The alien wood made excellent tinder. With his torch blazing he quickly made his way to the shield, half a mile deeper into the forest.

Fortunately, Ryan didn't encounter any dangerous wildlife. He spent the next hour gathering wood into a massive pile against the shield, along with stones to use as weapons. He then arranged the kindling in a semi-circle about ten yards out from him and set it blazing. This accomplished, he sat with his back to the shield and began whittling two spears from straight, solid branches.

Twenty minutes later the gray-furred pack animals appeared.

Just as before they emerged from nowhere and began their telltale clicking noises, far louder and more penetrating than such noises had a right to be and completely unnerving. Ryan counted fourteen of them. They were respecting the fire, but they held their ground.

Rage swelled up in him. *"Leave me alone!"* he shouted at the top of his lungs. He hurled rocks into the pack as hard as he could, but even if he made contact, it didn't help. The animals would disperse for a few minutes and then return, as if nothing had happened.

He screamed at them again and turned to the shield, beating his fists against it in blind fury as if this would somehow open it. His hands were now in considerable pain but he didn't stop until he could barely lift his arms any longer.

After fifteen minutes of circling the fire—at a healthy distance—the pack sensed they wouldn't be getting at Ryan any time soon. But instead of leaving, they laid on the ground facing the fire. Their eerie silver eyes reflected the raging flames and their bared teeth conveyed an insatiable desire to tear out Ryan's throat. Their prey was surrounded, and they were going to patiently wait him out. It was an excellent strategy. Ryan wasn't going anywhere. No matter how much fuel he had gathered for his fire, at some point it would die out.

And when it did, there would be absolutely nothing he could do to stop them.

CHAPTER 15

Flying Bloodhounds

Alyssa Cooper returned home from school over an hour later than usual. Her grandmother promptly informed her that her mom wouldn't be coming home that weekend—and her grandma was *not* happy about it. Alyssa suspected her mother and grandmother had exchanged some very angry words.

Apparently, their mom had decided to attend a conference for the weekend and couldn't be reached by phone. Alyssa wasn't all that surprised. Her grandmother may have been angry, but at this point Alyssa was more relieved than disappointed. At least there wouldn't be the almost constant fighting that seemed to go on whenever their mother was around.

When her grandmother left the room, Alyssa removed a clear plastic container from her backpack, riddled with tiny air-holes. She had picked it up on her way home from school, which was why she was so late. Inside about forty honeybees crawled around, buzzing irritably. She entered the kitchen, placed the container carefully inside the refrigerator, and sat down at the table.

All in all, thought Alyssa, it had been a horrible day. On the plus side, her dentist appointment had gone well, and she had had a good conversation with Ryan Resnick who was cute, nice, and had a good sense of humor too. She had the feeling he was really smart, also, despite the fact he didn't often show it in their English class. She had talked to a few other kids about him and they all said the same thing. It was almost as if the courses he was taking weren't worth his time or effort. As if he was preoccupied with far more important matters than just high school. Sometimes he spoke and acted just like any other fifteen-year-old kid, but sometimes he spoke and acted a lot older. As though he had one foot in the kid world and one foot in a far more serious one. And he seemed completely resistant to stress. As if no issue that would trouble a normal high schooler could compare to what he had already been through.

Alyssa laughed at herself as she realized she was reading far too much into his behavior. Ryan Resnick was probably just a nice, smart kid who didn't try very hard and was so confident he didn't let anything bother him.

But as for herself, she was nearing the breaking point when it came to Brewster, Pennsylvania—and when it came to her mother. She couldn't take much more of this. And Kelsey wasn't doing any better.

Alyssa had been naturally cheerful all of her life. From a very young age when she was around the house and in a *really* good mood, which was often, she would burst into song—something that never failed to drive her sister crazy. But not anymore. Definitely not anymore. Only when she was at school could she manage to be like her old self. Only at school was she able to temporarily forget about her home life and her hatred of Brewster. But the moment she returned home all her frustrations and angers came rushing back, and her mood blackened instantly.

Alyssa was outgoing and had been performing in plays since she was eight. She started taking dance classes when she was nine and had won several competitions over the years. She was especially good at jazz and hip-hop. But that was back in Chicago. Back in a city that had numerous dance competitions and a thriving junior theatre. Not here in the sticks. Not in a place where there were no good dance instructors and little opportunity to perform at any level.

She hated it here. With a passion. And she hated what the move had done to her mother. Whenever she thought about it she felt like throwing something through a window. Or breaking into tears.

While Alyssa had channeled her athleticism into dance, Kelsey had become a tennis and soccer star. Even though there were fewer teams and fewer opportunities to play these sports in Brewster than there had been in Chicago, she would still be okay in this regard. But Kelsey was less cheerful than her sister by nature, so she was impacted by the strain of their parents' divorce and their troubled home life at least as much as Alyssa.

Alyssa was determined to get out of Brewster the first instant she had the chance—and that meant college. College would be her escape from this horrible place. Nothing would stop her from leaving because she would leave nothing to chance. She would work harder than she ever had to excel in school, so she could get into any college she chose. And if money became a problem, she wouldn't let that stop her either. She would get an academic scholarship.

And the Science Fair competition was her key to achieving this goal.

But she had recently come to believe her project wouldn't be good enough, which made her the most frustrated of all.

Alyssa was interrupted from her reverie by her sister charging down the stairs. Kelsey entered the kitchen pulling a blue hooded sweatshirt over her head. Alyssa remained seated with a frown on her face and didn't say a word.

"Where were you?" said Kelsey irritably. "I thought you wanted to do a practice run before our big field test tomorrow. Now it might get too dark and too cold."

Alyssa didn't respond. If anything her frown deepened.

"What's wrong," said her sister.

What *isn't* wrong, thought Alyssa, but managed not to say this out loud.

"Are you mad because Mom's not coming home again this weekend?" asked Kelsey.

Alyssa shook her head no. "Are you?"

"No," said Kelsey, now frowning as deeply as her sister. "It's probably a good thing." She paused. "So if that's not it, what *is* wrong?" she asked again.

"What's wrong is that I'm beginning to think my flying bloodhound idea is stupid. It's not good enough to win at any level."

Kelsey's eyebrows came together in confusion. "What are you talking about? It couldn't be going better. All of our tests have worked. I still can't believe it," she said in wonder. "The field test will work, too, Alyssa. You'll see."

"It'll work," said Alyssa. "It just won't matter."

The project *was* good. Even very good. But it wasn't great. And all Alyssa could think of for the past several days were its flaws. Flaws she should have seen from the very beginning.

Ever since their mother had told them about the famous Pavlov and his dogs years before, Alyssa had been fascinated by classical and operant conditioning and had been determined to use these ideas to create a winning Science Fair project.

Ivan Pavlov was a Russian scientist who had won a Nobel Prize in 1904. He was very interested in digestion and studied dogs to learn more about it. Whenever a dog was given food, it would start to salivate, or drool. The saliva made the food easier to swallow and contained enzymes that would help break down certain parts of the meal. This process was automatic, like breathing, and dogs had no conscious control over it.

It wasn't long before Pavlov noticed his dogs began to drool even *before* they were served a meal. In fact, after further study he realized the dogs began to drool whenever they saw a lab coat. He was fascinated, because the dogs' meals were always served by people wearing lab coats. Somehow the dogs associated a lab coat with food and their involuntary drool responses were activated.

Pavlov immediately began to study this phenomenon, now called classical conditioning, and did so for the rest of his career. In one of his first and most famous experiments, widely known as Pavlov's Dog, he rang a bell as he fed his dogs, meal after meal. Sure enough, before too long, his dogs began to drool whenever the bell was rung, even if he no longer gave them any food.

From the early days of Pavlov the field had expanded by leaps and bounds. While classical conditioning operated on involuntary responses, *operant* conditioning worked on voluntary behaviors, using rewards and punishments to actually change complex behavior.

Alyssa was determined to come up with an unbeatable project in this field. She started by surfing the web for interesting applications that she hoped would spark ideas—and soon, she found one.

An application that could be summed up in three words she never thought she would see together. *Bomb sniffing honeybees.*

Bomb-sniffing honeybees?

This had caught Alyssa's attention immediately. At first she thought it was just a bad joke. But after reading about it on several official web sites she knew that it was real.

It turned out that a honeybee's sense of smell was every bit as good as a dog's. Their antenna could detect unimaginably small amounts of a scent in the air, which helped them zero in on pollen. So in the 1990's, scientists, funded by the military, had trained honeybees to sniff out bombs.

Using sugar-water as a reward, scientists at Los Alamos National Laboratories were able to train individual bees to stick out their tongues whenever they smelled a bomb or plastic explosives. Since a bee's tongue, or proboscis, was even longer than its antenna, this was easy to detect. By harnessing three bees inside a small box with a camera trained on their tongues, the box was turned into a magical, bee-powered, bomb sniffing device.

Working with individual bees using video cameras was fairly advanced, but there were simpler techniques.

Earlier, scientists had used sugar-water to train bees to recognize the scent of a chemical left by a number of different types of bombs. The scientists then tried to train the bees to swarm around the source of this scent whenever they found it. And it had worked!

This had given Alyssa her idea.

She would train bees in this same way to find missing persons, be they fugitives, campers lost in the woods, or kidnapping victims. The bees could be turned into tiny, flying bloodhounds. They could be given the scent of people who were lost and rewarded with sugar-water when they found them.

Alyssa immediately began to research honeybees. She soon decided that early fall would be the perfect time to proceed. It was just before bees stopped being active. They wouldn't fly when the temperature was fifty or below, which could be a problem on certain fall days, but this was also a season during which pollen was limited. A time when bees turned to other sources of food, like open garbage cans at outdoor parks. In the early fall they would be less distracted by pollen and nectar and more desperate for a perfect food source like sugar-water.

Alyssa learned that John Grace, a farmer who lived only a few miles away, was also a bee-keeper. After explaining her idea to him he had agreed to let her use his bees as test subjects. He used a variety that was on the calm side and wouldn't sting unless they were threatened.

When their grandmother had taken the girls back to Chicago a month earlier for a brief visit, Alyssa had asked one of Kelsey's tennis opponents, a girl named Lexi, to collect some of her sweat in a vial after the match. Since Alyssa and Kelsey were doing the experiments, they couldn't use their own sweat or it would mess up the results.

Back in Brewster, Alyssa diluted her disgusting container of Lexi-sweat with water and filled a large perfume bottle. The bottle had a rubber bulb attached to it. Squeezing the bulb would cause a fine mist of Lexi-sweat to shoot from the container.

Next Alyssa used this sweat to train a hive of honeybees. For six days straight she stood by the hive and sprayed the diluted Lexi-sweat into the air just before putting out a pie-tin full of delicious sugar-water.

Then, for the past three days, she and her sister had conducted experiments to determine how well the bees had been trained. The sisters had ventured one, two and three-hundred yards away from the hive. Each time they would stand by a tree or large rock with their camcorder and document that the bees had no interest in the tree or rock at all. Then they would spray some Lexi-sweat on these objects, and within minutes the bees would come swarming—waiting for their reward. Thousands of them. Every time. It was the coolest thing ever.

Their experiment would have two parts. In Phase

One they would train the bees to swarm around the primary source of a scent. In Phase Two, which was far more difficult, they would train the bees to swarm twenty yards *above* the source rather than right on it. Alyssa had reasoned that any missing person who suddenly had thousands of bees swarming around them would be freaked out for sure. She wanted to use bees to find missing persons, not to give them heart attacks.

Tomorrow at noon they were set to videotape their first field test of Phase One. They would start at the hive and begin hiking, taking the perfume bottle of diluted Lexi-sweat with them. Every half mile they would spray minute amounts of the sweat into the air to help guide the bees to the source. After three miles they would stop and spray a far larger dose of the Lexi-sweat on a tree. If the bees were able to find this tree three miles away and swarm to the most concentrated region of Lexi-sweat, they would consider the test a success.

They had planned a practice run for this afternoon to make sure the bees behaved as expected, which would include the testing of different camera angles to be sure the video they took would be as polished as possible.

That was the plan, at least. Now Kelsey didn't know what was going on. Her sister was acting very strangely. "Alyssa, why are you so negative about our project all of a sudden? You were so psyched about it. What happened?"

"I've realized there are problems I didn't think of before."

"Like what?"

"Like even if the bees do find a missing person, how are you going to find *the bees* once they have? How are you going to keep up with them when they fly off miles away?"

Kelsey thought for several long seconds. "Didn't you say the military was attaching tiny radio transmitters to bees? What about doing that?"

Alyssa considered. "Yeah, I guess you could," she said. "Good thinking." She paused. "But there are other problems, too. In real life, when someone is missing, the police take one of their dirty socks or something and have a bloodhound smell it. Then the bloodhound begins tracking them. But the bees don't know they're supposed to swarm around *any* scent you put under their noses, just the scent they've been trained with. So are you going to spend a week or two training them to swarm for each particular person? By the time they're trained it will be too late."

Kelsey frowned. "How come we didn't think of that before?"

"Probably because it was a cool idea and we were amazed that it was working. I mean, the project will still be awesome. But not awesome enough. The judges will see the problems with using this in real life." She shook her head. "There's another thing we should have considered. You can load a bloodhound into a car and drive it fifty miles away, but how are you going to do that with an entire beehive?"

"So . . . what are you saying?" said Kelsey in disappointment. "That we shouldn't finish the project?"

"No. We should still do it. The judges will still be impressed. It's just that we have to come up with a second part. A part using *individual* bees, like they did at Los Alamos. We have to think of some other cool thing we can train them to do."

"Like what?"

"I have no idea," mumbled Alyssa. Then she brightened. "But I did find out today that Ryan Resnick knows a lot about conditioning," she said. "I'm thinking of asking him to help." She paused. "I think you know his sister, Regan."

Kelsey nodded.

"What do you think of her?"

"She's nice. Real friendly, but kind of weird in a way, too. I can't really explain it. And she seems to know a lot of things I don't think they teach in school."

Interesting, thought Alyssa. Ryan's sister sounded a lot like him. These two were definitely unique. For some reason a TV show popped into her head in which a brother and sister from another planet were attending school on Earth. Nah, she thought, they weren't *that* odd.

"I know what you mean," said Alyssa. "Ryan can be

a bit strange sometimes also. But still, I think I . . ." She paused for several seconds. "I think I like him."

"Like him, like him?" said Kelsey.

Alyssa smiled. "Yeah," she admitted. "A lot, actually."

"*Really?*" said Kelsey with tremendous interest. She raised her eyebrows. "Do you think he can really help the project?"

"Maybe. He doesn't think the same way everyone else does. Maybe that's what we need." She paused. "I'll ask him for ideas and see what happens. In the meanwhile, we can practice training bees one at a time. I got a bunch of them from Mr. Grace on my way home from school. They're in the refrigerator."

"The refrigerator?"

"Yeah. If you lower their body temperature they become dazed, so you can strap them into tiny harnesses without them getting away or stinging you. By the time we get back they should be numb enough for us to work with."

"By the time we get back from what?" said Kelsey.

"From our experiment. Like I said, it still makes sense to finish our project like we planned."

"What's the point? Isn't it too late now?"

"Maybe," said Alyssa. "But it's supposed to stay in the high fifties until about seven o'clock tonight. If it gets too dark for this to work, so what? We'll still get some practice for tomorrow and have a nice hike. I *hate* this house. The less time we spend in it, the better."

Kelsey nodded. "Yeah. You can say that again."

"Let's get out of here," said Alyssa, rising from her chair. She and Kelsey left the kitchen and began gathering what they would need for their immanent test.

A few minutes later they heard a surprised shriek coming from the kitchen—from their grandmother.

"Alyssa," she shouted angrily just after her scream had stopped. "Could you come here for a minute?"

Kelsey turned toward her sister and grinned. "Let me guess," she said. "You didn't tell Grandma about your new pets."

Despite being in a bad mood, Alyssa laughed. "Uh-oh," she said, rushing off toward the kitchen. Her grandmother had lived a long time, but Alyssa was willing to bet she had never found forty bees in the fridge before. "Coming Grandma," she shouted, a broad smile still on her face. "Whatever you do, make sure you don't eat any of those. I need them."

CHAPTER 16

From Bad to Worse

Regan listened as her parents discussed strategies for rescuing Ryan. But as clever as they were they could think of no way to cross the glowing molten sea. Finally they gave up.

Regan had never seen her father cry, but he did on this occasion. His son was in grave danger and he was powerless to help him. Her mother just became strangely silent and her eyes burned with a frightening rage.

Thirty minutes later the predators returned.

One by one they came, until more than a dozen different species were represented. Along with the gray wolf-things they had faced there were armored creatures, clawed creatures, and creatures with eight-inch fangs. There were reptilian creatures the size of hippos with heads crowned in twenty-inch spikes. Carnivores that lumbered like bears but had the faces and teeth of a *Tyrannosaurus rex*. Hairy spider-creatures the size of small dogs that shot bolts of electricity at the barrier. Tentacled animals with razor sharp claws at the end of each of their ten snake-like arms. Brightly colored creatures that expanded like accordions and shot poison at the barrier from glands on their throats. Large, furless predators with kangaroo-like legs whose powerful kicks would surely have broken through the barrier had not the electric shocks discouraged their attempts. Animals with powerful tails ending in massive balls of thick bone that could be used as devastating clubs. And even animals that launched projectiles, like porcupine needles, from slots in their heads.

And every single one of them had a common goal: get inside the barrier and kill anything human. The approach of nightfall did nothing to discourage them and their growls and roars and hisses and clicks and screeches and snarls were unrelenting. Each tried to throw themselves through the glowing green barrier and each received a harsh shock for their efforts. This seemed to only make them that much more eager to reach the humans.

Miguel and Cam were still lying on the ground about twenty yards from the rest of the expedition. The group thought leaving them alone, away from loud voices and at a range that wouldn't tempt them to weaken themselves by contributing to any conversations, would be helpful as they began to recuperate. And they were right, especially since the remaining, healthy members of the expedition were at each other's throats. Their endless bickering was loud, and savage in its intensity.

Regan knew the team was falling apart, just when they needed each other the most. Her father was detached, as if he didn't care anymore, and her mother was more combative than Regan had ever seen her, sticking up for her husband and family.

Strangely, the wildlife seemed to ignore Cam and Miguel. The predators focused on the main group. None of the assorted beasts tried to throw themselves at the barrier near the two members of security. Only when Amanda Resnick brought them food and checked on their bandages did a number of the snarling beasts peel themselves away to stalk that part of the barrier—leaving as soon as she did.

Regan wanted to check in on her brother in the worst way. But she was afraid of distracting him at just the wrong moment. That was the last thing he needed. Besides, he had said he would contact her to report.

She lifted her yellow and black backpack and wandered to the opposite end of the shield to be alone. She plopped down on the ground and pulled a small white wristwatch from the front pocket of the nylon bag. It showed the time in Pennsylvania. A place to which she would never return.

She frowned and thought of Ryan once again as the incessant arguing between the adults became even louder.

She would wait five minutes, no more. Then she would contact her brother.

Chapter 17

A New Hypothesis

"Ryan," broadcast Regan as loudly as she could. "*Are you still okay?*"

Several long seconds passed. "*I told you I'd let you know!*" he barked.

"*I'm worried about you, Ryan.*"

"*Well you should be!*"

"*What's happening?*"

"*You tell me.*"

"*Okay. Cam and Miguel are recovering a little but they're still really weak. Mom and Dad are worried to death about you and blaming themselves that you got cut off from us. And most of the team members are still acting like crazed idiots. Dad's still the leader, but I'm not sure how long that will last. Donna, Bob, and Eric all seem like they can't wait to take over.*"

"So you've got a Lord of the Flies thing happening, only with adults."

"Lord of the Flies?"

"It's a book," explained Ryan irritably.

"I haven't read it."

"You will," snapped Ryan, but as he thought about this further he laughed bitterly. *"Then again, maybe you won't. Unless someone brought a copy in their back-pack."* He paused. *"Okay. Thanks for the depressing report. Now go away!"*

"I'm not going anywhere until you tell me what's going on with you," insisted Regan, trying not to be hurt by her brother's words.

"Why do you even care?" he demanded. *"So you can put the right words on my gravestone! Okay, I'll tell you. I'm sitting with my back against the Isis shield with a ring of fire in front of me. And fourteen of those click-ing, gray wolf-things are waiting patiently for the fire to die. Once the fire dies . . . so do I."*

"I don't know what to say."

"Well I do!" snapped Ryan. *"I know exactly what to say. We're the biggest fools who ever lived. We're not ready for Prometheus. We should have just walked away from it."*

"We are ready," countered Regan. *"Dad and the others are being really careful. We just didn't count on a psycho like Nathaniel."*

"So you contacted me on my last night alive to ar-

gue with me!" he broadcast angrily. "Is that really what you want to do?" He frowned deeply. "Something bad was bound to happen, no matter how careful we're being. We shouldn't be messing with technology and science we can't understand. Not don't understand. Can't understand. Like how gravity can be controlled by a small cube. Like how the Teacher can turn solid objects into see-through ghosts. Like the fourth dimension. Impossible to find. Impossible to even imagine. We're way, way out of our league."

Regan gasped, both aloud and telepathically.

"What?" snapped Ryan. "What now?"

"That's it, Ryan!"

Regan paused for several long moments as her mind raced through the possibilities.

"What's it?" he demanded.

"What you just said. About us turning into ghosts—and the fourth dimension. They're the same thing! It's so clear to me now."

"You've lost it, Regan."

"No. I've found it. Hold on."

Regan removed a pad of paper and pencil from her backpack and hastily scribbled on the first page.

"Remember Dad's drawing of Flatland? Well, there's something obvious that we didn't think about. I've just drawn a picture and I'm going to look at it and transmit it to you telepathically. I think you'll understand right away. Here it is."

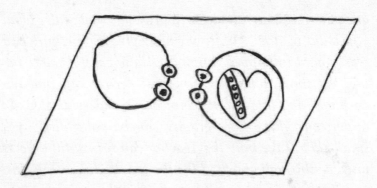

Regan didn't need to ask if her brother had received her mental image of the drawing. She knew he had.

"So here are two Flatlanders facing each other. I've drawn them like Dad did—you know, kind of like frog people. Anyway, I've shown the heart inside the one on the right. And inside the heart is a blood vessel. And inside the blood vessel are cells."

Ryan was having trouble concentrating, but even so understood where Regan was going immediately. *"You're right. I do get it,"* he broadcast. *"I wouldn't have drawn a heart like a valentine, but I get it. No Flatlander can see what's inside any other Flatlander. But we 3D beings can. Easily. We can see inside of everything in Flatland, at every level of detail, all at once."*

"Exactly," broadcast Regan excitedly. *"Dad was saying that Flatlanders could never understand up or down unless someone pulled them off the page. Well, what would happen if someone did that? They could look down for the first time. They could see everything*

inside of bank vaults and homes. And people. Their hearts, lungs and brains. They would think their fellow Flatlanders had all turned into ghosts. Remind you of anything?"

Ryan made no reply.

"Don't you see, Ryan! That's what the Teacher did to us. It pulled us in whichever direction the fourth dimension is in. If the two Flatlanders I've drawn were about to smash into each other, you could stop it by lifting one above the other. Not knowing about the third dimension they would swear that the only reason they didn't collide was that they had passed through each other. Just like we thought had happened with the Hauler. And the one on the left would be able to see everything inside of the one on the right. When the Hauler was about to crush us, the Teacher yanked us into the fourth dimension. While we were there we could see everything inside of three-dimensional objects."

"I get it," barked Ryan. *"I just don't care. I don't want to think about Qwervy science. I wish I'd never heard of them! Why don't you get out of my head and leave me in peace!"*

"I won't Ryan! Let me finish. I have an idea that might save your life."

"An idea? You think an idea is going to stop me from becoming dinner? No thanks. What I need is a machine gun. So unless you can get me one of those, leave me alone."

"I think we enter the fourth dimension whenever

we pass though a Qwervy shield," she continued, deciding to ignore her brother completely. *"That's why we felt the way we did—and why we could see inside of things again—when the tram passed through the Isis shield. Just like we could when the Hauler was about to hit us. Dad was sure a single crystal couldn't get us through every shield, no matter what the frequency. But it can. Because all the shields are touching the fourth dimension somehow."*

Regan scribbled another drawing.

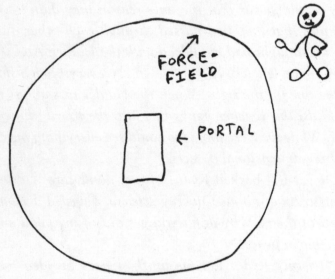

"Imagine you're a Flatlander. This is the shield surrounding the portal to Earth. You're the stick-figure. If you could just lift your foot a billionth of an inch in the up direction you could cross over the barrier. But you can't. I think that's where the crystal comes in. It gives

us just enough of a push into the fourth dimension to let us cross the barrier. But if we could just move a billionth of an inch in that direction ourselves, we wouldn't need the crystal."

Ryan didn't answer so Regan forged ahead.

"Before, we were just like everyone else. But things have changed. The Teacher lifted us off the page. We know what 3D objects look like when viewed from the fourth dimension. We know how our bodies feel when we're moving in that impossible direction. So all you have to do is find a tiny fourth-dimensional seam in the shield and go through. You can do it, Ryan. I'm sure of it."

"That's great, Regan," replied her brother sarcastically, finally responding. *"Can you come up with a theory of how I can flap my arms and fly out of here? That's just as likely. Or maybe I can click my heels together and say, 'there's no place like home.' "*

"Come on, Ryan. Why are we now suddenly able to see inside solid objects when we go through a barrier? Because our minds have been changed again. We've been shown the fourth dimension. So now we can recognize it when we're there. So press against the shield and find a way to move a billionth of an inch into the fourth dimension. And then go through it as easily as a Flatlander walking over a line."

"That's impossible!" barked Ryan. *"Dad said no human has ever been able to move into the fourth dimension. What part of that didn't you understand!"*

"No *human has ever been telepathic either. And yet we're using telepathy right now. Give it a shot,*" she broadcast as forcefully as she could. "*You have nothing to lose.*"

"*All right already! I'll give it a try. Just to shut you up! Just promise you'll leave when it doesn't work.*"

"*I promise.*"

Ryan rose and walked closer to the surrounding gray beasts, still inside the roaring semicircle of fire. He picked up his last three stones and flung them as hard as he could at the nearest three carnivores. "I hate this planet and I hate you!" he screamed at the top of his lungs. Then he stopped using words and just screamed at them as threateningly as he could until his throat hurt. None of the animals were the least bit intimidated.

Finally, he decided he was ready to make his ridiculous attempt. He pressed against the wall of force so he was touching it with as much of his body as possible.

If Regan was right, the barrier touched the fourth dimension. There was a crack he could pass through. Or step over. If only he could find an impossible direction in which to move.

He closed his eyes. He curled his hands into fists and fought to concentrate. He needed to move his body so he would feel the same stretching sensation he had felt twice before. He tried to recapture what this felt like in his mind. He visualized what he had seen before. The driver's insides. And inside the insides. And inside of that. For just a moment he fooled himself into thinking the sensation of being pulled apart had returned, but then he totally lost his concentration and knew he would never get it back.

It was over. He never had a chance of finding the fourth dimension and he knew it.

"I'm done," he broadcast to his sister. *"I tried your idiotic idea and I failed! Now go away!"*

CHAPTER 18

Through the Looking Glass

Ryan turned back around. To face the fire. And the vicious pack eagerly awaiting their chance at him. He opened his eyes.

The barrier was an inch in *front* of him!

He gasped. He blinked rapidly, not sure if he should believe his eyes. But the blinking didn't change anything.

He had made it through, after all. He had found the seam.

"Regan, I'm in! You were right!"

Three miles away, sitting by herself near the edge of a portable, green-tinted force-field, Regan beamed. *"Yessss!"* she replied happily. *"I knew it!"*

Ryan wasted no further time on celebration. He had to find a way to help the rest of the expedition. *"I'm looking for the other tram."*

He searched for several minutes within the shield perimeter and found the tram Nathaniel had stolen. He quickly inspected it. *"Nathaniel removed both the red and white crystals from this one too. And there aren't any more trams on Isis."*

"Why would he bother to do that? He thought there was no way we could get back through the shield to even reach the second tram."

"He's like Tezoc," replied Ryan. *"Very, very careful. If someone from Prometheus did try to rescue us, he wanted them to fail."* He paused. *"I'll be right back."*

As Ryan bolted through the portal the connection with his sister ended abruptly. Earth was just slightly beyond their telepathic range of fifteen miles.

Ryan looked around cautiously but no one was inside the zoo building. He shot through the nearest portal and used his knife to pry both a red and then a white crystal from the first tram he spotted. Returning to Isis he slid the white crystal into the small, hidden slot in the front of the tram and worked the controls.

Nothing happened.

"Regan," he broadcast. *"I can't get the tram to work. There must be some trick to inserting the white crystal, or maybe a white crystal from one tram won't work in another. I don't know."*

"That's okay. It doesn't matter anyway. You can't reach us until the lava river stops flowing and cools down. Or until we find a way around it."

"I'll go and get help," he assured her. *"But I need to do something first. I'll be back in five minutes."*

"Where are you going?" asked Regan.

But Ryan was just stepping through the portal as the thought reached him, and an instant later he was once again 25,000 light years away, back in the zoo building.

Ryan returned, right on schedule. *"I had to get another red crystal,"* he told her upon his return.

"Why do you need two?"

"You may be able to get through the shield the way I did, but who knows. I have no idea how I did it. And I'm not sure I could do it again. In case something happens to me and help never comes, I'm leaving a red crystal outside the shield for you and the expedition."

Regan considered this. *"Good thinking. And I get why you have two. So you can leave one outside and use one to get back across the barrier."*

"Exactly," replied Ryan. *"I'll bury the crystal right next to the shield. Look for a ring of ash by the shield where my fire was. I'll also mark its location with a few sticks."*

"How will you explain how you got through the barrier?"

Ryan thought for a few seconds. Having set foot back on Earth had done wonders for his mood and his powers of concentration. *"I'll say I was getting attacked and the barrier just opened for me somehow. Like this was another safety feature the Qwervy built in to protect zoo visitors that we didn't know about."*

Regan nodded. *"That should work."*

"Regan," he broadcast. *"Thanks. And sorry for being such a jerk. I owe you one. And I'm going to make it up to you."* Ryan paused. *"But before I go, I could use your help one last time. Remember in Nathaniel's letter he said something about gravity being an insanely weak force. A force that isn't a force."*

"I remember."

"I might be facing a weapon that controls gravity. So the more I understand it, the better."

"So you want me to ask Dad about that part of Nathaniel's letter?"

"Yeah. And any other thoughts he might have about this weapon."

"It isn't really a weapon, Ryan. It's a device that could change the world in some really great ways. Nathaniel is just misusing it."

Regan told him she'd be back in ten minutes and ended their connection.

She returned just five minutes later. Ryan was surprised. Once their father began talking about science it was usually hard to get him to stop.

"Okay," began Regan. *"Nathaniel called gravity ridiculously weak. That's because it is. There are only four known forces in the universe. Two of them are called the strong and weak nuclear forces. These do things like keep atoms from flying apart and . . . I don't*

know, something else. I only took notes when Dad got to gravity. The third is the electromagnetic force. And the fourth is gravity."

"So why did Nathaniel say it wasn't a force?"

"I'll get to that," replied Regan. *"Anyway, gravity is by far the weakest of the four forces. Dad says magnetism is . . . "* She looked down at her notes. *"Well, he doesn't remember exactly. But it's something like a thousand trillion trillion trillion times stronger than gravity. Which he says would be a 1 followed by 39 zeros if you were gonna write it."*

"Are you sure you heard that right?" asked Ryan. *"That doesn't seem possible."*

"That's what I thought. But it's true. Dad reminded me that the gravity produced by an object depends upon its mass. So the gravity we feel on Earth is produced by the mass of the entire planet." Regan glanced at her notes once again. *"Dad says the Earth weighs about twelve million billion billion pounds."*

"Really," commented Ryan, amused. *"I'll bet it was hard finding a scale big enough for that weigh-in."*

Regan smiled. *"The point is, even when the weight of the entire Earth is trying to hold a paperclip down, a tiny little magnet can lift it off the ground."*

Ryan thought about this and nodded. His dad made a good point. He had never thought about it that way. *"Okay. Magnetism one, gravity zero,"* he broadcast.

"Which means that if you did have the technology to affect gravity, there's a lot of room to strengthen it."

"I guess."

"So why is it not a force?" asked Ryan.

"Well, some scientists classify it this way, some don't. According to Einstein, gravity isn't so much a force as it is a change in the shape of space-time."

"What's space-time?" asked Ryan.

"Dad says it's like space and time rolled into one. But Dad told me when he was explaining not to worry about that. To think of it as the same thing as just space. Anyway, he told me to think of space as a gigantic sheet of rubber. Or a gigantic trampoline. And objects dent this trampoline, causing other objects to roll toward them. That's what gravity is."

"What?" broadcast Ryan uncertainly.

"Let me give you an example." She consulted her notes once again. "Suppose you spread marbles out on a large, circular trampoline. Then you set a hundred pound bowling ball in the very center of the tramp. If you did, the bowling ball would stretch the tramp down, creating a crater-shaped pocket, and the marbles would roll toward it. But even the marbles dent the tramp some, creating their own little indentation to sit in."

Ryan thought about this. "Okay. I sort of get it. So space is like a trampoline. And everything pushes into it. Light things dent it just a little. Heavy things, like the

Sun, dent it a lot. And the heavier an object is, the bigger the crater it creates, so the more other things are forced to roll toward the bottom of this crater."

"Right. So gravity isn't really a force. It's what happens when objects stretch space."

"Interesting," noted Ryan. *"But I can't see how any of this is going to help me stop Nathaniel."* He paused. *"Did Dad say anything else about the Enigma Cube?"*

"I tried, Ryan. But we got interrupted. There's a lot going on right now. He said he would tell me more at another time."

After another few minutes of telepathic conversation the siblings ended their connection.

Ryan took a deep breath and crossed the barrier again to leave a red crystal for the expedition. As had happened earlier that same day the first time he had crossed the Isis shield—could it really be true that only four or five hours had passed since then?—he felt the stretching sensation that meant he was brushing against the forth dimension. Now that he understood it—a little—he fought to open his mind as wide as he could to the experience.

Ryan buried the crystal and stabbed the two spears he had been making deep into the soft soil beside it to mark its location as he had promised. He shoved the other red crystal into his pocket. "Better luck next time, wolf-things," he said with a sneer.

With that, he crossed though the shield and headed to the portal back to Earth.

CHAPTER 19

Pinned

Ryan peered around the zoo exit cautiously. Not seeing anyone he emerged from the building, keeping an eye out for surprises.

A body was stretched out like a human speed bump on the ground twenty yards away. No one else was in sight.

He rushed over to the body and knelt beside it. It was Lieutenant Lebron Williams, and he was sprawled out like a snow angel on his stomach. He had been assigned to guard the entrance to the zoo. His automatic weapon was lying next to him, and every square inch of his body that could possibly be touching the ground was pinned there.

The guard's eyes were closed but he was still breathing.

"Lebron, it's Ryan Resnick. What happened?"

The guard managed a shallow grunt but that was all.

Ryan grabbed one of Lebron's hands that was palm-down against the floor and pulled. He was able to move it, but it was far heavier than a hand should have been. Nathaniel must have used the Enigma Cube. The gravity of the ground on which the guard was glued hadn't changed at all. The gravity of his *body* had changed. It was as if Lebron was wearing a bodysuit made of powerful magnets and the Earth was made of solid steel. To Ryan, the gravity around Lebron was the same as it had always been.

Nathaniel had chosen the setting on his weapon carefully. He didn't change the guard's gravity so much that his heart stopped or he could no longer breathe. Just enough so that every movement was a battle. Ryan suspected Lebron had been strong enough to drag himself this distance away from his post before he became too exhausted and was forced to give up.

There was nothing Ryan could do for him. "I have to go, Lebron," he said apologetically. "But I promise I'll try to find a way to help you."

Ryan checked several more buildings and the security headquarters but it was all the same. Everyone inside of Prometheus was now pinned to the floor. Nathaniel must have set the Enigma Cube to a broad enough radius that the gravity effect had hit all life within the city at the same time.

He calculated that he was only two or three hours behind the deranged physicist and his hostage. And if

Nathaniel had further business within Prometheus after using the gravity device, or had been delayed for any reason, Ryan might be almost on his heels.

Ryan entered the manmade cavern that abutted Prometheus and rushed to the elevator. Everyone in the cavern was anchored to the ground as well. When he reached topside it was the same story. The guards protecting the elevator were down. Everyone appeared to be alive, but all of them had their eyes closed tightly. Whenever Ryan stayed up really late—or when he was even a little tired and Mr. McPherson was boring him to death in chemistry class—his eyelids seemed as heavy as lead and it was a struggle to keep them open. He could only imagine what it must be like to have eyelids that actually *were* as heavy as lead.

Ryan exited the concrete bunker that housed the Prometheus elevator and entered the lobby of the decoy building that surrounded it. A clock on the wall read 6:14 and the sky was beginning to darken. He carefully peered outside.

Anyone within Proact who had been outside on the grounds when Nathaniel had used the Enigma Cube, probably a dozen in total, were spread-eagle on their stomachs. Whatever they had been doing when the wave hit, they had used all of their strength to change their body position so they were as flat on the ground as possible, lessening the strain on themselves. Hundreds of creeping and flying insects that had been caught in the wave were also glued to the ground, along with eight or nine birds that had had the misfortune of being in the gravity weapon's path.

It was a scene straight out of some psychotic nightmare, yet it was very, very real.

Ryan had little doubt that he would find the same scene, without the insects, within every Proact building, but he didn't have time to investigate further. Before he considered doing anything else—including going after Nathaniel—he had to leave this eerie war zone and find a way to bring back help for the rest of his family and the stranded Isis expedition.

As Ryan crept around the chemistry building the parking lot just inside the main gate came into view.

He stopped in his tracks!

Four very fit and very dangerous looking men were huddled there.

Mercenaries! While they weren't in uniform, each soldier held an assault rifle as though this were the most natural thing in the world. After Tezoc's attempted invasion the year before, Ryan knew a professional soldier-for-hire when he saw one. Nathaniel had promised mercenaries in his letter and he had clearly delivered.

Dropping to the ground, Ryan crawled behind a grove of trees that adorned the grounds nearby so he wouldn't be spotted.

The parking lot was nearly empty of cars, which meant that Nathaniel had trained the Enigma Cube on the Proact facility only recently. He had waited until after closing when the majority of employees had gone home for dinner and the weekend. A smart move, thought Ryan.

Under the mercenaries' watchful eyes, six large SUVs were idling next to each other, facing outward in a circle. A few of them began to turn slightly. One now faced Ryan head on!

Had he been seen?

Ryan's breath caught in his throat and he tried to stay as still as a statue behind the trees. If he had been seen, he was all out of options.

Ryan was bracing himself for being discovered when the four mercenaries suddenly jogged through the wide open gate and spread out around the large gravel area just outside the Proact grounds. They quickly surveiled the surrounding woods and then gave the all clear signal to the vehicles.

The six SUVs immediately began to exit the grounds. The one facing Ryan turned away and Ryan finally allowed himself to breathe. He crept closer to the gate, hoping to memorize a license plate belonging to at least one of the six off-road vehicles.

But he was too late.

All six of the SUVs immediately drove into the woods. Each went in a different direction, carefully maneuvering their way between trees and finding paths that would allow them to proceed.

The four remaining mercs regrouped at the most distant end of the gravel area abutting the Proact grounds, so Ryan continued moving until he was through the gate. He stayed well concealed and was confident none of them would be able to spot him.

Unfortunately, he didn't count on the two mercenaries who were approaching him from behind.

CHAPTER 20

Pursuit

R yan got lucky. Just as they rounded a corner, one of the two approaching mercenaries coughed.

Ryan whirled around and spotted them an instant before they spotted him. Adrenaline surged through him as he raced through the gravel, past the tree line, and into the woods. One of the mercenaries sprinted after him, but Ryan had a considerable head start. He was also one of the fastest kids at his school.

Unfortunately, the merc chasing him was even faster.

Ryan darted around trees and over fallen logs. He was racing against the mercenary but also against time. While there was enough light for him to see well now, this would not be true for long.

He saw two figures ahead in the distance. As he ran they began to take shape. One was tall, with long blond hair and wearing a yellow sweater, and the other was shorter, with darker hair and a hooded sweatshirt. The short one was holding a plastic thermos bottle and a pie-tin. The taller one had binoculars around her neck and was holding a small camcorder in front of her face. She lowered the camera.

It was Alyssa Cooper! And her younger sister. What could they possibly be doing here?

Whatever it was, Ryan realized he was leading the mercenary solider behind him straight toward the two girls. The man was gaining fast! Ryan knew he would be caught soon, but somehow he had to find a way to warn Alyssa and her sister to stay quiet and hidden.

Ryan made a sharp turn to the right, sprinted for another fifteen seconds, and then stopped abruptly. Far enough from the two girls that the merc couldn't see them, but close enough for them to hear what was going on.

"Okay, I surrender," he yelled loudly in the direction of the oncoming soldier, gasping for breath. "Don't shoot!" he bellowed. "Please don't kill me!"

That should do it, he thought. If that didn't put Alyssa on alert, nothing would.

Ryan put his head down and focused on slowing his breathing and heart rate after his long sprint. The merc caught up to him seconds later, his weapon drawn. The man was short and squat, with a neck as thick as a tree, but he ran like a track star.

"Where did you come from?" barked the soldier-for-hire, barely breathing hard. "And how is it you weren't affected by the gravity weapon?"

Ryan scratched his head. "Gravity weapon," he said in confusion. "What are you talking about?"

The merc smiled broadly. "You're not going to make it as an actor, kid. Look, if you cooperate you won't get hurt. But the boss will want to know your story." He paused. "My name is Tony. Tony DeMarco. What's yours?"

"I'm Cole," said Ryan, using the name of the first classmate that popped into his head. "Cole Johnson."

Ryan surveyed the landscape behind the merc, but made sure to do so very, very carefully so the man wouldn't follow his eyes. There! He found what he was looking to find. Alyssa and Kelsey crouching behind a wide birch tree. One whose numerous low-hanging branches were densely covered with leaves that had just turned yellow. The two girls were well back and to his left. As he had hoped, they had heard him and had—cautiously—come to investigate. When the merc marched him back to Proact they would be safe, as long as they left the woods immediately and took care to stay out of sight.

In a flash, Ryan realized that their presence nearby gave him the chance to escape. But if he involved them any further he would be putting them in danger. Even as he thought this he decided he didn't have a choice. He had a duty to warn security about Nathaniel and to get help for the stranded Isis expedition, something that was impossible to accomplish while a prisoner—or dead.

Ryan set his jaw in determination. His only hope was to get this Tony DeMarco to leave him in the woods alone. But how? Nothing was coming to mind.

"Okay, Cole," said the squat soldier. "Come with me. Cooperate and everything will be all right."

Ryan began to panic. He still hadn't thought of anything. Was there a way to stall for time? The answer came to him immediately.

Ryan took a step and collapsed to the ground with a startled groan.

The merc looked at him in confusion. "Get up!" he ordered.

Ryan shook his head. "I must have twisted my ankle when I stopped to surrender. Putting my full weight on it made it worse. I can't walk."

"I'm not buying it. Get up," said Tony DeMarco once again, waving the automatic weapon menacingly.

"Look, you can carry me. I can hop on one foot while you hold me up. Or you can shoot me," added Ryan defiantly. "But what I *can't* do is move quickly."

While Ryan was stalling a plan finally formed in his mind. He looked over the soldier's shoulder and pretended to be scanning the area, frantically searching for something. He had to make it obvious, but not *too* obvious.

The merc caught his eyes. "What are you looking for?" he barked.

Ryan gulped guiltily. "I don't know what you're talking about."

The merc pressed the nose of his rifle into Ryan's jean-covered thigh. "I really don't want to hurt a kid. But no more lies. You have five seconds. If I find out you lied about any detail, you will very much regret it. Five . . . four . . . three . . . two . . ."

"Alright!" shouted Ryan frantically. "Don't shoot. I'll tell you what you want to know." He shook his head in disgust as though he were betraying a trust. "My dad is a Proact guard. I was with him and five other guards when the gravity wave hit. But somehow it wore off on all of us. My dad told me to stay put while they went to the store room for better weapons." He shook his head dejectedly. "I should have listened."

Tony DeMarco searched the direction in which Ryan had been looking but saw nothing. He doubted the kid's story was true, but it paid to be cautious. The boss had said the gravity effect wouldn't wear off for three hours. On the other hand, this had obviously not been true for the kid. So maybe he *was* telling the truth after all. Was it possible that, even now, one or more of these revived guards were stalking him?

"Hop over here," whispered the merc, who was standing beside a slender hickory tree. "Quickly. Say a single word and I'll shoot you."

Ryan did as instructed.

"Sit down and hug the tree," whispered Tony, continuing to look nervously in the direction of Proact.

Ryan sat with his legs on either side of the trunk and encircled it with his arms.

"Cross your wrists."

Ryan did as he was told. The merc pulled a long, hard-plastic strip from the vest he was wearing and zipped it closed around Ryan's wrists, effectively hand-cuffing him to the tree.

"Don't go anywhere," whispered the short, muscular soldier, reaching into another deep pocket of his vest, which contained spare clips for his weapon, a combat knife, and a small roll of silver duct tape. He pulled out the roll and taped Ryan's mouth shut. Then, without another word, he headed off in the direction of Proact.

As soon as the man was out of sight, Alyssa and her sister made their way over to Ryan. The binoculars were hanging around Alyssa's neck and she was still holding the small camcorder. Kelsey dropped the pie-tin and white thermos bottle she had been holding to the ground while Alyssa crouched down and ripped the tape from her bound classmate's mouth.

"Ryan," said Alyssa anxiously, "what's going on? Who *was* that guy?"

"Shhhhh," he cautioned, his voice barely audible. "Whisper." He blew out a relieved breath. "Boy am I glad to see you," he said excitedly, but his mood darkened almost immediately. "Sorry to get you involved," he added with a frown. While it was true that the stakes couldn't be higher, if anything happened to Alyssa or her sister he would never forgive himself.

Ryan's face was pressed against the side of the tree trunk but both sisters had placed themselves within his line of sight. "Don't let your guard down," he cautioned. "We're up against soldiers who couldn't be more dangerous. There's a pocketknife in my right front pocket. Reach in and pull it out. *Hurry.*"

Alyssa did, but when she removed her hand she held two items. Her eyes widened as she recognized the second one. It was a lighter. "You smoke?" she said in surprise.

"No," whispered Ryan, shaking his head. "But you never know when you'll need a torch," he added with a wry smile.

"What?" mouthed Alyssa as she started sawing through the tough plastic handcuffs with Ryan's relatively dull pocketknife.

"Long story," replied Ryan.

"Do you know my sister Kelsey?" whispered Alyssa.

Ryan nodded. Both sisters were light on their feet and athletic, but they shared few similarities after that. Kelsey had dark hair, cut shorter than Alyssa's, and her features weren't quite as soft. "You're in Regan's class, right?"

"Right," mouthed Kelsey as Alyssa continued sawing.

"Put down the knife!" boomed a male voice coming from deeper inside the woods. A towering mercenary, well over six feet in height, followed the voice. And so did his automatic rifle.

Alyssa dropped the knife to the ground.

"Now turn around!" he ordered the sisters. "Carefully. Make one wrong move and I'll put a bullet in both of your heads," he added with a scowl.

CHAPTER 21

Sweating it Out

Neither girl could breathe. What was going on! Where did these soldiers keep coming from! The woods were crawling with them.

"Tony radioed me and told me to move in on this position," said the towering soldier. "Seems he didn't completely trust our boy Cole here. Tony has good instincts that way."

The mercenary slung his automatic rifle over his shoulder and pulled a machine pistol from his vest, set for single shot. "Give me the camcorder!" he barked at Alyssa.

Alyssa was so petrified with fear she could barely move. Finally she extended her arm, which was shaking, and the mercenary snatched the camera from her hand and slid it into his vest.

He pointed his weapon at Kelsey. "Let me see your hands," he ordered.

Kelsey removed her hands from the large front pockets of her sweatshirt. As she did so a bulky object fell out of her pocket and to the ground.

"What is that?" said the tall mercenary as he studied the object now on the ground at Kelsey's feet. "Is that a *perfume* bottle?" he said in disbelief as Kelsey picked it up. He roared with laughter. "I've faced men carrying knives, guns and even rocket launchers. But I've never faced a dreaded perfume bottle before. Is that an automatic or single shot?" he said, and then laughed again at his own joke.

Alyssa may have been paralyzed with fear but there was nothing wrong with her mind. "Don't wait for Phase Two," she croaked to her sister, barely able to get the words out given her petrified tongue and shortness of breath. "We *want* the missing person to freak out."

"What missing person?" said the merc, his thick eyebrows coming together in confusion.

Ryan had the same puzzled look on his face.

Kelsey, on the other hand, looked anything but confused. She was concentrating for all she was worth, running Alyssa's words through her mind until she understood exactly what Alyssa was trying to communicate to her.

The soldier glared at Alyssa. "What are you talking about?" he demanded.

"Nothing," she replied weakly. "I'm just really scared. I was babbling."

Kelsey blew out a huge breath. It was now or never.

"Here," she said, taking a few steps forward and extending the perfume bottle toward the massive mercenary. "You can have it."

The merc shook his head scornfully. "I don't want it," he barked. "Get it away from me."

Just as he was finishing his sentence Kelsey pumped the bulb several times as forcefully as she could. A heavy rain of mist sprayed on the merc's face and hair.

Furious, the merc hit the bottle out of Kelsey's hand with the butt of his pistol and then placed the barrel just over her shoulder. He squeezed the trigger and a single shot was fired, deafening the three kids. Kelsey screamed in fear and pain as a shallow groove appeared in her shoulder and began bleeding into her shirt.

"Do you think this is a game!" shouted the merc. "You think you're going to blind me with perfume! That was just a warning shot. The next time you try something cute I'll put a bullet right through your shoulder."

He wiped some of the mist from his face with the back of his hand, turning up his nose in disgust. "That has to be the worst perfume I've ever smelled. What is it called, essence of sweat socks?"

Alyssa was stunned. Kelsey had been shot! This guy wouldn't hesitate to kill them all. "What do you want?" she said. She tried to say it forcefully but the words almost stuck in her throat and came out in a whisper.

"I want to know where you two came from. And I want to know why Cole here wasn't affected by the gravity weapon."

"Leave them alone!" said Ryan. "They don't have any idea what this is about. Let them go and I'll tell you what you want to know."

The merc laughed. "Wow. That's like a line from some really corny movie. But I'm afraid it doesn't work that way in real life. Believe me, I have no doubt you'll tell us what we want to know. But these girls have seen my face." He smiled cruelly. "And we can always use two more hostages."

Kelsey had tears in the corner of her eyes from the pain and terror of being shot—even if the merc had only grazed her. Alyssa's legs felt weak and she had to fight to keep tears from her own eyes.

And then a surge of electricity raced through Alyssa as she saw two bees flying around the merc. They circled him a few times and then rushed off. Hopefully to find some friends. Or was it getting too cold and too dark for this to work? They would find out in minutes.

"You!" the soldier barked at Alyssa. "Pick up the knife and free the boy. We need to get moving."

Alyssa did as she was told, but she did everything she could to stall. Her hands were shaking anyway, so it was easy for her to pretend to drop the knife on multiple occasions. Several minutes went by and Ryan was still bound to the tree.

Finally the soldier's patience was at an end. "If you don't hurry it up," he hissed, "I'm going to *shoot* through those plastic cuffs. Might not be too good for your friend's hands."

"Where are you taking us?" asked Alyssa, now sawing at the hardened plastic with all of her strength.

The soldier gestured in the direction of the Proact grounds. "That way," he said. "Now hurry up!" he snapped.

"We can't go that way," said Kelsey anxiously. "We were here earlier today. There's a huge hive of killer bees in that direction. Those things could sting an elephant to death."

The merc rolled his eyes. "What is this," he said. "Some kind of circus act. First you attack me with perfume. And now you try to scare me with killer bees. Unbelievable. There are no killer bees in Pennsylvania."

But even as he was saying this six bees flew around his face and head. As if on cue.

He glanced up nervously.

And eight more arrived.

He waved his free hand to shoo them away. Killer bees? That was impossible. They liked warmer climates. But even as he thought this twenty more bees arrived and began landing on his face and hair.

Panicked, he slapped at his face, killing a number of them but agitating even more. Several stung him, causing him to forget about everything but the bees. More and more of them now arrived at a furious pace, like a living cloud. They landed on his face and hair until his face could no longer be seen. He now had an ever-moving ball of thousands of buzzing yellow insects sitting on his shoulders where his head should have been.

Screaming, he dropped his machine pistol and began to run, completely forgetting where he was. He had only gone about twenty yards when he cracked his head against a thick, low-hanging branch. He fell to the ground like a sack of bee-infested cement, completely unconscious.

It had all happened in less than a minute.

The mouths of all three kids fell open as if they were unable to believe what they had just seen. No one spoke for several long seconds.

Finally, Kelsey broke the stunned silence. "It worked!" she said excitedly. "You did it, Alyssa. Great job!"

"*We* did it," corrected Alyssa. It had been her idea but Kelsey had done the hardest part—and had paid a price. "How's your shoulder, Kel?" she asked worriedly.

"I'll be fine," said Kelsey bravely. "He barely nicked me."

Alyssa glanced over to where the merc was lying unconscious under a tree, his head still a crawling ball of wings, antenna, and tiny feet. "They're suffocating him," she said with a frown. "We can't let that happen."

She picked up the thermos bottle from where her sister had dropped it and rushed over to the fallen soldier. She poured its contents onto his shirt and dropped the bottle onto his stomach. The swarm immediately left the soldier's head and traveled the short distance to his stomach, hungrily drinking in their sugar-water reward.

The tall soldier had sustained about thirty stings, but he would live. Had he stayed conscious and continued to try to fight the mild-tempered bees the outcome would have been far worse for him.

"Good work guys," said Alyssa to the swarm as she raced back over to Ryan and her sister.

While Alyssa was saving the merc, Kelsey had picked up the pocketknife and had finished sawing through Ryan's plastic handcuffs. He rose, freed at last from the tree, as Alyssa joined them. "Thanks," he said to them both. He turned toward the fallen merc twenty yards away and shook his head in utter disbelief. "Wow. Did you *see* that! That was *so* lucky!" he said in amazement.

"Luck had nothing to do with it," said Alyssa, a proud smile coming over her face. "It's our project for the Science Fair. We've trained bees to respond to sweat. That's what we sprayed him with. A bee's sense of smell is as good as a dog's."

Ryan's eyes widened. Incredible, he thought. Now *that* was an impressive science project.

Ryan was about to tell them so when he spotted two mercenaries off in the distance through the trees, coming from the direction of the Proact grounds.

And the soldiers were heading straight toward them!

CHAPTER 22

The Hunt Continues

One of the two advancing mercenaries was Tony DeMarco, the man who had tied Ryan to the tree. He must have discovered that Ryan had tricked him and he was returning to retrieve his prisoner.

There was still some light, but Ryan knew it wouldn't last long enough for them to risk running for it. Luckily, neither merc had seen them yet.

"Let's go," whispered Ryan, so faintly that his two companions read his lips more than they heard him. "No noise. Don't step on dried leaves or sticks."

Ryan carefully picked his way among the trees and the two girls followed his lead. When he found an area in which the undergrowth was especially thick he lowered himself to his stomach and motioned for Alyssa and Kelsey to join him. They disappeared within the dense patch of green leaves.

"Don't move an inch," whispered Ryan.

And then he realized that he recognized this particular undergrowth.

It was the thickest bed of poison ivy he had ever seen.

Perfect, he thought miserably. He was really showing the girl of his dreams a great time. If he didn't get them all killed, how could Alyssa *not* go for him? What girl didn't like lying in poison ivy while being hunted by professional soldiers?

"Hey kid, listen up!" came a booming voice from where the towering mercenary had fallen. Most of the bees had had their fill of sugar-water and only a few remained on his stomach. "I know you're out there. You got me good, kid. And it looks like you got my unconscious associate here even better. I don't know how you did it, kid, but I'll tell you what—I won't hold a grudge. Surrender now and I'll go easy on you."

Ryan glanced at Alyssa and Kelsey and shook his head no.

Alyssa looked into Ryan's eyes and found nothing but resolve. Her first instincts about him were *not* just the product of an overactive imagination. She had been right. Ryan Resnick was *anything* but a normal high school kid. He was involved in something big. What it was she had no idea, but it was dangerous. And judging by the number of soldiers that were after him it was something important.

"Consider this," continued Tony DeMarco, his voice getting even louder. "We have two other men deeper in the woods, patrolling. You're boxed in, kid. And soon it will be pitch dark. We have night vision equipment and you don't. You don't have a chance."

Ryan knew they were right. But there had to be *some* way out of this. After thinking it through, Ryan decided their only chance was to reenter Proact. The soldiers wouldn't expect that.

Ryan quietly moved his hand and picked up a small rock lying nearby. He turned to the two girls, ignoring the poison ivy that was touching his face from all sides. "Get ready to move," he mouthed.

Alyssa silently removed the black binoculars from around her neck and placed them beside her. Ryan was impressed. She must have realized they would only slow her down or hit something and make noise.

"Look, kid. Here's the deal. All of us are ready to get out of here. If not for you, we'd be gone already. The gravity effect is set to wear off in three hours. No one wants Proact. We won't hurt you and we'll let you go when we're through. We just want to know how the gravity wave missed you."

Both men continued to advance, looking carefully in different directions. When neither was looking toward them, Ryan pulled himself to a silent crouch and whipped the rock as far as he could deeper into the woods. It didn't hit a tree but made a thudding sound when it landed on the ground. Just loud enough for the mercs to hear.

The two soldiers rushed right by them, racing toward the sound.

"Follow me," whispered Ryan as he jumped up and moved quickly and silently toward Proact. When the trio was far enough from the two mercenaries that they thought they wouldn't be heard, they began running. They passed through the Proact gate five minutes later without seeing anyone else.

It had worked!

While they had been moving, Ryan realized that they needed to go to the Prometheus bunker. There they would be totally safe from the mercs. Ryan's fingerprints and retina scans would get them inside and the mercs couldn't follow. Nathaniel could get inside, but Ryan was certain he was long gone in one of the six SUVs. If not, he would have used the Enigma Cube in the woods to pin Ryan to the ground. And the soldiers didn't have any idea who Ryan was. This was the best evidence of all that Nathaniel had left the grounds. The mercenaries probably didn't want to contact Nathaniel to tell him about Ryan until after Ryan had been interrogated.

Ryan led the two girls into the decoy building that surrounded the concrete Prometheus bunker. There were only a few small windows in the lobby area, strategically placed so no one could see who was inside at any time. Hopefully, the soldiers wouldn't think to look for them here. The receptionist impersonator had gone home for the weekend before the gravity weapon had been used, so they were alone.

"You two were *amazing*," said Ryan once they were inside, no longer feeling the need to whisper.

And they had been. It wasn't just that they had conceived such a great plan. It was that they had been able to bring themselves to carry it out. It was obvious they had been paralyzed with fear. But *everyone* became paralyzed with fear when facing a killer who was pointing a gun at them. The difference was that some remained that way, while others somehow found a way to think and act despite their fear. Until it happened, no one knew which category they would be in. Even the strongest, seemingly bravest man couldn't know how he would react to such a situation until he was faced with it. And Alyssa and Kelsey had come through with flying colors.

"Okay, Ryan," said Alyssa, white as a ghost, ignoring his compliment. "Tell us what's going on. Were those men going to *kill* you? Kill *us*?" she demanded.

Ryan took a deep breath. "Proact has been taken over. By professional soldiers." As he spoke he continued leading them behind the reception desk. He positioned himself behind a bank of video monitors that showed every possible angle of approach to the building.

"They said they don't want Proact," said Kelsey.

Ryan frowned. "Maybe they don't want it *anymore*. But they definitely have it right now."

"My mom might still be here!" said Alyssa in horror, her eyes wide. "She was going to a convention for the weekend but I don't know what time she was leaving."

Ryan winced at the mention of Michelle Cooper. He had to tell Alyssa and Kelsey the truth about what had happened to their mother. But it would take far too long, and now wasn't the time.

"Look, as far as I know no one has been killed," said Ryan. "I can tell you a lot more about what's going on—and I will. But right now I need to figure out how I can get a hold of someone."

Kelsey glanced at a light pink watch strapped around her left wrist. "Alyssa, Grandma's picking us up by the Proact gate in fifteen minutes. She'll freak if we're not there."

"That's *right*," said Alyssa, having momentarily forgotten all about their grandmother. "We have to tell her what's going on."

Ryan considered. "Alyssa, let's keep her out of this for now. Obviously you have to stop her from coming anywhere near this place. But don't tell her what happened just yet. It'll only make her worry and there's nothing she can do. Trust me on this one."

"Then what *do* I tell her?"

Ryan thought for a moment. "Tell her you ran into a friend and her mom and they invited you to dinner. Will that work?"

Alyssa tilted her head. "I think so," she said as she

removed a sleek silver cell phone from her pocket and dialed her grandmother. After a brief conversation she ended the call. "Okay, it worked. She doesn't expect us home until 9.00." Alyssa turned to Ryan. "Now we have to call the police," she insisted. "Right away."

Ryan shook his head. "They'd be way out of their league. I know who to call. It's just that he's in Colorado and I don't have his number."

"You're saying a guy in *Colorado* can help us more than the Brewster police?" said Alyssa doubtfully.

The corners of Ryan's mouth turned up just slightly into a knowing smile. "No doubt about it," he said with absolute conviction. "But I have to think of a way to reach him—and fast."

After a few seconds Ryan asked to borrow Alyssa's cell phone. Cell phones weren't allowed at Ryan's school and he had left his at home that morning. He took the phone she handed to him and considered what to do. Just to rule out the obvious he called information and tried to get Carl's number. It wasn't listed, just as he had expected.

Ryan concentrated for all he was worth until a desperate plan began to form in his mind. He flipped the phone open again with a frown. He would have liked to move to the absolute safety of the bunker or Prometheus, but cell phones couldn't get reception in these places.

He took a breath and exhaled slowly. Then he called information yet again.

"What city and state, please?" said a woman at the other end.

"Washington, D.C."

"What listing?"

"The White House," said Ryan simply.

"Please hold for that number," said the operator, unimpressed.

"Wait a minute," said Ryan. "Do you have a listing for White House Security?"

"There are only two White House listings: information and switchboard."

"Switchboard, please. Can you connect me?"

Alyssa and Kelsey looked on in dismay. Ryan turned away from them so that he wouldn't be distracted. He closed his eyes and took a deep breath. Soon there would be no turning back. What he was about to do was totally insane, but he couldn't think of anything else that could get Carl on the phone as quickly. He had considered asking to speak to President Quinn, telling the switchboard he knew him and that it was important—but he was certain this would get him nowhere. Ryan could only see one way to get the attention he needed.

Another women's voice came over the phone. "White House switchboard. How may I help you?"

Ryan winced. Could he really do this? But even as this question entered his mind, he knew the stakes were too high to back down now. "Can I have White House Security please?" he said. His voice had deepened over the past few years, but he tried to deepen it further. They would take him far less seriously if they thought he was a kid.

"We don't give out that number. You'll need to contact the Secret Service and—"

"Look, lady, here's the deal," barked Ryan, his pulse racing. "I've got a bomb set to blow the president off the planet! I have my finger on the detonator. Now how about putting me through to security!"

"What are you doing, Ryan?" shouted Alyssa from beside him. "You can't threaten the president! It's a crime to even *joke* about something like that."

Ryan ignored her. A man's voice came on the line. "Who is this?" he roared. "What is this all about?"

"Is this security?"

"You bet it is."

"Good. I know you're tracing this call. If you have a high enough clearance, you'll see that it's coming from a location more classified than Area 51. If your computer doesn't show you that, get someone higher up."

"And the bomb?"

"If you verify where I'm calling from, I won't set it off."

Three minutes later a different voice came on the line. "Okay, you're calling from a highly classified location. So classified that *I* don't even know what goes on there. So you've got my attention. *Why have you threatened the president?*"

"Look, President Quinn is the last person I'd ever hurt. I needed for someone like you to take me seriously in a hurry. I'm sorry to do it this way, but I didn't have another choice. I need to speak with Colonel Carl Sharp right away. It's an emergency. I'm guessing you can find a way to reach him."

There was a pause. "I'm looking him up now. But assuming he's for real, he'd better be able to vouch for you."

"He will. When you pull him up on your computer it should show that he has a direct line of authority from President Quinn. So even though he's officially a colonel, he can order around any general he wants. Do you see that?"

"Yes," said the voice with a mixture of amazement and newfound respect for this mystery caller.

"When you get him, tell him Ryan Resnick is on the other line and it's an emergency."

"Roger that," said the voice. "Hold on."

Alyssa and Kelsey had been listening to the entire exchange with their mouths open. "Who *are* you?" said Alyssa in awe.

No wonder he didn't seem stressed by anything going on in school, thought Alyssa. Here was a kid who had the nerve to threaten to kill the president to get a telephone number. And it was working!

Two minutes later yet another voice came on the phone. Finally, a recognizable voice. "Ryan, it's Carl," he said, and although he was a friend he was now *all* business. "I understand you're in the Prometheus decoy building. What's your situation?"

"Proact has been taken."

"We know. When security didn't check in on schedule forty minutes ago, the NSA automatically pointed a satellite at your location. They broke me out of my parents' anniversary party. The satellite showed nine guards and thirteen employees at various locations on the Proact grounds, all spread-eagle on their stomachs. We have to assume they're dead."

"They're not," said Ryan. "None of them."

There was a huge sigh of relief on the other end of the line. "Acknowledged," said Carl. "We're currently reading six armed men on site. Can you confirm?"

"That sounds about right," said Ryan. "They're mercenary soldiers."

"Do you know the status of Prometheus?" asked Carl, and he was unable to keep the worry out of his voice.

Everyone in the underground city may have been immobilized by the Enigma Cube, but Ryan was almost certain there were no mercenaries inside. "Prometheus is secure," he replied.

"Acknowledged," said Carl in relief once again. "Other than yourself, do you know of any friendlies within the Proact perimeter that are still active?"

"No," said Ryan, deciding it wasn't the time to tell Carl about Alyssa and Kelsey.

"Understood," said Carl. "We've scrambled a strike force of jet fighters from McGuire Air Force Base in Fort Dix, New Jersey. They're due to arrive within five minutes. I'll give them your location and let them know our people are still alive."

"Call them off!" said Ryan quickly. "The mercs are set to leave anyway. They said they don't want Proact. I believe them. Nathaniel Smith is behind this. He's the one you need. No one else matters."

"Nathaniel Smith," repeated Carl in dismay. "The shy physicist who works for your father?"

"That's right. He discovered the Enigma Cube controls gravity. And he's learned how to use it as a weapon."

Carl paused to consider this. "Controls gravity? So those bodies we see from the satellite are what . . . people who—"

"People who have had their gravity increased," said Ryan. "And are pinned to the ground." Ryan paused to give Carl a few seconds to digest this information. "A mercenary said they set the effect to wear off about three hours from now," he added. "Anyway, if Nathaniel is still here, he can make your jets crash with the push of a button."

"Understood," said Carl. "I'll be right back." He was on the line a minute later. "I called off the air strike.

But while air power is too easy to spot and bring down, a ground assault still might have a chance. I'm going to land an assault team about three miles from Proact. They'll move through the woods. They'll take longer to arrive but they'll have the element of surprise. And they'll have a chance of surviving an increase in gravity."

"Sounds good," said Ryan.

"Ryan, I've just pulled into Peterson Air Force Base here in Colorado. They're flying me to Fort Dix and helicoptering me from there to Brewster. Right now I need to get suited up, talk to the pilot, and get the military hunting for Nathaniel Smith. But I need to know how you happen to be where you are and how you came to be the last man standing. I'll call you from the air in twenty-five minutes."

There was a long pause. "Before I go," said Carl worriedly, his tone reflecting the concern and affection he felt for Ryan. "Are you going to be okay? Do you think your position is secure?"

"I think so," said Ryan. "But one way or another, I'm definitely going to find out."

CHAPTER 23

Starlight and Storm Clouds

Regan once again sat by herself as far away from the adults as she could manage.

Nightfall had come to Isis. But night had not fallen.

In some ways the sky seemed brighter now than when the sun was out.

Regan knew that when her brother had become separated from the group he had been very worried about the approaching night. If only someone had remembered to tell them that there was nightfall on Isis, but never darkness.

There wasn't exact agreement as to the number of stars in the Milky Way galaxy. Estimates typically ranged from 100 billion to a trillion. But there was one fact upon which scientists did agree fully: the Milky Way was shaped like an octopus, with a dense center and multiple tentacles spiraling outward from its center like a pinwheel. The Earth was located on one of these arms; a minor arm at the outskirts of the galaxy called Orion. Isis, on the other hand, was located at the center of the galaxy, in a region packed with uncountable stars. If stars were people, Isis would be located in the center of New York City, while the Earth would be located in a small farming community a thousand miles away.

Two or three thousand stars could be seen at night with the naked eye from a single spot on Earth. On Isis this number seemed infinite.

The night sky of Isis was spectacular. Stars crowded together so closely that it was hard to tell where one ended and another began. Regan knew the nearest ones were billions and trillions of miles away, but it almost seemed as though she could reach up and touch them all. The effect was beyond dazzling. As breathtaking as anything Regan had ever seen. But at the same time she was bathed in starlight, she felt as though there was an impenetrable storm cloud above her head.

How could everything have gone so wrong so quickly? She couldn't remember when her spirits had been so low. Ryan was back on Earth, but he could be in more danger there than the rest of them were on Isis. What if he had run into Nathaniel and the Enigma Cube just as he left the zoo building? Her inability to help him, or even know what he was up against, was maddening.

Regan rubbed her arms to warm them. It was getting

chilly. When she dressed for the trip she hadn't counted on having to set her only jacket on fire.

Ryan had left a red crystal for them outside the Isis shield. If he wasn't able to make it back in a day or two with help, she knew she would have to take matters into her own hands. She would have to convince the group to search for a way to cross the river of lava. To make their way to the shield.

But how would she convince them? At this point, if she told them about her telepathy and that Ryan had escaped and left them a crystal, they would be sure she had lost her mind. Or she could say nothing about Ryan and try to convince them she could get through the shield *without* a red crystal. How? By finding a fourth dimensional crack in the barrier. Oh yeah, *that* would do the trick.

The carnivores outside the shield seemed tireless. And while only the occasional newcomer would still throw themselves at the shield, none of the creatures took their eyes off the humans inside for an instant. Their eagerness to get at the members of the expedition had not lessened at all.

Since her brother had left to get help the fighting within the group had only gotten worse. There were now basically five factions. Donna, Bob, and Eric were each their own faction and were now spread out as far from each other as they could get. If not, a fistfight would surely have broken out by now. Miguel and Cam formed a fourth, neutral faction—the severely wounded. And the remaining three members of the Resnick family formed the fifth. All five factions had staked out their own territory within the portable shield. Regan had temporarily left the Resnick faction because her parents were busy arguing.

Regan wasn't sure who would tear the group to pieces first; the hostile wildlife or the group itself. It appeared to be a race. If Ryan couldn't send help, she had no idea how she could convince any of them—including her parents—to follow her to the Isis shield.

Regan saw her father from the corner of her eye separate from her mother and walk slowly in her direction carrying a blue, woolen blanket. He draped it over her shoulders and then sat down beside her, putting his arm around her.

"Thanks, Dad," she whispered.

"Are you okay, Sweetheart?" he asked warmly.

Regan attempted a half-hearted smile without success. "Yeah, Dad. Who wouldn't be?"

"You're doing great," he said sincerely. "Better than any of us, in fact. You saved all of our lives in the rainforest and you've been incredibly strong. I couldn't be prouder."

"Thanks, Dad," she said.

Her father looked away and a profound sadness came over his face. Regan guessed he was thinking about

Ryan. She was the only one who knew he was no longer on this lethal planet.

"I'm so sorry that I got you into this mess," he said, lowering his eyes.

Regan shook her head. "You didn't. No one could have seen this coming."

Her father didn't reply for some time. It was his job to keep his kids safe and he knew he had failed miserably. He should never have allowed them to join the expedition. A primitive alien planet was unpredictable and inherently dangerous. He wanted to scream in agony over the almost certain loss of his son. He wanted to lie down and sob and beat himself up for everything that happened, and for being so helpless to protect his wife and daughter from the nightmare to come. But he didn't. Instead he tightened both his jaw and his resolve. He would not give in to despair. He would find a way to stay calm, and strong, for his daughter. This was the least he could do. "Well, I'm sorry anyway," he said at last. "I should have been more prepared."

They sat in silence for several minutes. Regan settled in against her father and appreciated his warmth, both emotionally and physically.

Mr. Resnick sighed. "I hate to do this, Regan, but I'm afraid I have more bad news. I need to ask you to be even stronger than before."

"What now, Dad?" asked Regan wearily.

"The portable force-field generator is running out of

juice. The lava did more damage to it than I thought. It's losing power faster than it should. And the hand-crank doesn't work."

"How much time do we have?"

"Three hours. Maybe less. When the shield gets low on power, I designed it to begin shrinking rather than failing. The perimeter has already moved in a few feet. I'm surprised no one has noticed. But they will. And soon."

Mr. Resnick stood. "Move in from the edge of the barrier, Sweetheart."

He held out his hand and pulled her up to a standing position. He looked more tired than she had ever seen him.

"I have to go tell all the others now," he said. "And they won't be happy, to say the least. We'll have to build a circle of fire around the center of the shield—the last part to go. We'll wait to start the fires until just before the force-field is gone so they will last as long as possible. Once the generator goes completely, I'll try to repair it. The trouble is in the low-tech part of the device, so I'm confident I'll be able to," he lied.

"What if you can't, Dad?"

Her father forced a smile onto his face, one of the most difficult things he had ever done. "Are you doubting my repair skills?" he said, trying to sound light-hearted. "Don't worry, Regan, even if I can't fix it for some reason, I have other tricks up my sleeve. We'll be okay."

Regan nodded, trying to pretend that she believed him, even though her father was a terrible liar. It was easy for her to guess the truths he was trying to hide: that getting the generator to work again was far from a sure thing, and that without the force-field they wouldn't last until morning. "That's great, Dad," she said. She tried to fake a smile of her own but failed.

Without saying another word, Mr. Regan hugged his daughter and then slowly walked away to tell the others the bad news.

CHAPTER 24

Secrets

Ryan took a deep breath and turned to Alyssa and Kelsey Cooper. They had probably saved his life in the woods. Their mother was being held hostage by a psycho. They had a right to know what was going on.

"All right," he began. "We don't have much time until Carl calls back. What I'm about to tell you is the most classified information on the planet."

Under almost any other circumstance imaginable, the two girls would have been sure Ryan was exaggerating. But after recent events they weren't about to argue the point.

Ryan spoke as quickly as he could because he had a lot to cover. He told them about the discovery of Prometheus deep underground and the Prometheus Project that was established to explore the abandoned city. He told them about the zoo building and the portals off-planet. He told them about the bizarre and fantastic architecture and some of the wondrous technologies they had found. Finally he told them that he and Regan had made some key discoveries and were offered the chance to join the team. He didn't go into any detail and he asked them to hold their questions until later. The infor mation he left out could have filled entire encyclopedias, but in less than five minutes they had at least learned the basics.

Alyssa realized this explained perfectly why Ryan and his sister behaved the way they did at school. Why they always seemed different—above it all. When you're a part of the most important, and secret, project in the world, it's hard to get too excited about pep rallies or math class. Both Ryan and his sister could have let their special status on the Prometheus team go to their heads; could have become arrogant, self-important jerks. But Ryan was always friendly and never acted as if he thought he was better than everyone else. Which made him all the more impressive in Alyssa's mind.

"So this city, this . . . Prometheus," said Kelsey, pointing. "It's right through this door?"

"Well, the Prometheus *elevator* is. The city itself is quite a ways down, of course."

"Incredible," said Alyssa. "And the Proact people don't know about it?"

"Everyone who works at Prometheus is 'officially' working at Proact. In the beginning only a very few Proact scientists were on the Prometheus team, but the team has really grown in the past year. Now, about half of the Proact people are really with Prometheus." Ryan raised his eyebrows. "And your mother is one of them."

Both Alyssa and Kelsey's eyes widened in surprise. They had set out only a few hours earlier to perform a practice run of their experiment and now their lives had been turned completely upside down.

As Ryan spoke he continued to glance at the monitors to be sure no one was approaching the building.

"When I was talking to you at school today," he continued, "I wanted to tell you. But I couldn't. Your mom is involved in the most incredible discovery ever. It's normal for scientists to get carried away their first few months. It's the chance of a lifetime. Your mom's a biologist. Can you imagine how great it must be for her to be able to explore the biology of other *worlds*? Only a few people in history—the ones on the team—have ever had that chance."

"Isn't your mom a biologist too?" asked Alyssa.

Ryan nodded.

"So they work together?"

"Yes. Since my mom was one of the earliest members of the team, she now ranks pretty high. So, in a way, your mom works for mine."

Alyssa shook her head. "This is all so incredible. Now I get why we never see Mom anymore. I'm not surprised she's working every minute." She frowned deeply.

"But I'd expect her to be loving it. And she's not. The few times she *has* been around she's been a *nightmare*."

"Alyssa!" said Kelsey sharply, not approving of talking about their mother in this way in front of a stranger.

"It's true Kel and you know it."

"That doesn't matter."

"Look, Kel, Ryan told us some things he shouldn't have. Now maybe I'm doing the same. But this is important. Since we moved here, he knows Mom better than we do. She was living this secret life that we knew nothing about."

Kelsey thought about what her sister was saying and nodded her reluctant agreement.

Alyssa turned back toward Ryan. "So is our mom only miserable when she's around us? Is she friendly and happy when she's at work? You know, in this alien city of yours."

Ryan considered his response carefully. Finally he shook his head. "Not really," he admitted. "But it's probably just lack of sleep—and stress. She's under a ton of pressure. Stress can make you act like an idiot." He frowned. "Earlier today, I was under a lot of stress." He thought back to his time on Isis and decided this was an understatement. "And I was a total jerk to my sister. A total jerk." He didn't mention that she was trying to save his life at the time, which made his behavior even worse.

Ryan sighed. As much as he would have liked to stall forever, he had to tell them the rest. "I need to move on for a second. There's no good way to tell you this," he said, "so I'm just going to come out with it. Your mom has been taken hostage. By Nathaniel Smith, the man behind all of this."

Kelsey reeled from this revelation as if from a physical blow, reaching out and holding her sister's arm as if to steady herself. "No," she mumbled numbly. "That can't be true."

"I wish it weren't," said Ryan earnestly.

"Why her?" asked Alyssa, as a tear began forming in her eye.

"I don't know," said Ryan softly. "She was just at the wrong place at the wrong time."

"What does this guy want?" said Alyssa. "Has he asked for anything in exchange for letting her go?"

"No. He may just have wanted her in case he ran into trouble leaving Prometheus. Now that he's in the clear, she may still be a hostage or she may not be. He has this gravity weapon, so he doesn't really need a hostage, but he's very careful and likes the idea of having one anyway. If she isn't slowing him down, he probably still has her."

"Or she might not be useful anymore and he's already killed her," said Kelsey, her eyes now moist as well.

Ryan lowered his eyes but made no response.

Alyssa shook her head in horror. "This is a *night-*

mare. Since we've moved here *everything* has gone wrong. Mom and Dad divorced about a year ago. It was terrible. Hard on all of us. But after a few months, Mom seemed to be okay. Then, after the move, that changed. She must have been fooling herself. The divorce, the move, the new job, the longer hours. No wonder she's been like she has. It was too much for her to handle all at once."

"We shouldn't have been so angry at her," said Kelsey.

Alyssa nodded her agreement as a single tear rolled slowly down her cheek. "We've done nothing but fight the few times we've seen her, and these might be the last memories of her we'll ever have."

Ryan had never really thought about what might have happened if he and Regan had never become part of the team, but they might have ended up just like this. He never realized how hard the Prometheus Project must be on families.

"Look," said Ryan, "as far as we know, your mom is still fine. Nathaniel could have killed everyone inside Prometheus and Proact—but he didn't. When he decides he doesn't need her anymore, he'll probably just let her go."

Alyssa visibly fought to get control of her emotions. She took Kelsey's hand. "He's right, Kel. Things might work out. And when they do, we'll make it up to Mom. We won't be so selfish."

"You're *not* selfish," insisted Ryan. "How could you

not be mad at your mom? Regan and I were mad at our parents when we first moved here too. They moved us away from our friends. Away from San Diego, which we loved, to the most boring place on Earth. And my parents work all the time also. We were just lucky to have discovered the Prometheus Project and to join the team. If not for that, who knows how it might have turned out for our family, but I have the feeling it would have been really, really bad."

Alyssa and Kelsey nodded gratefully at Ryan's words.

Ryan knew how important this was for them. He was giving them the chance to learn about their mother's secret life, and the chance to gain perspective from someone who had rare insight into their situation.

Ryan was amazed at Alyssa's ability to stay upbeat at school; amazed at how little she had complained. When he and Regan had moved here, they had complained loudly and often to whomever would listen—and their parents *hadn't* been eaten alive with stress and *hadn't* turned bitter the way Alyssa's mom had.

"I promise you we'll get through this," said Ryan with absolute conviction. "All of us. Including your mom. And when we do, everything will change. I'm sure of it. When your life is on the line, you suddenly remember what's really important. Believe me, right now your mom isn't thinking about Prometheus. She's thinking about the two of you."

Alyssa thought about this. Ryan was right. If they

were lucky enough to get through this, things *would* change with their mom. Now they knew what she was really doing here. Why she had felt the need to move. If they could all survive this ordeal, Alyssa had no doubt they would become closer with their mom than ever.

Kelsey also agreed with Ryan that their relationship with their mother would change for the better if she survived. But his promise that their mother would get through this meant *nothing*. He had no idea what would happen. And he had no control over any of it. It wasn't as if he could do a single thing to stop Nathaniel from doing whatever he wanted to do.

Ryan read the skepticism in Kelsey's face and guessed what she was thinking. He knew that she was right. He shouldn't have made such a hollow promise. He had only wanted to make the sisters feel better, however he could, but the truth was their mom's chances were *not* good.

He thought about the contents of Nathaniel's letter.

No, he realized grimly, Michelle Cooper's chances were not good at all.

CHAPTER 25

Full Briefing

Colonial Carl Sharp called Alyssa's phone a minute later, right on schedule.

"Ryan, I've got you patched through my headphones," he said as he hurtled toward the East Coast. "Are you still safe and undetected?"

Ryan confirmed that he was. He could hear the roar of the jet in the background but Carl must have been using noise canceling technology because his voice came through quite clearly.

"My strike team is on the ground and estimated to arrive at Proact in forty minutes," continued Carl. There was a pause. "Ryan, President Quinn has been patched in with us as well."

"Hello, Ryan," said the president. His famous voice was unmistakable. "Nice to talk to you again. I wish it could be under better circumstances."

Alyssa and Kelsey were close enough to hear both ends of the conversation and both of them gasped. It was really the president! And he knew Ryan Resnick!

It was a wonder Ryan's head hadn't grown too big to fit through a door, thought Alyssa. It was remarkable that he was *ever* able to act like an ordinary kid. At first she had just liked him, but now she had come to admire him as well.

"Ah . . . hello, Mr. President," said Ryan. He gritted his teeth and winced. "Sorry about threatening to blow you up, sir."

President Quinn laughed. "Just try not to make a habit of it," he said wryly. "Can you give us a full briefing?"

Ryan did so. As he spoke, Alyssa and Kelsey hung on his every word, intent on learning as much about their mother's situation as they possibly could.

Ryan told Carl and the president how Dr. Harris was found shot in the Enigma building and everything that happened since. He told them how Nathaniel had tricked them and left them stranded on Isis. How he had taken Michelle Cooper hostage. About the contents of Nathaniel's letter. About the sea of lava that had surprised them and split Ryan from the rest of the expedition. About how the shield had opened on its own when Ryan was being attacked by vicious animals. "Probably a safety feature," he had lied.

Ryan spoke rapidly and Carl and President Quinn

asked very few questions. Even when he told them how he had escaped from the mercenaries in the woods—and just who it was that had helped him—they said nothing. Finally he finished and waited for them to respond.

"So I assume Michelle Cooper's daughters are there with you now," said Carl.

"Yes. Alyssa and Kelsey."

"Just to be sure I heard you right," said President Quinn. "Did you really say they took out a professional soldier with . . ." He hesitated as though he couldn't believe what he was about to say. "With a trained swarm of *honeybees*?"

"Yes, sir, Mr. President. I know it sounds crazy, but that's what happened."

"Incredible," said President Quinn. "Tell them I'm very impressed," he added appreciatively. "I sure am glad the kids of Brewster are on *our* side."

The girls glanced at each other in amazement. The President of the United States was talking about *them*. He was complimenting *them*. It seemed far too fantastic to be reality. Yet it was.

"I know I broke the rules by getting them involved with Prometheus," said Ryan. "I wouldn't have done it if there was any other way. But even if I hadn't been there, they would have run into the patrolling mercenaries before too long."

"That's okay, Ryan," said Carl reassuringly. "You

did nothing wrong. We'll worry about that later. Your safety is our main concern right now."

"Ryan, thanks for the briefing," said President Quinn. "I have to sign off now. Colonel Sharp, I'm going to keep this in your hands for now. You'll have absolute authority to command any part of the military you need. But keep me fully informed. Is that understood?"

"Yes sir, Mr. President."

"Ryan. Colonel Sharp. Good luck." And with that the president left them.

With the president no longer on the line, Ryan wasted no time in changing the subject. "Carl, I know you have other things to worry about right now," he said, "but my job is to get help for the Isis team."

"Understood," said Carl. "But there is nothing anyone can do for them right at the moment. I realize they think they're stranded and they've sustained some bad injuries, but they'll be safe within the portable shield until we can get to them."

"How will we do that?"

Carl paused in thought. "We can take a small, two-man chopper through the portal in pieces," he said finally. "Once we put it back together we can use a red crystal to get it through the shield. Then all we have to do is airlift the Isis team over the lava one at a time."

Ryan was relieved. This sounded like an excellent plan.

"There's a lot going on, but we can probably have

the chopper ready to go on Isis by Sunday night," finished Carl.

"Thanks, Carl. I'll tell Regan to have everyone waiting."

"Tell her how?"

"Oh yeah. I don't know what I was thinking. Never mind."

"So let's get back to Nathaniel," said Carl. "In his letter he boasted about running the world. So we know his end game. But did the letter give you any insight as to what his specific plans might be?"

"None."

"Well, he's very, very smart. Everyone on the team is. You can bet he's in one of those six SUVs. He knows the satellites can't track them through the woods. Even so, he was careful enough to send six of them in six different directions, just to be sure."

"Any way you can find them after they leave the woods?" asked Ryan.

"Very unlikely. He's being far too smart and cautious. You can bet he and his people will park the SUVs at the edge of the woods and exit on foot, jumping into cars that are waiting for them. We'd have to be extremely lucky to spot him. But we have one advantage he didn't count on."

"What's that?"

"You," said Carl simply. "He thought he stranded everyone who knew he was behind this. But you made it back from Isis to tell us who to look for. His SUV trick still might work and he still might disappear without a trace, but at least now we have *some* chance."

"It doesn't seem like his plan is to capture Prometheus," noted Ryan. "At least not right now. Which doesn't make sense to me. In his letter he said that capturing Prometheus would be the first thing he did, and he planned to hold it to make sure we were stranded on Isis forever."

"I don't know. Maybe he just liked the idea of you thinking you'd never get home. A cruel mind game. You said you were supposed to be gone until Sunday night. So maybe he planned to come back and control the city before anyone realized you were stranded. Given that he has the Enigma Cube, we'd be hard pressed to stop him even now that we know who to look for."

"But he already *had* Prometheus," said Ryan. "Why didn't he keep it?"

There was a long pause. "Again, because he's smart," said Carl. "Holding Prometheus would have been a dumb move. The ideal situation for him would have been to sneak the Enigma Cube out of the city without anyone knowing. But he couldn't. Because our sensors would have detected its alien energy signature. And the second it was missing the city would have been locked down.

"So he knew he would have to *use* the weapon to be able to get it out," continued Carl. "And yes, he could have held Prometheus, but if he did, we'd know where he was. Even with his weapon that would give us a big advantage. We could sneak in and mine the entire area without him knowing. We could plant bombs that we could activate with a remote. He'd have a great prize, but he'd trap himself at the same time."

Ryan's heart sped up as he thought he detected movement on one of the monitors, but it was only some leaves blowing in the wind.

"So his plan is brilliant," continued Carl. "He gets out of the city with the Enigma Cube and loses himself. We get Proact and Prometheus back, but now he has all the time in the world to plan how he wants to use the weapon. And we have no idea where he is. He can come at us at any time, from anywhere." Carl paused. "If I were in his situation, I'd have played it the same way," he finished, almost with a hint of admiration.

"I know you screen everyone very carefully before they join the team," said Ryan. "To make sure they're stable and . . . well, not like Nathaniel. How did he pass?"

"I wish I knew. We quizzed him hooked up to the best lie detector equipment we have. Like everyone. I supervised the test myself. We asked him what he would do in different situations designed to test his morals and ethics. He passed with flying colors."

"Well, lie detectors aren't perfect," noted Ryan.

"True, but the people who can fool them are really, really bad. People with no conscience, no sense of good and evil, right and wrong. Since we know the lie detector won't weed out this type of psychopath, we look into everyone's life history very carefully before we ask them to join Prometheus. A true psychopath always has something in their background that is suspicious. But not Nathaniel. Anyone psychotic enough to completely fool our lie detector *and* smart enough to hide any sign of this behavior in his past is doubly dangerous."

Alyssa and Kelsey continued to listen to every word. They were able to hear Carl's booming voice almost as well as Ryan could.

"Ryan, I need to go. I have a lot to do before I reach you."

"One last thing before you do," said Ryan. "When you went to Isis the animals ignored people completely. Now every last one of them wants us dead. Any idea why that is?"

"I thought about that when you were briefing us," said Carl. "Did your mom tell you what happened on our last trip?"

"Yes. About the animals that look just like lava rocks."

"Right. There were five of them in all. They only noticed us because I crushed one by accident. So the only thing that I could think of is that they alerted the other animals about us. But they couldn't have. They were all dead. And even if they were *alive* they couldn't have. After all, none of the species on Isis are intelligent. It's the same for all zoo planets. The Qwervy would never let us visit if this weren't true."

"I agree," said Ryan. "It's impossible. Even if they were alive. Even if they were intelligent. Even if *all* species were intelligent, they couldn't have spread the word that well. So it has to be something else that triggered it."

Ryan shook his head in frustration. He would probably never solve this mystery. But as long as they could get the Isis expedition back home, he decided he didn't care.

"It doesn't make sense," agreed Carl.

Ryan took a deep breath. There was one other point he needed to address. "How are things between you and, ah . . . my mom?" he asked hesitantly.

Carl sighed. "Not great, Ryan. She lost of a lot of respect for me after what happened on Isis."

"I know," said Ryan. "She thinks you killed two of the animals out of revenge. I told her she was wrong. That you would never do that. That you had saved her life."

There was a long pause. "No, Ryan. The truth is that your mom is right."

"What! How could that be?"

"I don't know," said Carl miserably. "After the injury I just lost it. I hated those animals for what they did to me. More than I've ever hated anything. And the thing is . . . well, the thing is that it was my own fault. They were minding their own business and I killed one of them. Who could blame them for what they did after that? Not that I still didn't have a right to defend myself—and the others—but those last two animals were backing away. They couldn't have hurt us."

Ryan couldn't believe what he was hearing. He had been so sure his mom was wrong about Carl.

"I lost my mind for a while," said Carl. "I wanted those animals dead," he admitted. "I'm not proud of that."

Ryan still refused to believe Carl could have acted in this way. "The pain must have been responsible," he said. "From what my mom said, your calf was nearly ripped from your leg. I can't even imagine how painful that must have been. When I stub my toe on the couch, I even hate the couch for a while. And that's because of a stubbed toe."

"I appreciate what you're trying to do, Ryan, but I've seen a lot of combat in my time and I've been in a lot of pain, and I've never lost control like this. But who knows? You could be right. I have to admit, once your mom hit me with the Med-Pen and the pain went away, I realized within five minutes that I had been out of control." He paused. "But I won't make excuses. I don't blame your mother for being disappointed in me."

"Ryan, look!" said Alyssa Cooper urgently, pointing to the monitors.

Ryan was so caught up in his conversation with Carl he had forgotten to look at the monitors for some time now. Good thing Alyssa had stayed alert. All six mercs were converging on the door to the lobby, their automatic weapons drawn.

"Gotta go, Carl," said Ryan anxiously. "We've got company."

CHAPTER 26

Inspiration

"I'm going to enter Prometheus," said Ryan. "The mercs can't follow us there."

"Hurry!" said Carl. "My men will be at Proact in eight minutes for the ground assault. Call me when you resurface. Your cell phone should have recorded my number."

Ryan was already moving to the door leading into the Prometheus bunker with the Cooper sisters as Carl spoke.

"Got it," said Ryan, closing the phone.

Ryan wondered how the mercenaries had found them. He guessed they had finally thought to check for cell phone activity in the area and had zeroed in on his signal.

Ryan hit a small button under the lip of the counter and a retina scanner slid out from a hidden compartment in the wall. He put his head against it and a tiny laser light crossed his right eye. The massive vault door opened with a loud click.

"Hurry," said Ryan, leading the girls inside and closing the door behind them.

They were safe. After a fingerprint scan and another retina scan they were standing in the massive Prometheus elevator. Ryan entered a password into a metal keypad in the elevator and it began its rapid descent.

The girls were horrified by the guards they encountered still pinned to the ground like insects in a bug collection. But when they stepped through the cavern and into the city their mouths dropped open and stayed there.

Ryan led them to one of the oversized golf-carts and had them slide in. He began driving as quickly as the cart would go.

"Ryan," said Kelsey, her eyes still wide. "This is fantastic! That building over there," she said pointing. "It looks like it's floating."

Ryan nodded. "That's an optical illusion. It really isn't. But if the builders of this city had wanted to have a floating building for real, I'm sure they could have pulled it off."

Alyssa pointed to yet another building. "And that one seems to be . . ."

"Sorry Alyssa. Kelsey," interrupted Ryan. "But I have this idea beginning to form in my head, and I think it's important. You don't know how much I'd love to show you around and answer questions—but I really need to concentrate."

"No problem," said Alyssa, but she was unable to completely hide her disappointment.

Ryan frowned. Just perfect. Win a dream date with Ryan Resnick. He'll have you running for your life and then he'll ignore you.

Ryan forced himself to return to the train of thought he was pursuing. The more he reasoned things through, the more convinced he was that he had hit on something important.

He stopped the cart in front of the zoo building and jumped out. "Wait here," he said excitedly and then rushed into the building.

He stepped through the Isis portal as quickly as he could.

"Regan!" he called out telepathically.

Several long seconds passed.

"Ryan?" came the surprised reply. *"You made it!"* Ryan could sense just how worried his sister had been about him. *"Are you okay? Did Nathaniel take over Prometheus?"*

"I'm fine," answered Ryan. *"I'm in no danger at the moment. Nathaniel got through security and escaped aboveground pretty easily, but he made no move to capture the city."*

"Really?" broadcast Regan, suddenly hopeful. *"That's great news."*

"*Yeah. Unfortunately, Earth is still in a lot of trouble. He recruited a bunch of mercenaries just like he said he would, and he's already used the Enigma Cube as a weapon. But at least he hasn't killed anyone so far. And there's more good news,*" added Ryan, brightening. "*I managed to contact Carl. He thinks we can be ready to pull you out of there by Sunday night.*"

Ryan waited for his sister's excited reaction but was greeted by nothing but silence.

"*What's wrong?*" he asked.

"*There's just one problem with that plan, Ryan.*"

"*What's that?*"

"*The generator is failing,*" responded Regan simply. "*We'll all be dead long before Sunday night.*"

CHAPTER 27

A Missing Device

"**W**hat's *your exact situation?*" asked Ryan urgently.

"*The shield is shrinking,*" replied Regan. She looked around. "*We have about half the area we had before. We're setting up wood in a circle around us to light on fire in an hour or so.*"

"*Good, then there's still time,*" broadcast Ryan. "*I asked Carl why all the animals went from ignoring humans to wanting us dead. He didn't know, but I've figured it out. And it has nothing to do with the lava rock creatures.*"

Ryan explained his theory as quickly as he could. In the beginning, Regan thought he was crazy, but the more he continued the more powerful his arguments became. By the end his conclusion was bizarre but inescapable.

And if he was right, he had saved all their lives. *If*

he was right. But it was still just a hypothesis, and even the best theories sometimes failed when put to the test. *"Okay, Ryan. I'm going to end our connection and give this a shot. I know you'll be trying to help Carl stop Nathaniel, so be careful."* Regan paused. *"I guess if there's anyone still alive here for you to rescue on Sunday,"* she added as bravely as she could, *"you'll know that this worked."*

Ryan shook his head. *"Regan, I'm not going any-where. Not until I know that you've succeeded and the expedition is safe. I'll stay out of your head,"* he told her, *"but I'll be right here if you need me."*

There was a pause. *"Thanks Ryan,"* she replied softly.

Ryan sighed deeply. *"Good luck,"* he whispered tele-pathically as their connection ended.

Regan wasted no time. She walked to where the emergency kit was lying on the ground next to Miguel and Cam. They were getting stronger and had been able to move on their own power closer toward the center of the circle as the force-field had receded.

She opened the emergency kit without saying a word. Even in the ever-shrinking confines of their camp, the five factions were still as far apart as they could get.

The Med-Pen she was looking for was missing.

She frowned deeply. Why couldn't anything ever be easy?

"I need everyone to come here," she said loudly. She got some angry looks but everyone came closer from their separate camps to satisfy their curiosity. Her parents moved the closest to her of anyone.

"Regan, what's going on?" asked her father.

"The Med-Pen is missing," she said, loudly enough to be heard by the entire group. "Who has it?" she demanded.

Everyone glared suspiciously at everyone else. Her parents drew even closer to her.

"How do we know *you* didn't take it?" barked Donna Morgan.

"Because I'm the one who discovered it's gone."

"That means nothing," said Bob Zubrin suspiciously. "You're a clever kid. Or maybe your family put you up to this. Steal the device and then sound the alarm to throw us off. There are *three* Resnicks in our cozy little group, after all. The odds point to you or your parents."

"Why would anyone take it?" said Ben Resnick. "It's for all of us to use."

"You really are a Boy Scout, aren't you?" said Donna contemptuously. *"It's for all of us to use,"* she repeated in a false, high-pitched voice, mocking him. "That's easy to say now, but all bets are off when the shield goes down. What if the group is forced to split up? And *someone* has to carry the emergency kit. What if that person is killed and dragged off?" She shook her head fiercely. "No, the device won't be there for all of us to use. I only wish I had thought to take it first," she finished cynically.

"Look," pleaded Regan. "Whoever has it, just give it to me for thirty seconds. I'll give it right back. I promise."

No one came forward. The stars glowed like a million fireflies above their heads but none of the stranded humans paid them the least bit of attention.

"Look, I know why the animals want to attack us," said Regan. "I can save our lives. Here's what's going on. The animals here . . ."

"Shut up already!" screamed Eric. "No one here has to listen to a *kid* anymore. And we're not! If I hear one more sentence from you I'm going to vomit. I don't care about your saving-the-world fantasies. We're done putting up with it!"

"Talk that way to my daughter again," hissed Amanda Resnick, "and I'll see to it it's the last thing you ever say."

"You think you can take me?" yelled Eric defiantly.

"What are you all doing!" screamed Miguel from the ground. He had lost so much blood that the effort of speaking this loudly made him dizzy. "Stop this!" He waved his hand limply at the dozens upon dozens of deadly predators outside the shield as they continued to pace anxiously. "Save it for them," he said.

"Oh great, security has finally decided to come back to life," said Eric. "Brilliant idea, Miguel. We'll save it for them. I've got news for you—nothing we save for them will help us. You know what *would have* helped us? If the lieutenant in charge of security had brought an actual *weapon* with him instead of a toy dart gun."

Regan couldn't bear to listen to any more. She snatched the silver remote control for the force-field generator and ran to the edge of the shield ten yards away. Donna, Eric, and Bob began to go after her.

"Stop!" she yelled, holding up the remote. "One more step and I lower the shield! *I'll do it!*" she screamed.

All three stopped at once.

"Regan, give me the remote," pleaded her father. "Get away from the edge. It's still receding."

"Sorry, Dad," she said sadly. "But this is something I have to do."

Regan wanted to burst into tears. To throw herself into her father's arms. She was so weary. But this was their only chance and she refused to give up.

"Listen to me, everyone," she yelled. "I'm going to tell you my theory. And you're going to listen. If I even see a single one of you not paying attention I'll lower this shield. You'll have no time to start the fires. The beasts of Isis will be on you before you can reach in your pocket for a *lighter*. *I'll do it!*" she screamed with a frightening intensity. *"I swear it!"*

As they looked into her eyes, blazing with desperation and crazed conviction, not one of the members of the stranded Isis expedition had any doubt at all that she would carry out her threat.

CHAPTER 28

Sixth Sense

"Alright, already!" growled Bob Zubrin. "If having the stage means that much to you, tell us this theory of yours. *Save our lives*," he said mockingly. "We're all ears."

Regan was momentarily elated, but she made sure not to show it. Her ploy had worked! She had been sure they would call her bluff, but they hadn't. She quickly changed gears, knowing that she had a very limited time to get through to her unwilling audience. There wasn't a second to waste. "The wildlife of Isis doesn't have a sense of smell," she began evenly. "But they have a sense that we *don't* have." She paused. "They can sense emotions. Negative emotions. It's a kind of telepathy I think."

"Are you kidding me," snapped Eric, rolling his eyes. "I think I'd rather get torn to shreds by the predators than have to listen to your lunatic nonsense."

Regan ignored him. "All animals give off primitive emotional energy. So among other things, the wildlife of Isis can use this sense to determine what is alive and what isn't. And when they are being threatened. But when we first came here we gave off emotional energy on a different frequency. Mom brought a group of calm scientists here to do what they love doing, so they radiated either no emotions or positive ones. Since human emotional energy was alien, and positive, the Isis wildlife couldn't sense us."

"You know what *I'm* really good at sensing," said Donna scathingly. "Stupidity. And this has to be the dumbest idea I've ever heard."

A scowl came over Regan's face and she was about to respond angrily when she caught herself and forced herself to relax. She took a deep breath and her expression softened. Their lives depended on her not getting sidetracked. "So humans seemed like trees to Isis animals," she continued, as if Donna had never spoken. "When they see a tree, they know it isn't alive. So they ignore it. They might walk around it or scratch their backs on its bark, but they don't think of it as a threat or something they can hunt for a meal."

"You can't compare us to a tree," said Donna irritably. "They don't move. *We* do."

"So do rocks rolling down hills," pointed out Regan. "Or leaves. But to these animals, anything that doesn't radiate emotional energy isn't alive. It's something to ignore—unless it's about to hit you."

"What an imagination," said Donna, shaking her head in disgust. "You should be a fantasy writer."

"Would you shut up already, Donna!" barked Bob. "Let her finish. This is torture enough without you prolonging it."

The two glared at each other angrily but said nothing else.

"Everyone here knows what happened the last time a team from Prometheus visited Isis," continued Regan. "Carl accidentally killed an animal, one that must have been able to disguise its appearance *and* emotional energy. Michelle Cooper had her feet resting on one of them for a long time, but it didn't react at all. Only when Carl's foot crushed the animal's chest did it pay any attention to humans. Why? Because Carl was totally shocked when this happened. Powerful negative emotions must have been *pouring* out of him. Fear. Guilt. Surprise. The animal's "emotional energy" sense was bombarded by it. Carl was a not-alive thing it suddenly sensed as being *very* alive."

Regan paused. "So what did this animal do? It used its sharp teeth to attack back, which caused even stronger negative emotions in Carl, followed by powerful negative emotions from *all* the humans. Fear, disgust, horror, hatred. It all poured out."

"Okay, we get it!" snapped Eric. "So they realized we humans were living things and attacked the group."

"Yes, and were killed because of it," said Regan. "By Carl. He shot them all." She continued to clutch the force-field remote tightly in her right hand. "But I overheard Carl a few weeks ago talking with another member of security about it," she said.

This wasn't true, but she wanted to relay the information Ryan had given her minutes before and this was the only way she could do it.

"I didn't understand what it was about at the time, but I do now."

"Get to the point!" demanded Eric.

"Carl said he was ashamed of himself for killing two of the lava-rock animals that weren't a threat anymore. Even *he* couldn't understand why he had reacted the way he did. He said he had been in a state of total rage more powerful than any he had ever felt before. That's all I heard. I didn't know what it meant at the time, but now I get what must have happened. Human emotional energy and Isis emotional energy aren't compatible. The animals were hating Carl and this somehow affected his mind, causing him to *hate them back*. The hatred bounced back and forth between them, growing as it did."

"This is nonsense," said Bob, glaring at Regan. "There are far simpler explanations. You don't have to resort to your ridiculous theory. I was *there*. Carl sticking his foot through an animal's chest put him and the rest of us on their radar screen. Period. Then he went berserk for a while because he was in massive pain. End of story."

"If only the one animal he stepped on suddenly noticed him, I'd agree with you," said Regan evenly. "But *all* the creatures noticed him, and not just him but the entire group of humans—humans not a single animal on Isis had ever reacted to before."

"This still could have been due to any number of other factors," persisted Bob.

"True, but I'm not finished. The best evidence is what's been happening to *us*. When we got here we saw lots of wildlife, but it completely ignored us, the way it always has. No animals tried to approach the trams. No animals circled us when we stopped. No animals attacked. Despite what happened to Carl, we felt perfectly safe walking around outside of the trams, which we did for ten minutes or so without the slightest problem. So when was the first time any of them *did* pay attention to us?"

"Come on Regan," snapped her mother irritably. "The first time we were noticed was in the rainforest, when the pack surrounded us. That's obvious. So what's your point?"

"My point is that this was right after we heard the tape-recorded screams," said Regan. "Which surprised us and scared us half to death. We were afraid and nervous. Everyone raced into the woods while these strong negative emotions were bursting out of us, and *this* is the reason we were noticed. Three of the wolf-things picked up this powerful new emotional 'scent' and came out to investigate. Seeing them made us even more afraid. Which caused more of the pack to investigate. Which caused even more fear in us humans. From there things snowballed, and there was no turning back.

"The emotional energy of Isis animals and humans isn't compatible," continued Regan. "Like fingernails scraping across a chalkboard. Like a bright light shined in your eyes. Like an ice pick being stabbed into the emotional centers of both their brains and ours. Incompatible emotional frequencies basically driving both groups mad. We first began arguing with each other when we were being attacked by the pack. Miguel yelled at Mom. She yelled back. Cam called Bob an idiot for not testing the tranquilizer. Remember?"

Regan remembered asking Ryan for his makeshift club to use as a torch. He had sensed the absolute urgency in her telepathic request, yet he had not given it to her or asked her why she needed it. Instead he had barked at her to get her own.

"You're nothing if not creative," said Eric. "I'll give you that. Yes, we've been on edge. No doubt about it. But not because of what you're saying. Because we were attacked and almost killed. Because scores of unstoppable killers are stalking us and want us dead. Because we've been stranded on a primitive planet by a *madman*. *That's* what's causing us all to be edgy."

Regan shook her head in disbelief. "*Edgy?* Do you really think that word covers how we've been acting?" said Regan. "How about incredibly hostile, bitter, and hateful. How about filled with uncontrollable rage." She paused. "Believe me, *I know*. When we were fighting off those wolf-things I was insane with rage. I love animals. And we invaded *their* space. Yes, I should have wanted to do whatever was needed to get away, that's understandable. But getting away wasn't enough. I wanted all of them *dead*. I wanted to set them all on fire. I wanted to rip them apart with my *bare hands*."

Mr. Resnick nodded. "I felt the same way," he admitted.

"I've been in combat before, and in a number of high pressure situations," said Cam weakly. "But I have never felt the level of blind hatred I did during that fight."

Miguel nodded his agreement. "Regan is right," he said.

A surge of adrenaline coursed through Regan's veins. She was beginning to get through to them. She decided to use an example involving sweat that Ryan had made up when he was convincing her of the truth. He said he thought of it because people naturally started sweating when they were afraid, and a swarm of bees had shown him that sweat could be dangerous. She had no idea what he meant by *that*.

"Imagine a planet full of carnivores with an incredible sense of smell," said Regan. "But they can't smell humans so they leave them alone. The only human scent they *can* smell is sweat, and this smell drives them out of their minds with rage. When they smell it they have to destroy the source at all cost. So everything is perfect between humans and these animals until one of the humans sweats for some reason."

"Then the carnivores smell it and come after them," said Mr. Resnick.

"Right. Which causes the humans to sweat some more. Which causes more animals to pick up the scent and attack. Which causes the humans to sweat even more. It's a never ending cycle. But what we've been dealing with is far worse, because what the wildlife is bringing out of us isn't sweat. It's fear. It's hatred. It's rage. It's a kind of madness."

Even though the eyes of many in the group burned with the exact rage of which Regan was speaking, she knew she was getting through.

"Hostility between us and the native wildlife is mirrored back and forth and amplified," said Regan. "Have any of you ever remembered being *this* angry? For *this* long?"

Mrs. Resnick shook her head. "No. Not even close. But I can't shake it. You're my daughter and I know I love you. But every time I hear your voice I want to scream at you to shut up. It's been taking all my self-control not to try to rip the arms off everyone in the group."

There were murmurs of agreement from several members of the expedition.

"This team is as good as it gets," said Regan. "Everyone here has been tested and selected because they're great scientists. Or the best military people in the country," she added, nodding in Miguel and Cam's direction. "Calm. Smart. Good at working with others. Yes we've been under a huge amount of pressure. But look at us! We've been at each other's throats since we were attacked in the rainforest."

She had even more evidence, but it was evidence Ryan had given her that she couldn't pass on. Evidence that had helped Ryan piece everything together. She and her brother had been in some tough spots. And the tougher things got, the closer they became. Ryan had always kept his cool under pressure. But not this time. This time he had turned into a hateful jerk. In addition to some of the hurtful things he had said to Regan, he told her how he beat his fists against the shield until he couldn't lift them. How he had hurled stones at the pack and screamed at them until his throat hurt. Ryan had gone insane with rage also. But just a few minutes back on Earth had helped him regain his emotional balance.

"There are four of us who have been in a state of constant hatred," continued Regan. "And four of us who haven't. You all know who you are."

Everyone surveyed everyone else and it became instantly obvious. Four sets of eyes were rational. Four sets were burning with barely contained fury.

"Eric, Bob, Donna, and Mom are filled with hatred," said Regan. "Miguel, Cam, Dad and I aren't. So what's different about these two groups?"

"Just tell us!" thundered Donna, further demonstrating Regan's point. "You're right. You must be. These animals *are* driving us mad. Which makes it hard to concentrate. So get on with it!"

"The difference is that Miguel, Cam, Dad and I were all injured," said Regan. "We were all dosed with the Med-Pen. The four of you weren't."

Her father tilted his head in thought. "So the Med-Pen must interpret the changes to the emotional centers of our brains as infections. Infections it can cure."

"Exactly," said Regan.

Ryan had told her that when their mom had finally used a Med-Pen on Carl, it had rebalanced him emotionally within about five minutes. Regan's own experience had been similar.

"I felt normal about five minutes after I used the Med-Pen," said Regan.

Mr. Resnick nodded. "Me too. I was finally able to remain calm."

"So that's why you needed a Med-Pen," said Eric. "You wanted to dose us all and cure us of this emotional poisoning."

"Yes. And I think when we do the animals will go back to ignoring us."

"It won't happen," said Donna. "We're far past the point of no return."

"We *aren't*," insisted Regan. "Have you noticed that none of the animals threw themselves at the shield trying to get at Miguel and Cam? That's because they couldn't 'smell' them emotionally. So we need for everyone to be cured by the Med-Pen. And then we have to relax. Be super calm. Generate no emotions, or even positive emotions. Let the animals of Isis go back to not being able to sense us, to thinking we're harmless trees or something."

"Okay, already," said Eric Morris, nodding. "I took the Med-Pen," he confessed, pulling the alien device from his pocket. "Let's give it a try."

Eric pointed the Med-Pen at Donna, Bob, Amanda Resnick and himself, pressing the appropriate control each time. "You had better be right!" he hissed, unable to control his hostility even knowing what was causing it.

Regan blew out a mouthful of air in relief and lowered the silver remote. "In five minutes or so you'll all be able to think clearly again," she said. "We'll be able to work as a team again."

No one spoke for three or four minutes, waiting to see what would happen.

Mr. Resnick broke the long silence. "Your analysis is excellent, Regan," he said. "But do you have any idea how this ability to transmit and receive emotional energy could have developed."

Regan thought about it for a moment. "Not really," she said.

"I think I do," said her mother, already beginning to feel more like herself. "I think it has to do with the volcanic nature of the planet. We've seen that lava can sneak up on you. Maybe in the early days of life on Isis this happened all the time. Rare animals were born with the ability to sense emotional energy at a distance. Negative emotional energy. Because they could sense the panic and fear of hundreds of other animals running away from lava many miles away, they could save themselves. Evolution rewarded this trait. These animals survived to have offspring while many animals without this trait didn't."

"An interesting hypothesis," said Eric, also now feeling more like his old self. "We wondered why the animals surrounding us had left when we were about to set up the portable force-field. Now we know."

"Right," said Mrs. Resnick. "They knew the lava was coming—ten or fifteen minutes before it reached us. They sensed the collective panic and fear of the animals that were closer to the lava source and *hadn't* been warned. While the lava river was on us before we had any warning, *they* had plenty of time to get away. They left calmly. Orderly."

"A very unique survival mechanism," said Bob.

"From its early start as a natural disaster warning mechanism, this sense probably evolved a variety of uses. And the animals evolved the ability to send as well as receive emotions."

"The sense probably takes the place of smell in many situations," said Mrs. Resnick. "Predators on Earth use scent to track prey. Prey animals can smell hidden predators approaching. Isis animals must have developed a complex system to use emotional energy to sense or to deceive other animals."

Regan grinned. This was more like it. The three biologists were working together again. Without the slightest hint of hostility. They were back to acting like enthusiastic scientists rather than deranged serial killers.

After just a few more minutes there could be no doubt: the cure had taken complete effect. For the first time since being attacked in the woods, all eight of the human beings still stranded on Isis were calm and rational once again.

Although the predators were still circling, still itching to get at them, the humans stayed relaxed and unafraid. Gradually predator after predator wandered off, as if not sure why they had been there in the first place. Suddenly freed from the overwhelming compulsion to stop the source of the brain-splitting emotional energy being directed toward them, the wildlife returned to normal. Animals that were natural enemies woke up as if they had been in a trance, and fled from each other or attacked each other violently.

Within five minutes every animal had dispersed.

"Ryan?" broadcast Regan questioningly once the crisis was over.

"I'm still here," came the immediate reply.

"You did it!" she told him excitedly. *"It worked!"*

"Fantastic," he replied, finally letting out the emotional breath he had been holding for almost an hour.

If his theory had been wrong his family would have surely died on Isis. Worry had eaten at his insides like battery acid as he waited to hear back from Regan. It had been the longest wait of his life.

"I can't tell you how glad I am that being on Earth brought you back to your senses," broadcast Regan.

Ryan thought about how he had acted before he had left Isis and winced. *"Yeah, me too,"* he broadcast sheepishly. *"I was the biggest jerk ever."*

"Yeah, you were," agreed Regan with a grin. *"But it wasn't your fault. And you saved all our lives—so you've got that going for you."*

Ryan smiled. *"Hey, I owed you one. I told you I'd make it up to you."* He paused. *"Well, it's a huge relief everything worked out. Hopefully we'll be able to get you off Isis by Sunday. But I have to get going. I left Alyssa and Kelsey Cooper outside the zoo building almost an hour ago."*

Regan smiled. *"Good one, Ryan. It's nice to see your sense of humor come back."*

"I'm not kidding."

"Come on, Ryan. Alyssa? Inside Prometheus?"

Ryan chuckled. *"It's a long story, Regs. But I have to get going. Next time you're on Earth I'll tell you all about it."* With that Ryan stepped through the portal and severed their connection, wishing he could see the startled look he was certain was now frozen on his sister's face.

CHAPTER 29

A Lethal Decision

Ryan rejoined Alyssa and Kelsey and apologized for leaving them alone for so long. They hadn't minded at all. The unique architecture of the city had continued to captivate them the entire time.

As he drove away from the zoo building Ryan considered telling Alyssa that he had lied that morning when he said he was an expert in classical and operant conditioning. He had done it so he would have something in common with her, but it was still a lie. He was getting very good at making up elaborate stories. It was true that much of the time he didn't have a choice, and telling creative lies had saved his life on a number of occasions, such as when he had bluffed the mercenary in the woods earlier that evening. But just because there were many times he *had* to lie didn't mean he should make it a habit. It meant that he should make even more of an effort to be honest when he was able to be.

Just as he decided he would tell her, he realized it wouldn't matter anyway. Carl would be sure to use his amnesia inhalant on her very soon. This inhalant, developed by a team of scientists at Carl's insistence, would erase the previous ten hours of a person's memory. Carl thought something like this was vital to protect the secrecy of Prometheus. When he used it on the Cooper sisters, they wouldn't remember anything about Prometheus. If he used it soon, Alyssa wouldn't remember her dentist appointment or her earlier conversation with Ryan either.

Ryan sighed. This was unfortunate, but there was no use dwelling on it.

He decided he should turn his attention to another matter anyway. Something was bothering him. Something Regan had broadcast to him when he had gone back to Isis, although for the life of him he couldn't quite put his finger on what it was. He had a nagging feeling it was something critically important, though, and he had learned to trust these strange hunches of his in emergency situations.

Hopefully he would figure it out, but right now they needed to reconnect with Carl. His ground assault team should have arrived long before to secure both Proact and Prometheus. Given that certain air force jets could travel well over a thousand miles per hour, Ryan wouldn't be surprised if the decorated colonel was already back in the city.

Sure enough, when they arrived at the entrance to Prometheus, Carl was facing a group of about twenty soldiers, issuing orders. Each was wearing full commando gear and carrying assault rifles. Although Carl was in civilian clothes, he carried himself with such confident grace and easy authority he had the instant respect of the soldiers. If not for the streaks of silver in his hair, no one would have guessed he was in his fifties. When he had finished giving orders the soldiers quickly dispersed to carry them out.

"Ryan!" said Carl warmly upon seeing him, his eyes lighting up. "Boy am I glad you're okay." He clapped Ryan on the back affectionately and turned to his two companions. "And you must be Alyssa and Kelsey." He leaned forward and shook each of their hands. "I'm Colonel Carl Sharp. But please call me Carl."

The girls shook his hand and said hello.

"Good timing," said Carl. "I just entered the city a minute ago. I need to reset electronic security down here. Follow me."

Carl began walking toward the security headquarters building that was very near the entrance to the city. The building projected a different holographic image around itself every day so it never looked the same twice. Today it was white and shaped like a tear-drop.

"I'm relieved you made it down here before your

unexpected company came calling," said Carl as they walked. "Where did you go?"

"We stopped off at the zoo planet," replied Ryan.

Carl nodded. "I thought as much. Hoping the expedition somehow made it across the lava. I assume you didn't see them waiting just outside the shield or they'd be with you."

"No. I'm afraid not." The corners of Ryan's mouth turned up into a slight smile. "But I'm glad I went anyway. I have the feeling they'll be just fine when we finally get to them."

They had entered the security headquarters and now stood in front of Carl's office. He had kept it locked during his trip to Colorado and now entered a code into a touch-pad nearby. Several dead-bolt locks disengaged and they entered.

Carl motioned for the trio of kids to have a seat around a large oak roundtable in the middle of his office. They plopped into three of the four cushioned black chairs surrounding it. Carl sat behind his desk a few yards away and began entering commands on his computer, rebooting all security protocols.

Once he was done, Carl turned toward Alyssa and Kelsey. "Do you know about your mother?" he asked grimly.

"Yes, she's a hostage," said Alyssa.

"You have to get her back," insisted Kelsey.

"Believe me," said Carl. "If we have any chance to

do so we'll take it." He frowned. "But I won't lie to you. Her odds are not good."

"But there has to be *something* you can do," pleaded Alyssa. "If you find this Nathaniel, can't you just give him what he wants to let her go?"

"I wish we could, but our hands are tied. Nathaniel has been classified as a terrorist," explained Carl. He shook his head somberly. "America has a firm policy of not negotiating with terrorists."

Both girls were stunned. They couldn't believe what they were hearing. This Nathaniel could announce he was killing their mother and no one would lift a finger to stop him. How could this be?

"I can't tell you how sorry I am this has happened," continued Carl earnestly. "Your mother is a valuable member of our team, and her safety is my responsibility, which I take very seriously. If I could trade places with her, I would. But I'm afraid her best bet is if Nathaniel realizes a hostage won't do him any good and decides to let her go."

"What are the odds of *that* happening," spat Kelsey in frustration and despair. "Even if he doesn't want her as a hostage anymore, he'll probably just kill her, won't he?"

Carl lowered his eyes and nodded. "Maybe," he said. "I could sugar-coat this, but I won't. I don't think that would be fair to you." He paused. "As long as your mother is still alive there is always hope," he added. "I only wish I could offer you more than just this."

There was silence in the room for several long seconds. Both girls were horrified at their mother's slim chances of survival and angry with Carl that he couldn't—or wouldn't—do more to save her.

"Any problems retaking Proact?" asked Ryan, deciding to change the subject.

"None," said Carl. "The mercs who were closing in on you must have realized you were out of reach almost immediately. They were gone when the assault team arrived."

"What is your team doing now?" asked Ryan.

"A thorough security sweep of Prometheus. I want an exact inventory of everyone who is pinned down by the Enigma Cube. If you're right, the effect should wear off in an hour or so. I also need to be certain there are no mercenaries still hiding down here. Next we'll do the same for Proact."

Carl had recalled seven of his men who had been off duty on this particular Friday evening. He had also drawn from the thirty special forces troops that were part of Prometheus security but were always stationed outside the alien city. Because they were stationed outside of Prometheus, if the city were taken, these commandoes would be available to move in at a moment's notice, not having to obtain security clearance or be brought up to speed on this highly classified project.

"Any news on Dr. Harris?" asked Ryan.

"Yes," said Carl, brightening. "He's in the hospital.

They think he's going to be okay. I'm sure our miracle medical device had a lot to do with that."

The landline on Carl's desk rang and he snatched the receiver from its cradle. He listened intently for a long while, interjecting a question or two every so often. He seemed excited but at the same time extremely troubled.

"Prepare for an action along the lines that we spoke about earlier," said Carl into the receiver. "Call me back when you're in position." With that he ended the call.

Carl stared at the three kids around his table for several seconds and rubbed his chin in thought. Finally, reaching a decision, he turned away and used a walkie-talkie to summon the nearest member of his team.

"I need to confer with Ryan alone," explained Carl apologetically to Alyssa and Kelsey.

The man he had called, Lieutenant Chris Malcolm, arrived two minutes later and entered the office.

"Chris," said Carl, "can you escort these two young women upstairs to the decoy building and stay with them."

Alyssa and Kelsey stood up and said goodbye. Ryan caught Alyssa's eye. "I'll be up as soon as I can," he said reassuringly. This seemed to lift her spirits immediately. Seconds later they and the lieutenant were gone.

"You've fallen for Alyssa Cooper pretty hard in the past few hours, haven't you," said Carl.

Ryan winced. "I didn't realize it was *that* obvious,"

he said. Then, with a sigh he added, "Actually, I've liked her for a few months. She's pretty and smart, but there's a lot more to her than just that. I mean, she's really incredible."

"And she likes you back," said Carl. "That's obvious to me too." He frowned deeply. "Which is only going to make this harder than it already is."

Ryan was instantly on alert. "What's going on, Carl?" he said guardedly.

"Thanks to you, we knew to look for Nathaniel." Carl walked over and sat at the table across from Ryan. "And I put several plans of action into place in case we found him."

Carl seemed reluctant to continue.

"And?" prompted Ryan impatiently.

"Well, I just got the call. We found him. We fed the coordinates of his face into the computer grid and a traffic camera found a match. We tracked him from there with satellites. He ditched the original SUV and now he's in another one. Different make, model and color. He's in the passenger's seat. The driver is a well known mercenary. We couldn't identify anyone else in the car."

"Okay," said Ryan cautiously. "That sounds like fantastic news. So what am I missing?"

"I just put one of our contingency plans in motion. I've decided I can't afford to wait until he's totally isolated to take him out."

Ryan thought about this. "So you're saying some innocent people might be caught in the way?"

"He's driving through fairly rural country," said Carl, "and we'll do everything we possibly can to avoid this. But there are no guarantees." He locked his eyes onto Ryan's. "Here's the problem. If Michelle Cooper is still a hostage, she could well be in that car." He pursed his lips and shook his head grimly. "If she is . . ."

Carl stopped, not really needing to finish the thought.

"So *that's* why you asked the girls to leave," said Ryan in outrage. "Because you're planning a strike that will probably kill their mom."

Carl frowned deeply. "Ryan, this is the toughest call I've ever had to make," he said, and his eyes revealed such a depth of pain that Ryan had no doubt that it was true. "But Nathaniel will be traveling through an unpopulated area in about ten minutes and this is the best time to strike." He sighed. "We just have to hope that Michelle isn't with him."

"You can't do this, Carl."

"Believe me, I wish there were some other way. This decision will haunt me the rest of my life," he added, and anguish and guilt were written all over his face—but only for a moment. All evidence of his internal ethical struggles soon vanished as his leadership instincts took over. He didn't have the luxury of coming across as anything but strong and decisive during a crisis. "But I don't have a choice," he continued firmly. "This guy is a psychopath. He now has the most dangerous weapon the world has ever seen, and has already used it. He boasted about ruling the world. If we wait to attack, and he somehow slips the noose, we might never get another chance. He could kill hundreds before this is through. Millions."

"He hasn't yet," argued Ryan. "And he could have. Easily."

"He shot Dr. Harris and left him for dead. He stranded all of you on Isis. You're the only one of us who heard his letter, so you tell me. Did he write that he just wanted to *borrow* the Enigma Cube and no one would get hurt? Or did he sound like a power mad psychopath who would stop at nothing to achieve his goals?"

Ryan said nothing, but his defeated expression was answer enough.

"We can't risk him getting away. Yes, there is a great risk Alyssa and Kelsey will lose their mother. It makes me sick to even think about. And I'm going to have to go upstairs afterwards and look them in the eye. But if we don't stop him now, he could orphan more kids than we could ever count."

Ryan was horrified, but he knew Carl was right. What if you could kill an Adolph Hitler, but it would cost an innocent life? Should you do it? For Ryan at least, the answer had to be yes. Ryan also knew that

Carl could have reminded him that Michelle Cooper had very little hope of survival even if he didn't strike. But he hadn't. Probably because it would have sounded like he was trying to rationalize his decision; like he was trying to take the easy way out, which wasn't Carl's style. He took full responsibility for his actions.

"Does President Quinn know about this?" asked Ryan.

"Yes. He has authorized me to do whatever I believe is necessary to stop this threat."

"If she *is* in that SUV, is there any chance she'll survive an attack on Nathaniel?"

Carl frowned and shook his head. "None. This guy controls *gravity*. In a twenty mile radius according to what you told me. We've already seen the power of this weapon. With it, as you said earlier, there is no doubt he could destroy jets at the touch of a button. He could ground tanks and entire armies. So we have no choice but to go for broke."

"What does that mean, go for broke?"

"It means high explosive missiles. The most potent we have that aren't nuclear. We've scrambled a jet that will fly straight above him, but at a high enough altitude that he won't see or hear it. We're lucky, because he can't possibly have any idea we're on to him already. When I give the word we'll launch three missiles straight down. It's possible he won't be able to react before they hit, but if he does see them in time and increases their gravity, they'll just fall *faster*. Or *implode*. We're modifying them so that an implosion will also prove fatal to anyone beneath them."

"What if he reduces the gravity on the missiles to zero?"

"It won't help him. Even at zero gravity they're being steered downward by rockets." Carl shook his head miserably. "If we thought anything short of this type of attack would work, we would try it."

They sat in silence for several minutes, dreading a call that could come at any moment. A call informing Carl that the missiles had been prepared and the jet was in place.

"There may be another way," said Ryan suddenly, breaking the long silence. He reached in his pocket and pulled out a red crystal. "I just had an idea. I think this crystal might make you immune to the effects of the Enigma Cube. Counteract it."

Carl knew better than to take Ryan's ideas lightly. "I'm listening," he said.

"We know that gravity is a change in the shape of space-time."

Carl stared at him blankly. "I sure didn't," he admitted. "But I'll take your word for it." He paused. "What exactly *is* space-time, anyway?"

"I'm not positive. I guess space and time rolled into one. The important thing is that gravity indents space." Ryan paused. "In higher dimensions, though, it might not have the same effect, and I think this crystal has something to do with higher dimensions."

"You've totally lost me, Ryan."

"It's complicated, and I don't understand much of it either. But I think there's a chance the crystal could make you immune to the gravity effect."

Carl considered. "Can I assume you've been carrying the crystal since you returned from Isis?"

Ryan nodded.

"Did you inspect anyone who was hit with the Enigma Cube?"

"Yes. Several of them."

"And when you were standing or kneeling over them, did the crystal counteract their higher gravity?"

Ryan frowned. Carl had a point. He would have made a great scientist. "Maybe you have to be holding it when the wave hits," said Ryan. Or else have had your mind opened to the possibilities of the fourth dimension, thought Ryan.

"I'm sorry, Ryan," said Carl earnestly. "More sorry than you'll ever know. But I can't risk Nathaniel getting away on the hope that the crystal will work. On an untested theory."

Ryan pursed his lips together in frustration and shook his head sadly. There was nothing to say. He hated what Carl was doing. Carl hated what Carl was doing. But Ryan knew the security chief had no other choice.

And while Carl would have to face Alyssa and Kelsey, so would he. Ryan had promised them their mom would be okay. While Carl had given them nothing but the truth, Ryan had given them false hope; a fantasy.

The phone rang. Carl took a deep breath and picked it up.

Ryan's eyes widened!

At just that instant he realized what he had been missing. What his sister had broadcast that had made him uneasy. It was just before he left Isis to rejoin Alyssa and Kelsey at the zoo building.

Regan had told him she was glad being on Earth had brought him back to his senses.

That was it! Returning to Earth *had* cured him. Almost instantly.

But returning to Earth *hadn't* cured Carl.

It had taken Ryan's mom about twenty minutes to find a Med-Pen. Yet Carl's emotional state had not improved during that time.

What did this mean? Had Carl's emotional state been worse even than Ryan's? Was it somehow of a different quality? And if so, why?

And if a Med-Pen had never been used on Carl, would the negative emotional effects of Isis have *ever* worn off?

Ryan's every instinct told him the answers to these questions were vitally important. As Carl discussed strategy and tactics with the pilot of a jet fighter flying many miles above Nathaniel Smith—and Michelle Cooper—Ryan's mind raced.

His mouth dropped open as he came to a startling conclusion. Could it really be true? He needed to think it through. Be *absolutely* sure he was right.

"Alright, Captain McGann," said Carl. "Arm the missiles. Wait until he's clear of cars and farmhouses and then commence firing. I repeat, you have a green light to engage. Do you copy?"

"Copy that, sir," said the captain.

"Stop!" screamed Ryan. "Call it off."

"Ryan, we've been through this," said Carl irritably, his ear still pressed against the phone. "My decision has been made."

"No. You don't understand. Nathaniel isn't the one behind this."

Ryan leaned forward intently. "You're about to bomb the wrong person."

CHAPTER 30

Decoy

"Have you lost your mind," said Carl.

Ryan stared at the security chief with a blazing intensity. "Carl, if you've ever trusted me before," he said evenly, "trust me now. You're about to make a terrible mistake."

Colonel Carl Sharp looked deep into Ryan's green eyes and saw nothing but certainty. Ryan and his sister had shown themselves to possess excellent instincts time and again. He made up his mind in an instant.

"Abort, abort, abort!" Carl barked into the receiver. "Stand down, Captain McGann. I repeat, stand down. Do you copy?"

"Copy that, sir. Standing down."

"Hold position and await further instructions," said Carl. He reached over and hit the mute button on the phone so the captain couldn't hear their conversation.

"Only because it's you, Ryan. Only because it's you. You had better make your points quickly."

"Nathaniel is a decoy," said Ryan breathlessly. "Michelle Cooper isn't *his* hostage. Nathaniel is *her* hostage."

Carl tilted his head in confusion. "What?"

"I told you the wildlife of Isis was relentlessly hostile to our expedition. You and I discussed why that might have happened. Well I figured it out. They can receive and transmit a kind of telepathic energy that hits the emotional centers of human brains. It drives us into a rage. *Our* emotional energy does the same to them."

"Ryan, get to the point. This has nothing to do with your theory that Nathaniel is a decoy," said Carl.

"It *does,*" insisted Ryan. "Just let me explain. You told me you were in an insane rage on Isis when you shot those creatures. Well everyone on *our* expedition experienced a similar rage." Ryan spoke as quickly as he could, racing to finish before Carl ran out of patience. "And after you shot the animals, when you were retreating in the tram that day, Mom was in a rage too. She told me. One she couldn't understand. And Bob Zubrin told me the same thing."

His mother and Bob had never really said this but Ryan knew from experience that this almost *had* to be true.

Carl nodded. "Now that I think of it, you're right. Everyone *was* screaming at everyone else. We all acted out of character, even for an emergency. Not just me."

"What about Michelle Cooper?"

Carl paused, searching his memory. A few seconds later he frowned deeply. "Your mom was yelling that I shouldn't have shot the last few animals. Michelle leaned over and hissed in my ear that she wished *she* had shot them. Or ripped the things apart with her bare hands."

"Is that something you would expect Michelle to say?" said Ryan. "No matter what was happening?"

"No," said Carl, a troubled look coming over his face. "I wouldn't." He paused. "I've tried to put that day out of my mind. Until you jogged my memory just now, I had forgotten she had even said this."

"When I was on Isis," said Ryan, "I couldn't have been angrier. But this stopped when I got back to Earth. Very quickly. As soon as I removed myself from the field being generated by the Isis animals. It must have been the same for my mother and Bob Zubrin. But it was different for you." He paused. "How long were you back on Earth before Mom could find a Med-Pen?" asked Ryan, already knowing the answer.

"Fifteen or twenty minutes."

"You told me your emotional state didn't improve during that time. And it wasn't because of the pain. The Med-Pen relieves pain instantly. But you said you didn't feel emotionally normal until five minutes *after* the device had been used. That's because the changes in your brain were like an infection, and the Med-Pen took five minutes to cure you."

Carl considered this. He had to admit Ryan was making some good points. But Nathaniel would be entering a populated area again in eight minutes. Carl's window of opportunity was closing fast. "Ryan, I need to order the strike."

"Just a little longer," said Ryan, and then he hastily continued. "The way I figure it there are two levels of crazy you can get from the animals of Isis. The first level is just from the energy traveling through the air and hitting your brain. The second level is far more intense. It's when you are actually *touching* one of them when their hatred explodes. Like both you and Michelle were doing. You stepped on one of the creatures. Michelle was resting her feet on one of them. When their hate-filled, poisonous emotional energy surged, you two received it full blast through your legs. You both got massive doses through this point of contact. Far more potent than if it had traveled through the air."

"Hold on," said Carl. He un-muted the phone. "Captain McGann, are you still in position?"

"Affirmative, sir."

"Good. Continue to circle and maintain your position," he said and then muted the phone once again. He nodded at Ryan to continue.

"It's easier to think of this energy as an infection," said Ryan. "The rest of your expedition received a small dose that went away when they got back to Earth. You and Michelle Cooper received an *enormous* dose that seared your brains. Changed your wiring so much that the infection became permanent. So just leaving Isis alone wasn't enough to cure the two of you like it was for the rest of your group. But *you* were treated with a Med-Pen. Michelle Cooper never was."

"So you're saying she was infected on Isis but never cured." Carl thought about this for a few seconds and then shook his head. "It doesn't fly. I've been around her since. She's not in a constant rage."

Ryan paused in thought. "Her mind probably couldn't take the constant anger and hatred," he said. "It drove her insane. Insane enough to experiment with the Enigma Cube. Insane enough to plot to steal it. The insanity took the place of the pure hatred. But not entirely. Have you ever seen her smile, even once, since you returned from Isis?"

Carl shook his head. "Never," he admitted. "And before that she smiled and laughed often."

"And don't forget, what she said into your ear on Isis is proof she had turned totally savage. That's because she had been severely infected with this incompatible emotional energy. From then on she became a much different person."

Carl's eyes narrowed as he considered what Ryan had said. "It's an interesting theory Ryan. But you could still be wrong."

"I'm *not*. Our Isis expedition returned to a sabotaged tram and Michelle Cooper and Nathaniel Smith were gone. One of them left a note. A *typed* note. Michelle could have written it just as easily as Nathaniel could have. She could have easily forged his signature at the end. None of us would know any better. She wrote the note to throw us off the trail."

Carl glanced anxiously at his watch but said nothing.

"Michelle joined the team four months ago. Regan and I met her and she seemed to really like us. She treated us like heroes for having defeated Tezoc. She knew every last detail about what had happened. Exactly what Tezoc had tried to do, and how he had done it. I told you the letter writer also knew a lot about Tezoc. Wanted to copy his strategies."

"Nathaniel could have known just as much about Tezoc as she did," pointed out Carl.

"Maybe," said Ryan. "But the strategy Tezoc is best known for is using exactly this kind of decoy."

Ryan could tell that Carl was almost convinced. He quickly pressed ahead. "Then she went from really liking me and Regan to really hating us. Just like that. We didn't know it, but it was just after she had returned from Isis! Exactly three months ago. She had changed! Ask Alyssa and Kelsey. They said the same thing. As of three months ago—exactly—they almost never saw her. And when they did she was a *nightmare*."

Ryan leaned forward. "They never saw her because

she spent every night experimenting with the Enigma Cube. She was a nightmare because Isis had turned her into a monster." Ryan shook his head adamantly. "The timing isn't just a coincidence."

Carl considered everything Ryan had said. It did seem to fit together perfectly, like a tight jigsaw puzzle. And Nathaniel had never added up. He aced the lie-detector test, and when Carl had checked his background, people said he was a saint. Kind to animals. Opposed to guns and any kind of violence. Donated his time to charitable causes. No psychopath could mask their true nature that effectively for that long. The same was true of Michelle Cooper. By all accounts she was a wonderful human being. But if Isis had truly made her insane, this would explain it.

Still, as good a case as Ryan made, he didn't have a single shred of hard evidence.

But as Carl thought about it further, he realized Ryan had all the hard evidence he needed. The evidence was Carl himself. Carl had been on Isis, and he remembered with horrible clarity how he had felt before being treated with the Med-Pen. As if all the hatred and fear in the world had been bottled up and concentrated inside of him. He knew from firsthand experience what Isis could do to someone. These memories alone didn't necessarily mean that Ryan was right. There could be other possible explanations for his temporary insanity. But when combined with the brilliant circumstantial evidence Ryan had presented, Carl was now convinced of the truth of Ryan's arguments to the very depths of his soul.

Carl un-muted the phone. "Captain McGann," he said. "Return to base. I repeat, return to base. We are scrubbing the mission."

"Roger that," said the captain. "Turning around and heading for home."

Ryan let out a huge sigh of relief as Carl hung up the phone. "Thanks Carl. I swear you're doing the right thing."

"I know I am," said Carl, "and it's you I should be thanking—for stopping me from doing the *wrong* thing."

The head of security spent a few minutes reviewing information he thought might be useful to Ryan and then asked him to continue his analysis.

"Here's what I think happened," said Ryan. "Michelle didn't count on Dr. Harris being there when she tried to steal the Enigma Cube. Shooting him wasn't part of her plan. But stealing the Cube and traveling with it to Isis was. She must have had it in her backpack, along with the letter she had written beforehand."

Ryan stood and tilted his head toward the ceiling as he tried to recreate her plan in his mind.

"So the trams stop and she tosses the tape-recorder into the forest. When we go after it she takes Nathaniel hostage, sabotages one of the trams, and leaves the note. Then, either because they picked up on her hostile emotional state and attacked her, or just for fun, she shoots four Isis animals. We found their bodies when we were making our way back to the tram."

Carl rose from his chair. "We need to go topside," he said. "Let's continue this as we walk."

"The letter makes it clear Nathaniel is responsible," said Ryan as they exited Carl's office and the security building and began walking the short distance to the Prometheus entrance. "If this happened under normal circumstances everyone would question why Nathaniel would write it and give himself away—give the nature of the *Enigma Cube* away. But no one does in this case because the letter also makes it clear he plans to strand the expedition on Isis forever. So it won't matter if he reveals his plans in every detail, no one can do anything about it."

"But Michelle never intended to capture Prometheus," noted Carl. "Meaning she always knew that the expedition would eventually be rescued, after all."

"Right. Michelle needed everyone to think Nathaniel had wanted to capture Prometheus but had changed his plans. That he had made a mistake. That the expedition was very lucky to get rescued. But it wouldn't have been luck. Michelle was *counting* on them coming back. She *needed* them to return."

Carl rubbed his chin once again. "Right," he said slowly, as the full extent of Michelle Cooper's deception began to sink in. "So they could identify Nathaniel as the villain." He shook his head at the sheer audacity of her plan. "And her as the poor hostage."

Ryan nodded. "Exactly. She didn't count on the animals becoming savage or the river of lava. She thought it was a harmless planet. So she was sure that once Prometheus was back online, sooner or later someone would realize the Isis group was missing and bring them back."

They stepped through the Prometheus entrance and into the manmade cavern.

"So she uses the returned Isis group to frame Nathaniel," said Ryan, "and now she has her decoy. Everyone is hunting for the wrong person. Which is brilliant enough. But if I'm guessing the rest correctly, her strategy was more than brilliant. It was *genius*. A strategy Tezoc himself would have been proud of. All she has to do is have a merc continue to hold Nathaniel hostage. Then she can pretend to escape. Or tell us Nathaniel let her go. In either case, she could come up with some clever insight that would lead us to where he was hiding."

"You're right," said Carl, almost in awe. "That *would be* genius. Then we bomb Nathaniel out of existence." A frown came over his face and he shook his head in disgust. "Which we would have already done if not for you," he added, gesturing toward Ryan. He paused for a moment, his jaw tightening, as he reflected on just how close he had come to killing an innocent man and playing right into Michelle Cooper's hands.

"When we searched the wreckage afterwards," he continued, "we'd be unable to find the Enigma Cube. We'd assume, incorrectly, that it was caught in the blast. After that we would think the crisis was over. No more villain. No more weapon." He shook his head in wonder. "And *she* ends up being the hero."

"And then she can return to the team," said Ryan. "Take her time. Make her plans. Continue building her mercenary army. And catch us completely off guard."

"I wouldn't be surprised if you're right," said Carl. "I'll bet this is exactly what she had planned."

They entered the Prometheus elevator and began the long ascent to the surface. "So what are you going to do now?" asked Ryan.

"With respect to Nathaniel, I have to call off the dogs. And I have to get a massive manhunt started for Michelle Cooper." He sighed. "But before I do I want to speak with her daughters. I think it's only right that I tell them before I tell anyone else."

"Tell them what? That their mother isn't a hostage. That she's really behind the whole thing?"

Carl nodded. "I'm afraid so."

"But why even bother? Aren't you just going to give them the amnesia compound anyway?"

Carl sighed. "It turns out the amnesia inhalant isn't fully perfected," he said. "A few of the mercenaries we used it on after the Tezoc incident ended up eventually losing several years of memory. We aren't sure why. I refuse to take that risk with these two innocent girls."

Ryan's eyes widened. Did that mean Carl might let them join the team. More importantly, might let *Alyssa* join the team.

Carl was frowning deeply as they stepped off the elevator and it closed behind them. "I'm afraid once we find Michelle we'll have to mount the same attack we had planned for Nathaniel. Which is a tragedy. Because even though she's responsible, it isn't her fault. It's the fault of Isis. She'll be every bit as much the innocent victim as she would have been had she really been Nathaniel's hostage."

They opened the door to the decoy building and stepped through. Chris Malcolm was sitting in a chair while the two Cooper sisters were pacing anxiously. Carl walked briskly toward the two girls while Ryan followed close behind.

Ryan buckled and collapsed to the floor!

He struggled to breathe, barely able to expand his lungs. He flattened himself spread-eagle on the ground. The pressure on every square inch of his body was enormous; as though an entire herd of elephants had decided to sit on him all at once.

He had been hit by a gravity wave!

Ryan used every ounce of his strength to pull his cheek off the ground and glance ahead for just a moment. He saw that Carl was pinned to the ground as well, along with Chris and the two sisters. Alyssa's pained face, flattened like a pancake on the floor, was the last thing Ryan saw as he lost the battle to keep his head upright and his eyelids open.

Ryan tried crawling toward the door to the Prometheus bunker, but moving even an inch was a mighty struggle, and after traveling only a yard or two he was too exhausted to continue.

His only chance was to find another seam to the fourth dimension. A dimension that wouldn't be affected the same by gravity's distortion of space. The crystal in his pocket had failed to protect him by itself. He concentrated for all he was worth and tried to recreate the feelings he had when the Hauler was about to hit him, and when he had passed through the Isis shield.

Nothing.

He continued to concentrate, straining to his absolute limit.

Still nothing. His gravity hadn't changed at all.

After five minutes of trying he was forced to give up.

This time his theory had been wrong. He was just as susceptible to the gravity effect as was everyone else.

Which meant there was nothing he could do but stay where he was, totally helpless, and await whatever might happened next.

CHAPTER 31

Deadly Encounter

Ryan wasn't sure how long he was pinned there. He had to use every ounce of his energy just to continue breathing. His heart was straining but somehow managed to pump blood through his body.

He felt duct tap being applied to his mouth, but he was unable to find the strength to open his eyes. If he had to guess, he would say that twenty minutes had passed since the wave had hit.

And then the crushing pressure was removed. Mercifully, between one instant and the next, gravity returned to normal. Ryan was exhausted and felt as if his muscles had been put through a meat tenderizer, but after experiencing many times the force of gravity for so long his ordinary weight had never felt so light. He rolled onto his back and opened his eyes.

Michelle Cooper towered above him, bathed in the

eerie, pulsing glow of the Enigma Cube, which she was holding lightly at her side. The smaller cube in its center was spinning less furiously than it had when Ryan had seen it before and the indentations spaced out along the edges of the outer cube now glowed in a rainbow of colors, each piercingly bright, with unearthly sharpness and clarity. The pulsing alien energy that they had somehow been able to sense before seemed tamer now, possibly because it was no longer powering the million-fold increase in gravity required to maintain the Cube at a weight of 200,000 pounds. Even so, the object still radiated what seemed like impossibly pure, concentrated light and was as hypnotic as ever.

Michelle Cooper was not alone. The five mercenary soldiers who had accompanied her ordered Ryan, Carl and the two girls to their feet. The mouths of all four of them had already been sealed with duct tape and they were now expertly bound as well. The mercs ignored Chris Malcolm who was still pinned to the floor by many times the normal force of gravity. Even though his eyes were shut tightly, Michelle was careful to stay out of his line of sight in case he managed to reopen them, and she remained silent so he wouldn't recognize her voice.

Alyssa and Kelsey squirmed against their bonds and yelled outraged questions at their mother—questions that were turned into muffled gibberish by the duct tape—while their eyes practically bulged from their sockets, expressing a horror and an anguish that only a profound betrayal could elicit. This was insane! Their mother was obviously no longer a hostage, so what was she doing? Why wasn't she acknowledging her own daughters? Why was she allowing this to happen?

Michelle Cooper stared at them callously, without the slightest hint of compassion, and then turned away as if they were of no further concern. Ryan saw the intense hurt this caused in every line of their faces and would have given anything to at least explain to them why their mother was acting this way, but there was nothing he could do.

The four prisoners were marched to two white SUVs parked outside of the building, their doors still open. Ryan and Carl were pushed into the back seat of one of the two vehicles while Alyssa and Kelsey were pushed into the other.

They drove through the woods for ten minutes, the going slow, until they reached a two-story wooden cabin with a modern satellite dish on its roof, which looked decidedly out of place. The cabin faced a tiny lake on one side and was surrounded by numerous trees on the other. The structure was totally isolated, probably for dozens and dozens of acres in all directions.

Carl and Ryan were ushered up wooden steps into one room while Alyssa and Kelsey were locked in another.

The cabin may have been rustic on the outside, but inside it was well appointed with a modern kitchen, a large plasma television and several laptop computers. Ryan's hands were freed and he was shoved onto a high-backed wooden chair. His ankles were bound a foot apart and he was loosely tied to the chair with rope, his arms at his sides. Carl was pushed into a standing position next to him, still bound as before.

"Go back to base camp and await my instructions," Michelle Cooper ordered the mercenaries now that the prisoners had been dealt with to her specifications.

All five mercs exited the cabin and drove off in one of the two SUVs. Only Michelle Cooper, her two daughters, Ryan and Carl remained.

"On your stomach, Colonel!" commanded Michelle icily, holding the Cube suggestively in front of her. Its brilliant luminosity made the brightly lighted room seem murky and drab by comparison.

Carl eyed Michelle and calculated his chances of mounting a successful attack. Even bound as he was he was skilled enough in combat to overpower her, but she was smart and was carefully maintaining a safe distance away. He had no other choice but to lower himself to the floor as instructed, knowing his risk of injury was far less if he was already pressed to the ground when the Enigma Cube was activated rather than collapsing there.

Michelle pointed the Cube at Carl and touched a small indentation on its edge that glowed a vivid blue. He was instantly pressed even further into the floor as if an invisible steamroller had parked on his back.

Michelle walked over to Ryan and yanked the tape from his mouth as hard as she could. Ryan thought his lips would come off in the process.

"*Ryan Resnick,*" she said in disdain. "My least favorite kid in the world. I'm going to leave *your* gravity alone for now. Because you and I need to have a little talk."

Michelle Cooper pulled up a chair and faced him from five feet away. She put the cube on the floor by her side and glared at him. Ryan's eyes were drawn to the Cube but he forced himself to look away and into the blazing blue eyes of the woman in front of him. "I stranded you at the center of the galaxy," she spat. "And even this didn't get you out of my hair." She shook her head in disbelief. "You have a lot of questions to answer."

"I'll answer them all," said Ryan. "Honestly and completely. If you'll answer a few of mine."

Michelle laughed maliciously. "Oh, I know you'll answer my questions, Ryan. But let's be very clear: this is *not* a negotiation." She lifted the Enigma Cube and pointed one of its twelve edges toward Ryan. "I touch this yellow indentation and your body collapses in on itself. Like a grape being hit with a sledgehammer."

She put the Cube down but continued to glare at him. "My mercenary friends finally told me about finding a kid coming out of Proact. From their physical description and the way you managed to escape, I had no doubt that it was you they had discovered. Which is impossible! The first thing I did after stranding you and the others on Isis was to incapacitate everyone inside Prometheus. So who rescued you?" she demanded.

Ryan told her the same story he had told Carl. That he had been helped by a safety feature of the Isis shield.

She considered him for a long moment, as if weighing his story. "I have no choice but to believe you. There's no other way you could have gotten through the barrier." She shook her head in disgust. "You truly are the luckiest person who ever lived."

At that moment Ryan didn't feel so lucky, but he remained silent.

"How did my daughters get involved?"

Ryan told her the truth, leaving nothing out.

"How were you able to see through my deception," she asked next. "How did you realize Nathaniel was a decoy?"

Ryan's eyes widened. So it wasn't just a coincidence that she had captured them when she had. But how could she have known Ryan and Carl were on to her. Ryan had just figured it out and they had not told *anyone*.

Michelle read Ryan's surprised expression. "You're wondering how I knew that I'd been discovered," she guessed. "Aren't you? Well, I'll tell you. After the city was mine, I planted bugs inside the headquarters of Prometheus and Proact security, inside the cavern, and inside the Prometheus elevator. To spy on all the idiots hunting Nathaniel." She grinned icily. "I bought this cabin last month. It appealed to me to hide right under your noses and keep Proact in range of the Cube. Close enough to take over again at a moment's notice if I had to." She smiled again, very pleased with herself. "Which turned out to be the case."

Ryan searched his memory to determine just what she had overheard. He had been in Prometheus security headquarters but had only spoken when he was in Carl's office. And she couldn't have planted a bug *there*. It had been locked securely while Carl was away.

So she had only heard them talking in the cavern and the elevator. In the cavern they had discussed her probable strategy. In the elevator, Carl had said he wanted to tell Michelle's daughters that she was behind everything before telling anyone else.

That was it! Of course Michelle had pounced when she had.

She must have been listening to her bugs from this very cabin. She had learned she had been discovered but also that she had a window of opportunity. So she had almost immediately sent a gravity pulse from the cabin outward—to Proact and beyond. Then all she had to do was drive calmly to Proact to capture them.

Michelle Cooper could see the understanding in Ryan's eyes. "That's right," she said coldly. "However you figured things out, I got to you before you told anyone. So everything will continue to go forward exactly as I planned. The gravity effect will wear off on everyone shortly. The rest of the Isis team will be rescued and tell everyone the tragic tale of the crazed physicist and his poor, helpless hostage. Then I'll appear with a heroic tale of escape and lead security right to Nathaniel, just as you guessed." She raised her eyebrows. "And they'll bomb him into oblivion. After that, everything will return to normal." A cruel smile came over her face. "At least they'll *think* it has. Until I'm ready to make my *real* move."

"What about me and Carl?"

"Are you really *that* stupid?" she said in disdain. "You can't possibly think I'm just going to let you go. No, I'll be using the Enigma Cube on such a high setting that you and Carl will be turned into *paste*. Later, I'm going to tell everyone how Nathaniel Smith tortured and killed you, probably becoming teary-eyed when I do. People will wonder why he went to the trouble of capturing you and Carl from the decoy building, but this will remain a mystery. After all," she said with a sneer, "who can possibly guess the motives of a psychopath like Nathaniel?"

Ryan knew she wasn't bluffing. Once she was finished interrogating him he was dead. He had a vision of a large cockroach being crushed by a hard shoe—of the insect's repulsive guts exploding through its shell accompanied by a sharp crunching sound. He shuddered, knowing this exact fate was in his immediate future. He forced himself not to think about it. When he did he couldn't breathe and his mind became paralyzed with fear.

While he was alive there was always a chance, always hope, as Carl had said. But he had mere minutes to come up with a plan and nothing was coming to mind.

"Look," said Ryan. "You're not yourself. Let me explain what—"

"Don't try to change the subject!" thundered Michelle. Then, calmly, as if her outburst had never happened, she added, "I think you were about to tell me how you knew Nathaniel was a decoy."

Ryan took a deep breath. "I figured it out because I realized you weren't yourself. Not since you returned from your visit to Isis three months ago."

"What are you talking about?" she spat. "How am I not myself?"

"Would the old Michelle Cooper shoot Dr. Harris? Strand innocent people on another planet?" He leaned forward intently. "You bound and gagged your own daughters!"

"There is nothing wrong with me!" she yelled. "There is something wrong with the pathetic species called *Homo sapiens*. I've grown. I realized now how much I *loathe* humanity. And my daughters are no different. I despise *them* just as much!"

"Think about it. This wasn't true before three months ago. Something terrible happened to you on Isis."

"Enough!" shouted Michelle Cooper, picking up

the Enigma Cube and pointing it at Ryan. "Answer my question! How did you know Nathaniel was a decoy? Tell me now or I'll use a gravity setting that will make the one I used before seem like a *picnic*."

"I'm trying to tell you. The Isis animals give off some kind of emotional energy that—"

"Time's up!" hissed Michelle hatefully, touching an indentation on the Cube.

Ryan felt as if he was hit by a falling wall of two-foot thick concrete.

With a sickening crunch he crashed through the chair, which splintered around him, driving a dagger-sized piece of wood two-inches into his thigh. The moment he landed his increased weight flattened him against his back on the floor. Gravity was so strong that blood refused to pour from his wound. Ryan's heart couldn't beat and one of his ribs fractured. He didn't scream or even grunt because he couldn't draw a breath to do so.

He was an instant away from blacking out when his gravity returned to normal.

"That was five seconds," said Michelle calmly. "I'll bet it seemed like a lot longer."

Ryan remained on his back and said nothing. Blood began pouring from his leg and onto the floor. And he couldn't think! Not through the agonizing pain that flooded his brain from his broken rib and gashed leg. His entire body felt as if it had been through a blender. Maybe it was finally time to give up: to face the fact that he would die here in this isolated cabin. He had finally come to a situation he couldn't trick or bluff his way out of. If only the pain would go away. But that wouldn't happen. If anything, it would get worse.

"I'm going to ask you one last time," said Michelle. "How did you know Nathaniel was a decoy? And I don't want to hear a single word about Isis."

Ryan's eyes were dead and defeated. But as he stared into the depths of Michelle Cooper's pitiless blue eyes, they suddenly sparked back to life.

Ryan laughed. He laughed as if he had heard a very funny joke.

"What are you laughing about?" she demanded.

"I'm laughing at *you*. I'm laughing because you're just as dead as I am. You just don't know it yet."

"How do you figure?"

"Carl rigged a boobie trap. In case he was captured. After I convinced him to call off the air strike on Nathaniel, he told me all about it—luckily in his office where you couldn't listen in. It's a high powered spray hidden in a shirt button. As powerful as a sneeze. While I had you distracted he was able to move just enough to activate it."

Michelle sneered at him. "Don't try one of your famous bluffs on *me*," she said scornfully. "I'm not a fool. And your bluff is insultingly poor. Maybe the great Ryan Resnick has lost his touch."

"It's not a bluff," said Ryan. "He got the spray from

the bioweapons people at Fort Dix. It's the most deadly virus ever designed, and the virus particles are so light they'll stay afloat even if their gravity is increased. Some of them have already reached us. We have about ten minutes to live."

She shook her head. "The U.S. doesn't do bioweapons research anymore. We've signed several treaties that prevent it."

"If you say so. Just do me a favor, kill me now before the virus starts eating away all my skin."

"You're making this up. You're acting too bravely for it to be true. You would never act like your own death meant so little to you. Why?" she demanded. "This bluff gains you *nothing*."

"I'm not making it up. You'll see."

Ryan was hit once again by a gravity wave. Just as intense as the last one. While it lasted the same five seconds, this time Ryan blacked out just before the effect ended, and at least one more of his ribs cracked under the strain.

Michelle Cooper waited patiently for Ryan to regain consciousness. When he did, thirty seconds later, she rose from the chair and held the Enigma Cube over him menacingly. "I'm only going to try this one more time," she said through clenched teeth. "Why are you bluffing?"

Ryan fought through pain that threatened to completely overwhelm him. "Do what you want to me," he croaked weakly. "It doesn't matter. We're both already dead."

"Yeah," hissed Michelle, touching another indentation on the Cube. *"Well you first!"*

Ryan felt bone crushing weight return. It wasn't as high a setting as the last time, but it was higher than she had used when she had captured them in the decoy building. He fought to stay conscious. If he blacked out he would be unable to fight for breath and he would die within a minute or two.

"You're helping me conduct a little experiment right now, Ryan," said Michelle calmly. "Once a scientist, always a scientist, I guess." She glanced at her watch. "You see I've never used this exact setting before. As a biologist, I'm making an educated guess that you can survive for about fifteen minutes." She sneered at him. "But do try to hold out for as long as you can. I want my data to be accurate."

Ryan fought through the enormous pain for what seemed like an eternity.

Finally, he could struggle no longer, and he collapsed into unconsciousness.

CHAPTER 32

The Return

Unconscious, Ryan was unable to draw even a shallow breath for his already oxygen depleted body. Starved for air, his body and brain began shutting down.

Suddenly, gravity returned to normal.

Although still unconscious, Ryan's breathing resumed. His heart—no longer struggling under a crushing weight—sped to pump oxygen to the trillions of cells in his body.

Two minutes later, Ryan returned to consciousness and forced his eyes open. An image slowly came into focus. Michelle Cooper. Kneeling over him and wrapping his thigh with bandages and gauze.

"Ryan," she said in surprise and profound relief. "You're awake."

Ryan nodded weakly.

"I'm so sorry for what I did to you," she said, looking a little dazed.

Ryan smiled thinly. "You used the Med-Pen on yourself after all," he rasped, barely above a whisper. Given that he no longer felt any pain, he knew she had used it on him as well.

"Yes," she replied. For some reason she was having trouble remembering further back than ten or fifteen minutes earlier. She wasn't even sure how she had gotten here. Or why she had been so intent on hurting Ryan Resnick.

"But you were sure I was bluffing," said Ryan.

She thought about this. "I don't know," she said with a shrug. "I remember you telling me we would both die from a deadly virus. And thinking you were bluffing. But I also remember thinking that since I had a Med-Pen, I might as well use it—just in case you weren't. That it would only take a second."

Michelle Cooper shook her head in confusion. "But what's going on, Ryan? I *hated* you. I wanted to kill you so badly I could taste it. Then all of a sudden I would have given anything for you to be okay."

"It's a long story," rasped Ryan weakly. "The short version is that you were infected on Isis. Your first trip there made you temporarily insane."

Michelle's eyes narrowed. Could this be true? She thought back to her first visit to Isis, and as she did so a dam burst open, freeing all of her memories of the past three months. They all came rushing back to her, crashing into her like a tidal wave. Ryan was right! She had behaved *horribly*. She had done vile, despicable things. She gasped, feeling sick to the very core of her soul.

"I feel like I just woke from some terrible nightmare," she said in horror.

"You did," whispered Ryan. "You weren't yourself. The Med-Pen cured you."

Michelle Cooper knew in her heart that this is exactly what had happened. The alien device had restored her mind to its normal state.

As she thought about the past fifteen minutes, her eyes widened. "So *that's* what your bluff was all about," she said in wonder. "You needed to trick me into *curing* myself." She stared at him in admiration. "Incredible." There was a pause. "I'll never be able to thank you enough."

Ryan had never come so close to giving up. It had been hopeless. The pain made it almost impossible for him to think clearly. But the pain had been the key to finding an answer because he had realized that the only way it would go away is if he had a Med-Pen. And then he remembered that Michelle had stolen one. That she had one with her. In a flash he realized what he had to do. If he could trick her into using it on herself, it might cure her. Ryan hadn't been sure it would still work since her mind had been in an altered state for such a long time, but he knew this was his only chance. And it had worked perfectly.

Maybe he *was* the luckiest person who ever lived.

Carl managed a grunt from his position on the floor. Michelle jumped up as if she had been electrocuted. "Sorry, Carl," she said as she trained the Enigma Cube on him. "Didn't mean to forget about you."

Carl's gravity returned to normal and he rose slowly from the floor. He knelt beside Michelle and inspected Ryan carefully. "Are you okay?" he said protectively, although he was far from fully recovered himself.

"Yeah," whispered Ryan. He managed a faint smile. "Although I've probably been better."

Michelle laughed, and instead of the chilling quality her laugh had had before there was now a cheerful, contagious quality to it.

Carl remembered this laugh and realized how much he had missed it. He caught Michelle's eye and nodded. "Welcome back, Michelle," he said warmly.

She returned the nod. Tears slowly formed in the corners of her eyes as she once again thought about the waking nightmare that had been the last three months of her life. About the unspeakable things she had said and done.

The Isis infection had somehow altered her brain chemistry in despicable ways, but even so, how could she ever forgive herself for not fighting harder to retain her sanity? For not fighting harder to stop the madness from consuming her? How could she ever forgive herself for the way she had treated those closest to her? She was ashamed and horrified and disgusted at herself for allowing the infection to so easily turn her into a psychopath.

At the same time she was overjoyed that she was now herself again and would be able to make amends. A kaleidoscope of emotions spun inside her. Extreme joy and extreme sorrow. Profound regret and profound hope for the future.

"I'll help you round up the mercs who were working with me and rescue poor Nathaniel," she said finally. "But can it wait fifteen minutes or so?"

Carl nodded.

Michelle Cooper smiled through tear filled eyes. "Thanks," she said, walking to the door.

Just before she left the room she turned back to face Ryan and Carl. "My daughters are in the next room," she explained. "Girls that I love more than anything in the world."

Tears now left her eyes and began streaming down her face. "It's time they got their mother back."

CHAPTER 33

Friends

It was Monday night and the four members of the Resnick family were seated at their dinner table in front of a large window. The window provided an excellent view of the thick woods just beyond their backyard, but this was the last thing any of them wanted to see just then. Everyone had had more than their fill of woods—both earthly and alien—during the weekend that had just passed.

Three of the four family members had spent the entire weekend off-planet. Once the portable generator died, the Isis team had set up the self-inflatable dwellings they had brought and enlarged their camp. They made sure to stay very calm and positive and they had no further encounters with any of the wildlife.

Most of the group had been certain they would be stranded on Isis for the rest of their lives. They believed they should begin exploring immediately in an effort to find an area for a permanent settlement. Regan was able to convince the group to wait at least two or three days before doing this. To give Miguel and Cam more time to recover from their injuries and to give Prometheus security a few days to take back the city and mount a rescue party. She argued well and her absolute conviction that this would happen was quite persuasive. Naturally, she didn't tell anyone that she *knew* the city was already back in the hands of Carl and that a rescue plan had *already* been devised.

Knowing they would be rescued, Regan was determined to keep her and Ryan's telepathy secret. Even so, she wasn't about to let her parents continue believing their son was almost certainly dead.

So she lied to them.

She told them Ryan had been feeling some pain so she had treated him with a Med-Pen ten minutes before he was separated from the group. That they had discussed the Isis wildlife and she was sure he was about to come to the same conclusions that she had. That he had told her after the Med-Pen had returned him to normal he was tired of being angry, and determined to be upbeat no matter what happened. She told them she and Ryan had developed a sixth sense of their own when it came to one another, and she was more certain he was alive than she had ever been of anything in her life.

She knew her parents couldn't share her absolute optimism, but she didn't stop trying to convince them until she had seen a reasonable measure of hope return to their eyes.

To stay emotionally positive, everyone decided to act as if Regan was right and they were very near rescue. The biologists stayed upbeat by studying the wildlife, designing experiments to test this new sense Regan had discovered, and discussing the probable evolution of the Isis biosphere.

Surprisingly, Ben Resnick and Donna Morgan were able to salvage their X-ray experiment. Although some of the structural parts of their X-ray detector equipment had been spattered with lava, making things more difficult, they still managed to set it up in time to get the readings they needed.

On Saturday night the dazzling stars came out again. In uncountable numbers. But now the group took the time to truly appreciate their magnificence.

In the wee hours of Sunday night, Pennsylvania time, a tiny, two person helicopter landed at their camp. They had been rescued! The joy and relief they all felt was beyond description. If the animals of Isis could have sensed positive emotions they might have felt *these* on the other side of the planet. But this was still nothing compared to the tidal wave of positive emotions that burst from Ben and Amanda Resnick when the pilot informed them that their son was still alive and well.

One by one the party was airlifted to the Isis shield. When Regan crossed it she experienced the same sensations and the same ability to see through solid objects as she had before. Unfortunately, she didn't have the chance to find out if she could now get through Qwervy shields without a red crystal like her brother. She vowed to make the attempt the very next time she visited the alien city.

Ryan was praised profusely for stopping Michelle Cooper while Regan was seen as the hero who had saved the Isis expedition. The ironic part was that Ryan would have never made it back to Earth to be a hero without Regan. He would have been killed by the gray pack animals when his fire went out. And she could have never saved the expedition if he hadn't solved the mystery of the unusual sixth sense possessed by Isis's wildlife. None of it really mattered. They didn't care if anyone ever knew the true story of what had happened that weekend. The fact that everything had turned out okay was the important thing.

Carl had seen to it that Ryan was taken to a hospital directly from Michelle Cooper's cabin. The gash in his leg had required eighteen stitches and three of his ribs were fractured. He had learned that the treatment for broken ribs was simply to manage the pain and let them heal. Other than these two injuries he had come through his ordeal remarkably well. Because he had been treated with the Med-Pen in the cabin, he would be as good as new in a week or so. He had also seen to it that Alyssa and Kelsey were treated with a Med-Pen. It was the least he could do for Kelsey's shoulder and to make sure they didn't get what he considered the ultimate curse: poison ivy.

After a long and tearful reunion with the loving mother who had been absent from their lives for the past three months, the girls pleaded with Carl to let them join the Prometheus Project. Carl denied them repeatedly just to see how much they really wanted it. It soon became clear they were just as passionate about pursuing this opportunity as Ryan and Regan had been years earlier, and their behavior during the crisis and their contribution to the team had been impressive. They had proved their mettle under fire, and Ryan and Regan had paved the way by demonstrating that bright, resourceful kids could become valuable additions to the team.

Ryan argued for them as well. He told Carl about Alyssa's success in the Science Fair the previous year, and about her and her sister's creative scientific minds. He made sure that Carl fully appreciated the contribution the two sisters had made by saving him in the woods, and how impressed President Quinn had been with them and their swarm of trained bees. Ryan didn't know how they would do in the Science Fair, but it was hard to say a project wasn't successful when it was praised by a president and used to escape from an armed mercenary. If not for Alyssa and Kelsey, Ryan would have almost certainly been killed. If that had happened Michelle Cooper's plan would have worked. And who knows how much death and destruction she would have rained on the world with the Enigma Cube.

After consulting briefly with the recovering Harry Harris, Carl had let the Resnicks know only three hours earlier they had decided to allow the Cooper sisters to join the Prometheus team.

With that settled, and all of the unbelievable events of the weekend now behind them, the Resnick family was relieved that things were returning to normal. And nothing was more normal for them than having a family dinner in the peace and comfort of their home.

Regan's spirits were high as she attacked the plate of spaghetti and meatballs in front of her. "Boy, I can't believe we missed another day of school," she said between bites. "Principal Lyons probably has steam coming out of her ears. Like in those cartoons."

After finally getting back to Earth, Regan and her father had visited the doctor early that morning, and both had received a number of stitches. Their parents agreed that both kids could use a day off.

"It's not just missing another day," noted Mrs. Resnick. "It's that we're sending you both back to school all banged up. Your principal must think we're the worst parents who ever lived."

"Yeah," said Mr. Resnick. "Who could blame her?"

"Well, if she asks what happened to us," said Regan with a grin, "I'm thinking of saying we were in a skydiving accident. Hey, if your chute doesn't open, walking away with a few broken ribs and some cuts and stab wounds isn't bad."

Everyone laughed. Everyone, that is, except Ryan. His head was tilted down and he was picking at his spaghetti gloomily.

"What's wrong, Ry?" said Regan. "You don't like the skydiving idea? How about I'll use that, and you say you lost a wrestling match with a Python."

Ryan just grunted.

"What's the matter, Ryan?" said his sister. "You should be the happiest person in the world."

"I'll say," said their mother. "Let me see," she began, ticking points off her fingers one by one. "All of us are alive and well—which is a miracle. Dr. Harris is recovering nicely. Carl rounded up all the mercenaries. Nathaniel is back, good as new. Michelle is cured and taking her daughters on a week-long vacation next week. And the Enigma Cube is back inside Prometheus and under guard." She tilted her head. "Am I missing anything?"

Regan grinned. "Yes. The most important thing when it comes to Ryan's happiness. Alyssa Cooper has been added to the team."

"Actually," said Mr. Resnick innocently, "*both* Cooper girls have been added."

"I *know*," said Regan, rolling her eyes, "and I'm sure Ryan is just fine with Kelsey joining us. But ask him how he feels about *Alyssa*."

"Oh, now I get it," said Mrs. Resnick. "You're saying Ryan thinks this girl is pretty special."

Regan laughed. "I'm not sure 'pretty special' would

be the exact words he would use to describe her, but yeah, that's what I'm saying."

Mr. Resnick turned to his son with an intrigued expression. "Weren't you talking to her on the phone just before dinner?" he asked.

Ryan frowned and nodded slightly.

"Uh-oh," said Regan, picking up on his body language. "What happened Ryan? You saved Alyssa's mom, so now you're *really* on her good side. And because of you, Alyssa and her sister get to join the team. Get to be part of the coolest discovery *ever*. So how could she not like you?"

Ryan sighed. "She does," he said. "A lot. In fact, she liked me *before* any of this happened. I was just slow to figure that out. Now she likes me even more."

"So then what's the problem?" asked Mr. Resnick.

"She said she thought a lot about it, and has decided it's important that we just stay friends for now. Since there are only four kids on the team, we'll be seeing a lot of each other for a long time. She figures if something goes wrong between us, our relationship could be really, really awkward." He shook his head miserably. "She's not happy about it either, but she thinks it's best for us."

"Interesting," said his mother thoughtfully. "I agree with her. Sounds like a very sensible girl. I'm impressed with her already."

"Let me make sure I understand," said Regan.

"So because you're the hero, because she likes you so much . . . you *don't* get the girl."

Everyone around the table laughed except for Ryan.

"Come on, Ryan," said his sister cheerfully. "Look on the bright side. Mom is right. It's a miracle we're even alive. And it's going to be awesome having other kids on the team. You'll be closer to Alyssa than you ever could have been before." She shrugged. "Be good friends with her and then see what happens. You never know what the future will bring."

Ryan stared at his sister for a long while. Finally, he raised his eyebrows. "You know, Regan, when you're right you're right. I don't give up easily. Who knows what will happen."

"That's the spirit, Ryan," said his father with a twinkle in his eye. "Your mother and I started out as just friends. For years. And look at us. We got married."

"*Married?*" said Ryan, recoiling in shock. "Who said anything about *that*? Alyssa's great and all, but that's a million years away."

"You never know," said Ben Resnick. "Stranger things have happened."

"Yeah," said Regan, raising her eyebrows. "Especially to *this* family."

"I'm not sure marriage would be a good idea, Ben," teased Mrs. Resnick. "Isn't it supposed to be bad luck to marry a girl whose mother has already tried to kill you?"

"Oh yeah," said her husband, playing along. "I think I did hear that."

"On the other hand," said Mrs. Resnick. "Maybe it's a good thing. Maybe she's gotten it out of her system."

"*Okay,*" said Ryan, shaking his head and then breaking out into a smile despite himself. "You win. You've cheered me up. We'll get to know each other as friends. See what happens. I'll just have to live with that." Ryan raised his eyebrows and added, "At least for now."

"Great," said Mr. Resnick. "Just make sure you don't let her distract you *too* much," he added light-heartedly. "Like your mother distracted me. After all, if disaster ever strikes again, we need you and Regan at your sharpest."

"Hey, I didn't let her distract me during *this* disaster," protested Ryan. A grin came over his face. "Okay, maybe just a little," he said, holding his thumb and index finger a centimeter apart. "But it doesn't matter. We've had more than our share of disasters. What are the odds we'll ever have another one?"

"I agree with Ryan," said Regan. "There's just no way."

"You're probably right," said Mr. Resnick. "But as you just said, Regan, you never know what the future will bring."

"That's true," said Regan, happily stabbing a meatball with her fork. "But I for one can't *wait* to find out," she finished with an enthusiastic gleam in her eye.

About The Author

DOUGLAS E. RICHARDS is a former biotechnology executive who has written extensively for the award-winning magazine, *National Geographic KIDS*, and also for *American Fencing Magazine*. He currently lives in San Diego, California with his wife, Kelly, his children, Ryan and Regan (for whom the main characters in his Prometheus Project series are named), and his dog Dash. After graduating with a BS in microbiology from the Ohio State University, he earned a master's degree in molecular biology from the University of Wisconsin and a master's in business administration from the University of Chicago. To learn more about Douglas and his work, please visit *www.douglaserichards.com*.